DIG TWO GRAVES

An absolutely gripping British crime thriller
with a massive twist

HELEN H. DURRANT

DS Hedley Sharpe Book 1

JOFFE BOOKS

Joffe Books, London
www.joffebooks.com

First published in Great Britain in 2024

Cover Design by Nick Castle

ISBN: 978-1-83526-492-8

For Peter and his never-ending patience and help.

CHAPTER ONE

Hedley Sharpe was an overweight, often foul-mouthed detective superintendent in his fifties. But this morning he looked slick and professional as he strode across the foyer of the Crown Court. The look belied the turmoil of emotion filling his head, the hard, fixed expression on his face giving little away as he approached his waiting colleagues.

"He's a bloody no show. So what happened? I thought we were watching the slippery bugger."

"We checked on him late last night, sir," a detective constable replied nervously, "and I can confirm that he was safely tucked up at home. We had a police guard on both the front and back doors. We also spoke to his solicitor, who was with him, and he promised faithfully to get him here on time this morning."

"Lying jokers, the bloody lot of them." Hedley turned and addressed the huddle of men to his right, the accused's legal team. "The star of this little show appears to have done a runner. Any of you lot know where he's gone?" Stepping up to one of them, Hedley gave him a sharp poke in the guts. "You're the idiot who fought so hard for bail. Now we know why, don't we. Dean Rawlins had no intention of attending this morning, and you damn well knew it. I hope he paid you well because you're going to earn it. You, laddie, have a shed load of questions to answer."

Caught off guard by Hedley's vicious jab, the man stepped back. "I wouldn't dare help the man in the way you suggest, Superintendent. As Mr Rawlins' solicitor, I'm paid to do all I can for him, but that doesn't include breaking the law. We tried our best, even to the extent of leaving one of our juniors to ensure that Mr Rawlins stayed put overnight. You're not the only one who'll lose out over this morning's débâcle."

Hedley sneered. "Don't make me laugh. When we find him — and we will, make no mistake — he'll talk. And then the law will come down hard on the bloody lot of you."

"You seem to forget, Superintendent, that everyone is innocent until proven guilty. Nothing has yet been proved against my client, and the evidence is weak at best."

Giving the solicitor a scowl, Hedley nodded at his DI, Stuart Vasey. "C'mon, let's go. The Rawlins house needs a visit, sharpish."

Hedley needed to get away from this bunch of know-it-all lawyers before he lamped one of them. Most of all, he needed to calm down. Getting angry like this would do his blood pressure no good at all. The medics had warned him enough times about what the outcome would be if he didn't change his lifestyle. The problem was, Hedley saw little wrong with the way he lived or conducted himself. True, he was overweight. He liked a drink and he had a temper, as everyone he worked with knew, but it was rarely an issue. Mostly he considered himself to be easy-going and fair minded with his team.

"It'll have taken some planning," he told Stuart as they walked down the steps and out of the courthouse. "We can be pretty certain of that. We've had uniform kicking about that house of his for weeks. I can't believe they didn't pick up on something."

"Give them a break, Hedley. Rawlins was biding his time. He waited until the very last minute," Stuart said. "He lulled everyone into a false sense of security, convinced us all that he intended to turn up and face the charges, and as soon as he had us all believing he meant it, he did one."

"What I don't get is where does a man like him go? His face has been plastered across the media for weeks. We have to find him. We must get justice for the poor buggers he's murdered over the years."

"*Allegedly* murdered, Hedley. Like his brief said, innocent until proven guilty."

"He did it all right," said Hedley flatly. "Put out an alert for him — you know, airports and the like. If he intends to leave the country, he won't get far."

"That's all well and good, but knowing Rawlins he'll have his bolthole well sorted. Don't forget who he is. With his resources he can buy himself all the help he needs, along with friends only too willing to supply it."

The last thing Hedley needed was reminding of how the underbelly of this city kowtowed to Rawlins. "D'you reckon Murray gave him a hand?"

Stuart shook his head. "I doubt it. That pair hate each other. If Rawlins has disappeared, Connor Murray will be all too delighted to have him out of the way. Still, it won't do any harm to talk to him, I suppose. At least we can satisfy ourselves that Murray had nothing to do with his disappearance."

"Murray wouldn't dare. He knows damn well we'd find out." Hedley checked his watch. "How long will it take us to get to the Rawlins house? Probably a wasted journey, he'll be long gone, but we should check it out anyway."

"He lives out Saddleworth way," Stuart said. "In a new upmarket housing estate above the village of Uppermill."

Hedley sighed. In that case it'd take a bloody age. "All I can say is, I hope we find something to make all this dashing about worth it. I missed my breakfast this morning, what with having to get done up like a dog's dinner and get to the court on time. Bloody Rawlins. I get my hands on him, he'll know about it."

Held up by heavy traffic and roadworks, it took them well over an hour to reach the quiet estate where Dean

Rawlins lived. Hedley was fuming, impatient for answers, fast.

Stuart eyed the collection of tall newbuilds. "Looks like any other residential area. With all the money Rawlins has put away, I imagined some huge stone pile up in the hills."

"It's upmarket enough," Hedley told him. "Rawlins is smart. He knows not to attract too much attention." He surveyed the large detached house in front of them. "Let's get this over with then. You go round the back and I'll get the front."

After several minutes of fruitless banging on doors, Hedley had got nowhere. Stuart had better luck.

"There's French doors round the back here," he called out. "They're wide open, just swinging in the breeze."

That didn't sound right. Hedley walked round and followed Stuart inside. All was silent and suspiciously tidy.

Stuart headed towards the hallway. "There's no one about. Something is wrong, all right. It looks like a show house, as if there's never been a soul here."

Hedley stood looking round the room, his hands in his trouser pockets, pondering the possibilities. "I wonder what's happened to that solicitor, the one who was supposed to be keeping an eye on the bugger? And what about our uniforms? We left two of them on watch."

"Whatever happened, you can bet it won't have been good. We should get forensics up here," Stuart said.

"Do that," Hedley agreed. "I don't like mysteries, don't like them at all. They make my teeth itch."

CHAPTER TWO

One year later

"Long time no see."

Simple words, but the sound of that voice sent a shiver of fear down Chloe Todd's spine. The greeting was accompanied by a broad smile that invited a reply. But no way could Chloe reciprocate. She and Selina Harris were way beyond polite conversation. Chloe had finished with her a long time ago and saw no reason why that should change now.

"Surely we can put the past behind us," Selina said, still smiling. "It's been years and I'm no longer the woman I was, Chloe. I'm a different person now."

"Well, I can't put it behind me. Not now, not ever," Chloe hissed. She turned away, not daring to look back and check if Selina was following her. Her nerves were jangling. She could deal with many things — and over the next few weeks would have to do just that — but not Selina Harris.

Chloe's breath came fast, shallow. She felt stifled. The small, crowded sitting room suddenly felt more claustrophobic than it had. There was no sign of Simon either. Where had he gone? He'd promised not to do this, he knew how she was with strangers, but what did he care? He had no heart, no compassion.

She couldn't wait to be rid of him.

"This is silly. We really should have that catch-up. Let's put things right between us, Chloe."

Selina was at her back. Chloe could smell her perfume, strong and cloying, just like she remembered.

"You haven't changed much. Neither of us have." She treated Chloe to another broad smile, displaying her perfect white teeth. "Someone told me you're pregnant. Congratulations. I bet Simon is thrilled."

"You've got that wrong," Chloe said, her meaning unclear. "Now, leave me be." She laid a protective hand over her belly. "I don't want to speak to you now, or ever." Having said her piece, Chloe hurried off into the adjoining room, but that one too was packed with strangers. Still struggling to breathe, Chloe felt the familiar twinge of panic in her stomach. She swallowed the bile that rose in her throat. Why did Selina always have this effect on her? No one else had such power.

"Sorry, Chloe." Simon spoke from behind her. "I had to have a word with Gerald over there — a spot of business that won't wait."

"I want to go home. I can't do this. I thought I could but I was wrong. There are too many people here and I'm not comfortable." She looked into his eyes, begging for understanding. They were cold, unsympathetic. He might pretend, but he had no idea how she felt He never would. This entire relationship was a huge mistake. "You know this is a bad time for me. You shouldn't have made me come."

"You're being silly. You knew Graham and how everyone liked him. He'd be thrilled that we're all here for him today. And as for taking you home, that's out of the question. They all know what happened to you and don't wish you any harm. C'mon, Chloe. It's a funeral, for heaven's sake, we can't just cut and run. Give it another half an hour at least." He gave her a peck on the cheek and was gone again.

"Not an understanding bone in his body, that man. He's always been the same. I don't know what you're doing with him, Chloe. He's not what you need."

Selina again. Damn the woman, why couldn't she leave her alone? "You have no idea what I need."

"I think you need someone, a friend, to confide in," Selina whispered, her breath warm on Chloe's neck. "Simon isn't easy to live with, not with the work he's in and the people he mixes with."

Chloe felt dizzy, hounded. She couldn't cope. She wanted to run back to the security of her own home, leaving Selina Harris far behind. She wanted to lock the doors against her old enemy so she couldn't creep up behind her and whisper poison in her ear. "Leave me alone," Chloe spat. "I don't want to speak to you. I don't even know what you're doing here. You're nothing to do with Gerald, you're not family."

"That's where you're wrong. It's only a matter of time before I *am* family." She had that familiar self-satisfied look on her face, the one Chloe recognised only too well. "Two months ago, Gerald and I got engaged. I have every right to be here. Surely Simon told you?"

No, he hadn't told her. Now Chloe felt stupid, upset that people were keeping things from her.

Selina leaned forward again. "Gerald needs taking in hand," she whispered. "Unlike Simon, he has all that money languishing in his bank, even more now that Graham has died, and he has no idea how to spend it. I saw my chance, and bingo. Like you, I will soon be married to the Firm." She flashed those perfect teeth again.

"You're a selfish bitch, Selina. You always were. I might not see much of him but I feel sorry for Gerald."

"No need. He'll be just fine with me. The first thing I intend to do is get him out of that slum he's got us living in and move somewhere nice. Simon has the right idea. He's just moved the pair of you into a place in Saddleworth, I believe. How're you liking it?"

"None of your business, and Gerald loves that little cottage. He's been there thirty years or more."

Selina smiled again. "Not for much longer."

"Like I said, you're a selfish bitch."

That made Selina's face fall. "Chloe, I came here today hoping things would be different between us. I was wrong. You're still the neurotic woman you always were. I'm not surprised Simon treats you like dirt, you play the victim so well. You need to get a life, Chloe. Learn to enjoy yourself."

Selina strutted off, her high heels tapping on the wooden floor, her long blonde hair swinging. Chloe watched the men's eyes following her across the room and hated her more than ever. The last thing she needed was Selina Harris back in her life.

CHAPTER THREE

Day one

Chloe Todd stood at the window and watched her husband, Simon, back his car off the driveway and leave for work. Finally, she was alone in the house. With just her own thoughts for company, she would have a few hours' peace.

Life with Simon was not easy. He was a complicated man. He had exacting standards to which he expected Chloe to conform. She'd been married to him for almost a year and during that time he'd made it his business to gradually exert his control over every aspect of her life.

What was worse, she'd let him. But what choice did she have?

She walked from room to room, distressed at the state of the place. There was a lot to do. They'd moved into this house late yesterday, but what with Simon's work and the fact that he'd forbidden her to unpack their stuff, everything was a mess. The furniture was in position but their belongings, the pictures, the knick-knacks, were strewn over every surface. Looking at the labelled boxes littering the floor of the sitting room, Chloe decided that despite Simon's instructions, she would make a start on the unpacking. Surely, he could have no objection to her at least putting the kitchen stuff in its proper place. The boxes sealed tight with tape and marked with a red cross were definitely not to be touched. Their contents were for Simon's eyes only.

A new home. Chloe should be thrilled, but she wasn't. Like everything else in their relationship, she'd had no choice in the matter. Without consulting her, Simon had found this house and they'd moved in at breakneck speed. He'd wanted somewhere away from the city but not so far that he couldn't commute. Which was all very well, but it meant that Chloe was more isolated than ever.

Did he even care that she'd left her old life and the people who went with it? Abby, for one, who'd been her friend for years and who had helped when she'd been at rock bottom and living rough. Abby had taught her a lot and Chloe would never forget her. The old Chloe, the Chloe of the days before Simon, had relied on friends like Abby to get her through.

As for the isolation, that was Simon all over. He was keen to cut her off from her past, and if he got his way she wouldn't have much of a future either.

Chloe was well aware that she was something of a liability to Simon. He had rammed it down her throat often enough. She didn't mix well, particularly not with Simon's business associates and his family — Graham's funeral was a prime example. Was this his way of sorting it, ensuring that she didn't meet them again? No time to dwell on it today. With Simon gone, she could spend the morning familiarising herself with her new surroundings.

Delving into a box that had obviously been mislabelled 'crockery', she pulled out an infant's white hand-knitted cardi. Her hands shook. Simon wasn't a nice man but he had promised this wouldn't happen. She held the tiny garment up to her face and breathed in the smell of fresh air and lemons. It brought tears to her eyes and made her think of Lily.

Outside, the sun shone brightly, inviting and warm. If only she could pop baby Lily into her pram, push her around the small estate and meet other mums. It was a simple enough thing to do. The pram was sitting in the kitchen where Simon had put it. But he had forbidden all contact with their new neighbours for the time being. Simon had to be the one to make first contact. To explain about her.

It wasn't natural. Things didn't need to be this way. All she wanted was to be in charge of her own life again. But that was unlikely to happen. Simon was very much the boss in this relationship.

She went to the front window and peered between the blinds at the houses across the road. The people in them were no doubt as curious about their new neighbours as she was about them. What were their lives like, she wondered with a pang of envy. They would be a far cry from hers, that was for sure. Normality hadn't been a feature of her life for some time. How could it be with a past like hers? Neither she nor Simon were ordinary in any sense of the word.

But she had to give him credit. Simon had found a beautiful house that must have cost a fortune. It was a large detached with four bedrooms and a spacious sitting room that stretched from the front through to French doors leading out into the back garden.

Perfect as it was, Chloe couldn't help thinking about the people she'd left behind. She didn't have much of a family but her mother was still around. Would she ask questions? Chloe couldn't decide. Dora had never been much of a parent. In fact, she hadn't given a damn about her daughter. Chloe had only been ten years old when her mother abandoned her for the local pub and the company of others like herself. While Chloe was growing up, Dora was drinking, leaving her daughter to suffer the bullying, the beatings she'd got from the likes of Selina Harris.

Chloe closed her eyes, as the memories of all those who had tormented her took control. Selina had been the worst. Because of Selina, her childhood had been one long misery. She shook her head. The nerves were back. One way or another, Chloe had to beat them or she was lost.

Simon had insisted that this would be a new start. She must leave the past behind and not look back. Easily said, but there were things in Chloe's past that she would never forget. Things that had made her the person she was today.

Chloe was out of her depth in the countryside. She was used to the bustle of city streets. Ardwick, where she'd grown up, was practically in the centre of Manchester. Saddleworth consisted of nothing but a string of villages abutting the Pennines. From her front window she could see the hills rising above the rooftops across the road. A beautiful view but foreign to her. Would she ever get used to it? She turned away with a shrug. Perhaps with time the area's rugged beauty might grow on her.

At the back of the house there was a landscaped garden bounded by high fencing. A row of trees bordered a dirt track that led to a road at the bottom. On a day like today the garden begged to be used. Chloe took a breath, flung open the French doors and wheeled the pram out onto the patio.

This act of wanton independence gave her a much-needed boost. She felt wicked, defiant, and it made her feel — well, normal. It was a rare feeling and one she enjoyed. She turned on the radio and hummed to herself as she worked. Three empty boxes and a leisurely coffee later, it was time to return to the status quo. Simon would soon be back for lunch.

Chloe went into the garden to bring the baby back indoors. Lifting the blanket, she peered into the pram to see if Lily was awake. She gasped in horror.

The nightmare was back.

CHAPTER FOUR

"Help! Someone, anyone. Please, you have to help me." Chloe stood in the middle of the avenue screaming her head off. "My baby's gone! My little girl, she's been stolen."

Within seconds the quiet road was full of people. Suddenly a pair of ample arms went round her and held on tight. A woman with dark curly hair was speaking — words came out of her mouth but Chloe couldn't make sense of them. Her head was full of Lily and the horror of what had happened.

"I'm Brenda. I live across the road from you," the woman with the arms said gently.

"She was in her pram in the garden, asleep. I went to bring her in and . . ." Chloe began to sob.

"Don't worry, love, we'll help you look for her."

Chloe gave the woman a shove. "She's twelve weeks old, for God's sake. She's not hiding or run off. Someone's taken her."

Brenda led Chloe back to the house. "In that case, we should ring the police straight away."

Chloe stared at her, eyes wild with panic. How would Simon react to that? Not good, that was for sure. But by the time they'd reached Chloe's front door, Brenda had already made the call on her mobile.

"All done," she said kindly. "Come on, let's get you inside."

"My husband will be home any minute," Chloe cried. "He can't find you in the house."

Brenda shook her head, dismissing the comment. "I know, you've just moved in. If it's the mess that bothers you, don't worry, we've all been there. Your husband will be grateful for the help once he hears what's happened."

Chloe shook her head — *no, he won't.* The familiarity with which Brenda walked through her home bothered her.

"I knew the couple who lived here before you," Brenda explained, seeing the look. "Me and Della were good friends. We were always in each other's houses. I didn't catch your name."

This was against all the rules laid down by Simon, but what could she do? She couldn't refuse to answer. "Chloe."

"I detect a faint accent, where're you from?"

"Manchester."

"You look very young to be married with a child."

Why did people always say that? They'd stare at forty-something Simon, look at her, a fragile-looking twenty-five-year-old, and start with the comments.

"You don't understand. No way will my husband approve of me allowing a strange woman to wander around his house asking questions," Chloe said. "Thanks for your help but I'll be all right now. Simon will be home soon."

"You've had a dreadful experience. Your child has been taken, you must be distraught," Brenda said, her eyes wide in horror. "I can't imagine how that feels. There's no way I'm leaving you alone."

"Please go. I need to tidy up, get Simon his meal."

"You're his wife, not his slave."

The look on Brenda's face said she wasn't impressed. It was a look Chloe was familiar with.

Brenda went into the kitchen and filled the kettle. "You sit down, love. He wants food, he can get his own. I'll get you some tea, just the job for shock."

Tea was the last thing Chloe wanted. What she wanted — no, *needed* — was to think, to come up with an explanation for this upheaval, something Simon would understand. If that was even possible.

Brenda was staring at her with the look she'd seen on other women's faces when she spoke of Simon and their relationship. She'd only just met this woman, but already Brenda had realised what sort of man she was married to. A man who liked to be in control. A bully.

"I'm just across the road, the house with the red door, if you ever want to talk." She put a gentle hand on Chloe's shoulder. "Remember that, Chloe. Don't suffer alone, it's not worth it. You feel the need to get out of the house, away from that husband of yours, fancy a good ole rant, I'll listen."

"It's not what you think," Chloe protested. "I just want my baby back."

"I know, love, and I wish I could do more to help. Anyway, the police will be here soon."

Though she wanted rid of this woman, Chloe couldn't help liking her. Brenda was comforting, easy to talk to. She might live in a huge house with an expensive car in the drive, but there was no edge to her. Brenda seemed like a down-to-earth, practical woman. But could Chloe trust her? Dare she take that risk? And if she made friends with her, what would Simon say?

"Chloe! What the hell's going on? Why's there a crowd of people outside the house?"

Simon Todd blustered into the kitchen, took one look at Brenda and scowled. "Who the hell are you?"

"I live across the road. Chloe has had a terrible shock. There's bad news, I'm afraid."

"Brenda's okay, she's helping me," Chloe explained through her tears.

"Helping with what? What's happened? Are you ill?"

There was a look of concern on Simon's face but it didn't fool Chloe. She knew what was going on inside his head. The concern was a sham, assumed for Brenda's benefit. He'd expressly said there was to be no drama. Drama meant strangers asking questions, and that was exactly what was happening now. She'd pay dearly for this.

"Your baby was taken from the garden," Brenda said. "Naturally, when Chloe found the pram empty, she was distraught. There was no way she could have coped on her own."

"Well, I've got this now," Simon barked. "Thanks for helping, now you can leave."

Brenda opened her mouth to respond when the doorbell rang. Chloe heard voices in the hall.

"Who's that?" Simon asked.

"That'll be the police," Brenda said. "They'll need to speak to you both, and no doubt Chloe will have to make a statement. I'll leave you to it." She passed Chloe a slip of paper. "My number. Remember what I said, I'm only across the road."

This only served to make Simon more angry. "Police! Who the hell called them?"

"I did. In case you didn't hear me, your child is missing," Brenda said, with a sarcasm that made Chloe wince.

Simon stood stock still, his hands on his hips, staring at her. "You stupid bitch. There is no fucking baby. There never was."

CHAPTER FIVE

Simon Todd stood outside the red door and rang the bell. Moments later, Brenda Howells, her ample arms folded tight, was standing in front of him.

"I thought I should explain," he began.

"How's Chloe?" Brenda asked.

"Sleeping. I gave her a couple of her tablets so she'll be out of it for an hour or two."

"You'd better come in," Brenda said.

"Firstly, I must apologise for the way I behaved earlier. You should know that Chloe isn't well. The doctor was quite clear, no dramas. Nothing to upset her." Simon spoke hastily, trailing behind her towards the sitting room. "You have to understand how strained things are between us."

She turned to face him, her eyes blazing. "Oh, I understand perfectly. I saw for myself how things are. You're nothing but a bully. The poor girl is terrified of you."

Simon shook his head. "No, no, you've got it all wrong. Chloe is ill and I have to take care of her. That means not allowing her to get worked up. I don't let her take on stuff she can't cope with."

Brenda didn't look impressed. "She isn't even allowed out, she can't explore or mix with anyone. That can't be good for her. We're your neighbours, surely she can talk to us."

"I told her not to overdo it, that was all. I didn't want her wandering around and getting lost. Like I said, I have to take care of her. Her mind wanders and she's easily confused."

Ignoring his explanation, Brenda said, "I saw how she was. She stood in your kitchen, scared to death of you coming home and finding out what had happened. The woman was a nervous wreck. How is that taking care of her?" Brenda shook her head, her expression full of disgust. "You're a piece of work. I can't abide men like you. You're a self-centred bully who doesn't give a damn for anyone's feelings, and particularly your wife's."

Ordinarily, Simon Todd would have had plenty to say about that outburst, put the woman in her place. But the time wasn't right. "You don't understand. Life with Chloe is complicated. Losing the baby was the final straw. It's as if her mind blotted it out, and sometimes she simply won't accept that it happened at all."

He saw Brenda's expression soften. The mention of a little baby had done the trick and averted a blazing row.

"So, there was a baby?" she asked.

"Yes, a little girl, born twelve weeks ago. Chloe named her Lily. She was stillborn. Chloe hasn't been right since. She has these lapses when she believes Lily is still with us, like today. It happens when she's stressed. I can only think that the move must have brought it on. She's even kept all Lily's things, clothes and baby paraphernalia. I boxed them all up ready for the move, intending to put them away until they're needed again. But Chloe wouldn't listen. While I was at work she had the lot out, even the pram. I believe the upheaval of moving sent her into a sort of meltdown." He averted his eyes from Brenda's gaze. "It's my fault. I shouldn't have left her alone, not on our first full day in the new house, but I had no choice. I still have to work."

"These . . . episodes. Does she usually recover?"

"A couple of days' rest and she'll be okay. I'll speak to her, explain yet again how things are."

"It might be an idea to take a step back. Let Chloe make friends around here. We're a pleasant bunch on the avenue and we all get on well. We don't have to talk about babies. We can keep the chat general. It will do Chloe good to have people around her that she can talk to when you're not here."

Simon stared at the woman. She wasn't going to take no for an answer. Now what to do? The last thing he wanted was Chloe gossiping with the neighbours. "Thank you, but we'll see how she goes on. I'm considering organising a trip away for her. She has family members that will be only too pleased to look after her for a few days." This was a lie. Chloe's mother certainly didn't want her around.

He saw the look. The woman wasn't convinced. What did it matter, anyway? He wouldn't be hanging around long enough to suffer much flak from the neighbours.

"I appreciate your help today," he said. "I know you meant well. You had no idea what you were up against. If you want to see her, I'm sure she'll be better tomorrow."

The woman nodded. Simon hoped she understood. He didn't want her going across the road and waking Chloe when he was out.

"She has my number. Tell her to give me a ring in the morning. We can have coffee and a chat. Being welcomed onto the avenue might make her feel better."

Simon nodded. "Thanks. You've been very helpful, but trust me, I know how best to handle her."

Simon Todd didn't like independent women. They made him angry, frustrated that he couldn't mould them to his will. This Brenda woman could be trouble, and he couldn't have that. Chloe would have to be persuaded to see sense. When she woke up, he'd speak to her, make her see that Brenda wasn't a good choice for a friend.

CHAPTER SIX

Day two

Detective Superintendent Hedley Sharpe slammed the fridge door shut. No milk. That meant no early morning coffee, which in turn meant a miserable start to the day. His eyes flitted to the clock on the kitchen wall. There was just enough time to nip to Abid's shop on the corner and buy some. Nip? Who was he kidding? His nipping days were long gone. His fifty-something-year-old body and ample build saw to that. But he would have to be quick. His inspector, Stuart Vasey, would be here any time to pick him up.

"Those lads were back last night," Abid said as he handed over the milk. "I went out to tackle them. I told them to get lost but they stood their ground, shouted stuff, obscene things I can't repeat, and threw eggs at the window. They're not local, I didn't recognise any of 'em. Mum got upset and had one of her turns."

"They're nothing but hooligans," Abid's mother, Meena Khan, said, picking up a loaf from the shelf before disappearing into the back room.

"Didn't realise she was there," Abid said sheepishly. "She's thoroughly sick of it. It's every night now, and often midnight before it stops. Do these kids have no homes to go to?"

"You shouldn't take them on alone, Abid," Hedley said. "Leave it to the professionals. You've got a camera on the wall outside. I'll have a word with the Community Policing team, tell them to call round and you can give them the footage. They recognise anyone and they'll act. Tell Meena I have her back."

"The doctor's put her on tablets. It's not just the kids, she's fed up with having us under her feet too," Abid admitted. "Wants me to take over the shop, and my brothers to get married and off her hands so she can go and live with her sister in Huddersfield."

Hedley could understand Meena's frustration. It wasn't easy having three grown sons still at home. "If she goes, this place won't be the same. Not that you don't do a great job, but Meena's been here for ever." Hedley fumbled in his jacket pocket. No money. "Sorry, can I give you the cash later? Time's tight this morning — got an early shout."

"No worries. I'll put it on your tab."

Hedley gave him a smile. Apart from the occasional spot of bother from the younger element, there was a lot to be said for living in this friendly inner-city backstreet. The inhabitants were a mixed bunch of folk from many ethnic backgrounds who all rubbed along and over the years had built up friendships. They trusted each other, something which was not to be sniffed at. Hedley, for one, had no desire to swap this street for a garden-fronted semi out in the sticks. Levenshulme might be busy and congested but it was home. Plus, it had the added advantage of being only a couple of miles from Manchester city centre.

Emily had kept on about moving. Had she lived, the pair of them would have ended up living near her mother in some posh job in Didsbury. Hedley smiled. Emily had always been ambitious. It was she who'd encouraged him to rise through the ranks. If it hadn't been for her he'd never have made it to superintendent. When they first met, he'd been a rookie copper in uniform. Emily had taken a keen interest in his career and helped him study for every exam he'd taken. Granted, he had a passion for catching villains and was good at it, so it wasn't all down to her. Once he'd attracted the interest of the higher-ups, there was plenty of opportunity for advancement, and Emily made sure he seized it. Losing her was like losing his right arm. But with no Emily to push him out, Hedley had been happy to stay put in Levenshulme.

One mug of strong, milky coffee later and he was ready to face whatever horrors the day threw at him. On cue he heard a shout from the hallway. It was Stuart.

"You should keep that door locked. I could be anyone," Stuart said. "The enemies you must have made over the years, you need to be more careful."

Hedley grinned. "None of my enemies know where I live. Anyway, I think you overestimate my importance. I'm hardly worth the effort."

"I can name a handful of Manchester villains who'd disagree. Rawlins and Murray, for example." Stuart cast his eyes around the pocket-sized sitting room, noting the discarded clothing on the ancient sofa and the empty fast-food containers stacked on the table. "You live like a slob. Ever considered doing a bit of tidying up?"

"What with the late nights at the pub plus the stress of the job, I have little time for housework," Hedley said. "Believe me, a widower's life isn't an easy one."

"Hedley, it's been four years since Emily died."

"Since Emily was murdered," said Hedley pointedly. "Let's have it right. I get by just fine. The job, a good whisky and a warm bed to flop into once the day is done, what more could I want? Anyway, you've no room to talk. I've seen your place just as messy. You want to get that Isabel wed so she can look after you."

"Not her. Isabel is a career woman. Job first, me second. She's made that quite clear."

Hedley shook his head. "Weird relationship, if you ask me. Any more complaints, or can we get going?"

Stuart nodded at the pile of empty cartons. "Looking at that rubbish, I'd advise you to watch your diet. You've got a cholesterol check next week and you don't want nursey on your case."

Hedley picked up a cushion from the sofa and tossed it at him. "Cheeky git. I'm working on it, all right?"

"But not fast enough, Hedley. I'm serious now. You're going downhill fast. You should take some time, look at your life and decide what's important. You'd hate it if you suddenly found yourself with no job. A heart attack would do that, and given the state of you it's a distinct possibility. You forget how many ambitious hopefuls are climbing the greasy pole trying to catch you up. One slip and some bright spark will be up there ahead of you."

Stuart was right. These days he seemed to be waging a constant struggle to stay one step ahead. The Rawlins case was still unsolved, and then there was Murray. In Rawlins' absence, he had been creating mayhem on the streets with his drug dealing, but the evidence Hedley needed for a conviction remained out of reach.

"Perhaps I will change my life. But not today." Hedley put on his jacket and checked the pockets — mobile and wallet present. "We should get going."

The pair got into Stuart's car and headed towards the A6 and the city centre.

"Go on then, Stuart, give me the gist."

"A body, male, dumped in the cellar of a disused building. You know, one of the empty shops at the top of Oldham Road. He had a grotty old duvet thrown over him and the body was well rotted. In fact, there's not a lot left of him but bone. This hot summer we've just had hasn't helped either."

"Any identification on him?" Hedley asked.

"Not that Rufus has found yet, but he's still got a suit hanging off his bones. One interesting thing. The building he was found in and the one next door belong to Dean Rawlins."

Interesting indeed, but did it mean anything in the scheme of things? Rawlins owned numerous buildings in this city. None of them were much cop and were mostly used as drug dens.

"Has Rufus determined how he died yet?" Dr Rufus Kane was the pathologist.

"Shot through the head," Stuart said. "One bullet, he says. He also said that it will be hard to tell if he tried to fight back. The flesh on the body is too far gone."

"Do we have any idea of a timescale?" Hedley asked.

"Rufus reckons he's been there at least twelve months, possibly more. The post-mortem will give him a clearer picture. One thing we do know, he was killed where he was found. The blood splatters on the walls tell us that. Although forensics will have to make sure it is the victim's blood."

"Perhaps he was one of Manchester's great unwashed? Some homeless bloke who'd found himself a dry place to doss down for the night and got unlucky?"

"Don't think so," Stuart said. "According to Rufus, that suit he's wearing is expensive, could even be hand-made."

"Sounds like a robbery, in that case," Hedley said.

"I've got Lou checking missing person reports," Stuart said. "She gets something, she'll call."

DC Louise Calvert was known as Lou to the team.

Despite the traffic, it took only minutes to reach the location. Stuart pulled up beside the taped-off area. Dozens of onlookers were watching the goings on from the sidelines, including a couple Hedley recognised as being from the press. One of them was Millicent Austin, a woman he knew well. She waved and shouted to him.

"Superintendent Sharpe! Hedley, how about a few words," she asked.

Hedley waved a hand. "Later," he shouted back with a nod.

"Any closer and you get covered up," Rufus insisted.

Hedley took the proffered paper suit, wriggled his bulk into it and approached the body.

"Got anything more?" he asked Rufus.

"I've given your inspector everything I have so far. Ask again when he's on the slab."

"Any belongings found on him? Nearby?" Hedley asked, casting his eyes around.

"We've found nothing in his pockets. There's the duvet, of course. I presume he didn't bring it with him. It's old and filthy, out of keeping with the way he's dressed. But the dirt on it isn't from the decomposition of the body, so it must have been thrown over him recently," Rufus said.

Hedley's heart sank. Just the body, no belongings, so nothing to go on. "Will we get prints?"

"His fingers are non-existent, but we will get DNA from the long bones if nothing else," Rufus said. "It's been hot, the flies and a myriad of other flying creatures have got in here. Over time they've feasted on the poor bugger; his hands were just another thing to nibble on."

In that case, they were reliant on DNA. Hedley frowned. All very well, provided there was a match on the database. If there wasn't, they were scuppered.

CHAPTER SEVEN

The Major Crime Division was housed in a sprawling police station in Ardwick. Some of it was newly built and state of the art, other parts dated back to Victorian times. Hedley and his team had their office in the old part of the building. He made his way up to the second floor and into his domain, a glass-walled office in the far corner of the room. He was gasping and rubbing his chest by the time he'd clambered up the staircase. The lift on this side of the building had been out of action for three months now. If someone didn't fix it soon, those stairs would be the death of him.

Hedley sat down, logged on to the system and stared up at the man standing empty-handed in front of him. "I thought you were fetching coffee. What happened?"

Stuart thrust a sheet of paper at his boss. "I thought this might be more important. Take a look."

A quick glimpse and Hedley shook his head. "This has nothing to do with us. It belongs to the local force out in the sticks, let them deal with it. It isn't even a genuine baby-snatch. It says here that the father told the uniformed officer who attended that there never was an infant, and that his wife has . . . well, problems."

"Look at the address, Hedley," Stuart said. "Now tell me the locals can deal with it."

It took Hedley a few seconds to take it in. "Bloody hell! That's Dean Rawlins' house in Saddleworth. What're they doing living there?"

"Rawlins has been missing for a year or more ever since he did a disappearing act the night before his court appearance. He simply melted into thin air, if you remember. I can only presume that the property has been sold or rented out. It'll have been tricky though, lots of legal jiggery pokery because it was probably still in Rawlins' name. And with him not being around to sign any documents — well, you take my point."

Hedley rattled the paper at his DI. "Check that one, will you? We've got the poor bastard from this morning to sort. He's lying in the morgue half eaten by insects. We can't just shelve him because of this."

"We can't just ignore it either. The Rawlins case is mega important, and it's still outstanding. He was up on a double murder charge, don't forget. And since he disappeared, we've had intelligence about that diamond robbery he was suspected of being involved in. Plus, there's the two officers charged with guarding him. One was battered about the head so hard he can no longer work, and the other is on light duties. That solicitor who was watching him has become a jibbering idiot."

"Okay, I take your point." Hedley checked the time. A trip out to Saddleworth and back would take a while. He picked up his desk phone and rang the morgue. He needed a quick word with Rufus Kane, to find out when he'd have the PM results.

"It'll be tomorrow morning," Kane confirmed. "Jack has ballistics on the job and his team is taking a close look at where the victim was found. He wants to make sure we've gathered everything that might possibly help us identify him." Dr Jack Lambert was a forensics expert who knew his job.

"Okay, we'll get on with our side of things. Let me know when you've got owt." Hedley put the phone down. "I hope for their sakes that this house sale or rental is all above board. Someone should have warned the buyer, told them what a psycho Rawlins is. I wish someone had warned me — look what happened to my Emily."

Stuart shook his head. "That was never proved, Hedley. We found no evidence that Rawlins had anything to do with your wife's death."

Hedley slapped his ample belly. "My gut tells me he did. You know what a piece of work he is. Getting at me through Emily is just the sort of thing he'd do."

"We'd better get on with it, the day's rattling on," Stuart said quickly.

Hedley got cumbrously to his feet. He'd just put his jacket on when DC Louise Calvert knocked on his door.

"There have been over five hundred reports of missing men during the last nine months, sir. Want me to check on them all?"

Hedley shook his head. "That'd take too long. We'll wait and see what Rufus comes up with. That suit the victim was wearing suggests he had money. If you want to narrow the list down, you might start there."

Stuart had taken the list from her and was studying it. All the surnames were in alphabetical order. "You know who's missing off here, don't you?"

"I added everyone that came up," Lou said.

"What about Dean Rawlins?"

Hedley looked up from his desk, a quizzical look on his face. "You're suggesting that the villain has been lying dead all this time?" he said. "Well, well. If that's true, it'll make my day."

CHAPTER EIGHT

"Why didn't you ever seek help, tell someone about Simon?" Brenda asked. "What he's doing is the worst type of coercive control. You don't have to take it, you know. There are counsellors, people you can speak to who will give you sound advice."

Chloe looked at her neighbour. It was all so simple to her, but she didn't know the whole story and no way could Chloe tell her. "He's always maintained that doing things his way is for the best."

Brenda looked mystified. "Best for who? Certainly not you."

Chloe shook her head. She'd said too much, had to make an excuse. "It's the tablets, they make me confused." She had already decided not to take them anymore. But hiding them under her tongue hadn't worked. Simon was on to that one. Yesterday afternoon, he'd taken her by the throat and shaken her until they went down. She'd waited until he'd left the house and then stuck her fingers down her throat and vomited them up.

Chloe didn't want Brenda interrogating her either. Why couldn't people leave her alone? It was too early, not yet eleven in the morning, and the questions were coming thick and fast. Brenda meant well but it was all too much.

"Simon means well," she said. "I should trust him more. What you said about control, that isn't right either. I often get things wrong, which annoys him. It's down to the pills. They make me see things that aren't always real."

"What about your child? Surely he realises that you can't just wipe her from your memory."

"He says I should forget Lily, get over her and move on. We'll both move on together."

"Yes, but that's not what's happened, is it? It seems to me that he's easily put it all behind him but isn't prepared to get you the help you need."

Brenda was right, of course. Like a lot of women, Chloe knew she needed help, but not in the way her neighbour meant.

"I might have just met him but I can see right through him. The man's a louse. Sorry, Chloe, but he is. He's no idea what you've been through. And if yesterday is anything to go by, you're still confused and upset over what happened with the baby."

"Simon is complicated. He does things that people don't always understand or agree with," Chloe said. "But he's usually right in the end. I just have to trust him."

But Brenda kept giving her these disbelieving looks. If only she'd just go away and leave her on her own. In her increasing agitation she was rubbing at her arm. Brenda glanced at her hand and let out a gasp.

"There's blood on your hand. You're hurt." Brenda reached forward, rolled up Chloe's sleeve and examined the injuries.

Chloe pulled away. "No. I don't want you to see."

But Brenda wasn't giving up. She stared in disbelief at the many small cuts running up her forearm. "You did this. You're cutting yourself, aren't you? A couple of them are recent, they're still bleeding. They need looking at."

"Don't fuss, they'll heal in time. They usually do."

"That arm tells me you definitely need help." The soft tone of her voice made Chloe wince. She didn't want this, didn't want her kindness.

"It's something I've never been able to understand. How can anyone want to hurt themselves, take a blade to their own flesh?"

Would Brenda understand if she told her the truth? Chloe decided not to even try. "I do what I must to get me through."

"But Simon must have noticed, surely?"

"He doesn't take it seriously. He says I'm a mixed-up idiot who deserves the pain I inflict on myself."

Avoiding Brenda's astonished gaze, Chloe turned her back and went into the sitting room, where she began to move things off the cluttered sofa so that she could sit down.

But Brenda followed her. "Seriously, you really do need help. Where is Simon anyway? He should be here. His car's not on the drive — in fact, when I think about it, it hasn't been there all night."

Chloe shrugged. "He has been back. He went out after the police had gone and didn't return until late, then he left again early this morning. He's a busy man."

Brenda's face clouded with disbelief, a look that meant more explaining, more lies. Chloe was tired of it all.

"He should be with you," Brenda said. "Look at the state you're in. Those cuts are recent, within the last few hours, if I'm not mistaken. You're in no fit state to be left alone. If he'd said something I would gladly have stayed with you."

"That's very kind but I took my pills and slept through." Chloe gave Brenda a small smile. More lies, but what else could she say? She couldn't tell her the truth, that was out of the question. Simon was a brutal, unforgiving man who scared the life out of her. But for now, she needed to stay with him. No way could she admit that to her new neighbour. Chloe wondered how long she could keep it up. Brenda was a perceptive woman. She'd already seen right through their so-called relationship. She mustn't see more.

She tried again. "Yesterday I allowed my emotions to get the upper hand, but I'm better now. I'll sort my head out and Simon will come back when he's ready."

"Sort your head out," Brenda scoffed. "Have you heard yourself? After what you've been through, that's rubbish and you know it. What you need is professional help, someone to talk things over with."

"I don't want to talk about Lily," Chloe insisted. "It's too upsetting for both me and Simon. I know he hurts too."

She spoke convincingly. Chloe was becoming adept at not telling the truth.

Lily was no lie. She'd been real enough. It felt like a lifetime ago since she'd held her baby, but if Lily had lived, she'd be twelve weeks old. There were times when Chloe could sense her presence, hear her cries, and then the need to take care of her was so powerful it hurt.

"D'you have keepsakes from the birth? Handprints, photos and the like?"

Chloe nodded. "Somewhere among this little lot. Which is why I want to get everything sorted and in its place."

"I can help you, if you like," Brenda offered. "And we have a brilliant medical practice in the village. You should register, make an appointment. They'll sort counselling for you. In fact, I work as a part-time counsellor there myself. I could arrange something for you."

"I'll see what Simon says when he gets home."

"You don't have to live in his shadow, you know. Even though I've only just met him, I can see he gives you no freedom."

Chloe didn't reply. How could she? Brenda was right, and if everything went to plan, Brenda's views on Simon could be extremely useful.

"Have you ever considered that you'd be better off without him?" Brenda asked.

Her words made Chloe smile. When had she not? However, life wasn't that simple. Brenda didn't know the half of it. "He'd never let me go. He's a possessive man, proud, too. His wife couldn't possibly leave him. How would he explain it to friends and family?"

"In that case, he should try taking better care of you."

Chloe sat on the sofa and stuck her feet up on one of the packing cases. She'd had a restless night and needed sleep. "I might go back to bed for an hour, give the day another go a bit later."

"Why not ring Simon's mobile, find out where he's got to?"

Chloe shook her head. The last thing she wanted was him coming back. Life was better with Simon out of the way. "He'll return soon enough," she yawned.

Brenda was staring out of the front window. "A car has just pulled up outside. It's not Simon's sleek number either. Who d'you think it is?"

Chloe didn't know what to think, and anyway, she was only half listening. She'd closed her eyes and was a mere whisper away from drifting off into another world when Brenda's words rolled around her head like red warning beacons.

Two strange men.

She was hauled back into the here and now by a sudden fearful thought. It was too soon, they couldn't know yet. This meant trouble.

CHAPTER NINE

The doorbell rang. Chloe, her heart in her mouth, waited for Brenda to answer it, praying it had nothing to do with Simon.

"This is Superintendent Sharpe and DI Vasey from the Major Crime Division," Brenda announced. "They'd like a word with you."

Chloe hardly knew Brenda, but she knew enough to realise that Brenda was deeply worried about this visit. Two detectives, so whatever this was about, it was serious, and therefore could only be about Simon. Chloe was suddenly afraid. She'd no idea what the two detectives were about to ask but guessed that their questions might be difficult to answer. There was so much about Simon and his life that she didn't know anything about.

"Is this, er, about my husband?" she asked.

"No, we just have a few routine questions," Hedley assured her, his tone measured.

"It's just that you're high-ranking detectives," Chloe said. "You wouldn't come here for no reason."

Hedley nodded. Bright woman. "You're right. We do have our reasons. We get the right answers and we'll leave you in peace. We're not here about your husband but about this house. Can you tell us who you bought it or are renting it from."

Chloe looked from one detective to the other. The tall one had his pen and notebook poised. The problem was, she'd no idea what to tell them, nor why this information should be so important. Worse than that, they were unlikely to believe her answer.

"I've no idea."

The words hung in the air for a few moments. Just as she'd thought, the detectives looked doubtful.

"You mean you never met the seller or landlord?" the tall one asked.

He had mousey blond hair and the most brilliant blue eyes Chloe had ever seen. She stared at them, transfixed, thinking about the implications of his question and the answer she was about to give.

"I didn't see the house until we moved in. My husband, Simon, dealt with everything." She'd said it as if it was the most normal thing in the world, but from the doubtful look on the two men's faces, she could see they didn't believe her. Fair enough; that sort of thing didn't go on in this day and age.

"And you went along with that?" Hedley asked. "Weren't you curious? Didn't you ask questions? At least you must have wanted to know where the house was located."

Chloe felt panic start to grip her. Even if she told the truth, this man would never understand. "I've been ill," she said. "My husband didn't want to worry me with the details of the move. We both wanted a new start in a new area, and I simply left everything to him."

Brenda butted in. "Chloe's right. That's what yesterday was all about." She gave Chloe an apologetic smile. "She had a blip, and not knowing the truth of what had actually happened to the infant, I called the police."

Hedley nodded. She wasn't telling him anything he didn't already know. "Given that you live in the avenue, perhaps you knew the people who used to own this house?"

"Yes. Dean and his girlfriend, Della Barlow," she said. "I didn't know Dean that well but me and Della were quite close, we often had lunch and shopped together."

"So she must have mentioned that they were moving out," Hedley said.

Brenda shook her head. "That's the odd bit. I didn't even realise they'd gone. Me and Della had appointments booked at the beauty salon that morning. I rang her to arrange when to meet but got no reply. Next thing I know, there's police and people in white suits all over the place. I never did get to the bottom of it."

"What was your impression of Dean Rawlins?" Stuart asked.

"He was a lot of fun. Never backward at putting his hand in his pocket. He treated the whole Avenue to a slap-up do a couple of Christmases ago. It must have cost him a packet."

"Didn't you ever wonder where all his money came from?" Stuart asked.

"His job, I suppose. He always seemed well-heeled — you know, big car and holidays abroad."

"Do you know what he did for a living?" Hedley asked.

"Della said he was in finance — whatever that means. I didn't pry." She smiled. "I didn't want to appear like some nosey cow."

Hedley turned to Chloe. "We will need to speak to your husband. I'd like to know how the house came under new occupancy when the owner hasn't been seen or heard of for over a year."

Chloe's stomach began to churn. She didn't need this. "I'm sure it'll be all right. My husband searched long and hard for just the perfect place. When he found this house, he knew it was the right one. He won't have made a mistake."

Chloe could see from his expression that the superintendent thought her a fool. Someone who was happy to have no say in what happened within her marriage. "You have to appreciate how things are. Simon is a busy man. He too works in finance and his job is pretty stressful. I often don't see him until late."

"Where is his office, Mrs Todd?" Stuart Vasey asked.

She waved a hand vaguely. "In town. Somewhere on the Quays."

"And the name of the firm he works for?"

Chloe said nothing. She looked away. Fancy not knowing such basic information. They must think her really stupid. But the fact was, Simon had never told her.

"Okay, I admit I don't know. Simon is used to getting his own way. He needed to get the move sorted, so I just went along with him." She smiled brightly at the detectives. "Simon is a good man, all he wants is for me to be happy. And he hasn't done too badly. This house is great. There's plenty of room and I'm sure we'll both come to love it in time."

"Make sure your husband rings me as soon as he gets in," Hedley said, handing her his card. "It is important. If I don't hear from him, we will be back."

This sounded like a threat. She had to get the next bit just right, and on cue the hot tears glistened on her cheeks. "I'm sorry. I've had a bad couple of days. My husband is protective. He keeps all the difficult legal stuff from me, and I'm grateful."

Chloe couldn't have the police becoming involved. She had to ensure they got the information they'd asked for. "I'll speak to him when he comes home. I'm sure he'll ring or send you a message."

Brenda showed the pair out. "It'll just be an admin mix-up. I wouldn't worry," she said when she returned.

"Things are never that simple with Simon. There will be a reason why he wanted us to live in this particular house, Brenda. I have no idea what that is yet, but I intend to do my best to find out."

The lie appeared to convince her. Chloe knew exactly why they were here. But it was important to have Brenda well and truly on her side.

CHAPTER TEN

Standing on the drive, Stuart gazed around and gave a little whistle. "Take a look at the property up here. This avenue alone must be worth a fortune."

"Yep," said Hedley. "Manchester's on the up — well, parts of it."

"If you're talking Ancoats, forget it," Stuart scoffed. "A mate of mine had his clobber stolen from the back seat of his car last week, in a secure car park, too. He's renting one of those swanky, warehouse-style apartments. Just goes to show, you can posh it up all you like but Ancoats will always be Ancoats."

Hedley smiled. "We live in hard times, don't forget. That's not an excuse but it doesn't make our lives any easier."

"Doesn't seem to be touching the folk around here much," Stuart said.

"What did you make of the bewildered wife?" Hedley asked, getting into the car. "How can a young woman move into a house she's never seen, in an unfamiliar area, without any idea of who they'd bought the property from? The whole thing stinks to me."

"Granted it's weird, but some relationships are like that."

"What you're saying is that he's just bossy. Makes her keep her nose out and her mouth shut."

"I reckon the neighbour has cottoned on to what things are like, sir."

"She could prove useful if we don't get the right answers from the bossy husband. We'll see what he has to say for himself first and go from there."

"You're thinking the husband is or was involved with Rawlins?"

"Could be the reason the Todds are living in the villain's house," Hedley said. "Rawlins certainly hasn't been around to sign any documents, has he?"

"I'll give the land registry a nudge when we're back at the station," Stuart suggested.

"You do that. And speak to that solicitor of Rawlins'. Most of all I want to speak to Simon Todd, get the measure of the man, weigh him up."

"What she told us, all that guff about knowing nothing about her husband's search for a house. D'you believe any of that?"

"Not a word," Hedley said. "She's obviously troubled about something. Did you see those cuts on her arms? A sure sign she's got problems."

"From what she told us, I'd say her problem is a controlling husband who discusses nothing with her," Stuart said.

Hedley wasn't so sure. "If her old man had been involved with Rawlins at any time, that's a good enough reason for her silence. Anyway, I'll reserve judgement until I know more about her."

"Well, I feel sorry for her," Stuart said. "She doesn't strike me as the kind of woman who'd be involved with someone like Rawlins."

Hedley didn't know what to make of her. Was she the bullied wife, scared of her own shadow, or was that all an act? Time would tell. "When we get back, organise a patrol car to take a few turns around that estate, keep an eye out. I also want Simon Todd's background looking at. Hers too. Get a complete profile and find out what both of them were doing prior to getting together — I want to know everything about that pair."

Stuart grinned. "You really have taken against them."

"She could be lying through her teeth. It's a strange set-up and I'm curious. There's no way what they've got can be called a marriage. If she's to be believed, that woman knows absolutely nothing about the man she married. Strikes me it's a marriage in name only. What I can't work out is why. Why live with a man like Todd if there's no proper relationship?"

"Her reactions might have been a little off beam, but for now I'll put that down to her being terrified of something or someone, possibly us," Stuart said. "Chloe Todd isn't stupid, you can see that, regardless of the impression she wants to give us. She must know or suspect something about her husband's life, and she might even know about Rawlins."

"What d'you reckon the baby thing's all about?" Hedley asked.

"She had an infant, stillborn. That's a huge trauma for any woman."

Hedley nodded. He reckoned Stuart was right. "Find out about that too while you're digging around in 'Todd world'."

It took them an hour before they finally pulled into the station car park. "Forget the pretty surroundings, now you know why I prefer to live local," Hedley said. "Imagine having to make that journey twice a day."

"Makes you wonder why the Todds moved all the way out to Saddleworth. According to the wife, our absent husband works on the Quays."

"Rawlins had an office there too until he disappeared, but it was merely a front. I would like to know if anyone else took that office on — our missing husband, for instance," Hedley said.

"Bit of a long shot. And don't forget the dead bloke," Stuart said as they climbed the stairs.

Hedley didn't need reminding. He was well aware of their workload. Nonetheless, Stuart had a point. The murder must take priority. Taking his mobile from his pocket, he rang the morgue. "Rufus, what've you got for me?"

"Shot in the head, as we know. I'd put him in the forty-something age range. He was tall, six foot. We'll test for drug use and let you know. I've sent off a sample of bone marrow for DNA testing."

All very thorough. "Anything to give us a clue as to who he was?"

"Not yet, but his clothing was on the expensive side, particularly that suit. I was able to make out the label; it was made by Axford's, the men's tailors on Deansgate. That might be a starting point. The suit is reasonably new, too."

"Thanks, Rufus. If I find out who he is, I'll let you know." Hedley wasn't too sure about how much help the suit would be. If the man had been homeless he could have got it from one of the shelters or been given it by a concerned do-gooder. He turned to Stuart. "The sod that murdered him knew what he was doing. It won't be easy to pin a name on our poor victim."

CHAPTER ELEVEN

On entering the incident room, Hedley scanned the board. There was still precious little on it. "Come on, you lot, you have to do better than this," he barked at the team. "I want solid information, facts I can use." He clapped his hands. "Shake a leg and get me the answers. Who is our body? What was he into that got him killed? And let's have a list of suspects."

DC Louise Calvert looked up from her computer. "I've gone through that list again like you suggested, but there are still plenty of names on it."

"Forensics is our best bet," Hedley told her. "Wait and see what they give us."

"That duvet," Stuart said, joining them. "Where did it come from, I wonder? The area around Piccadilly Gardens and the alleys off Oldham Road are a regular venue for rough sleepers, so it's feasible that one of them left it there."

"Perhaps we should have a word?" Hedley suggested. He turned to DC Ryan Ogden. "A task for you, lad. Take a wander round later and ask a few pertinent questions. Find out if anyone has used that cellar recently."

Hedley retired to his office, deep in thought. What were they looking at? Was this some elaborate hit cooked up by

Murray to rid himself of a long-time nuisance? And was that nuisance Rawlins? Or had someone else left the poor sod to rot in that cellar? A bullet to the brain was certainly Murray's style — problem was, it was Rawlins' too. One thing was obvious to Hedley: whoever the killer was, he wasn't keen for anyone to know who the victim was , or he wouldn't have hidden him away like that, removing anything that might identify the poor bugger.

Hedley needed a word with Professor Gabriel Stubbs, Jack Lambert's boss and the senior forensic scientist at the station. He and his team worked closely with pathology, operating from a suite of state-of-the-art labs down in the basement.

"The bullet from this morning, Gabe. Has it been found?"

"From the mess the bones of the face are in, I doubt it's still inside his head. I've got my people looking at that cellar and the surroundings. If it's there, they'll find it."

"If they do, would you check for matches on the database, particularly to any bullets found in cases where we've suspected either Murray or Rawlins have been involved," Hedley said.

"Rawlins. Now there's a name I've not heard in a month or so. Back, is he?"

"I certainly hope not, but my guts are telling me something's wrong, and his name's come up recently."

"Leave it with me, Hedley. You should have a word with Rufus. He's got some more results for you."

As Hedley put the phone down, Stuart entered the office bearing coffee and sandwiches, and with a printout between his teeth. Eyeing the snacks, Hedley decided to leave the pathologist until he'd eaten. An excellent pathologist, Rufus did tend to get a bit overinvolved in detailed descriptions of what had been done to the flesh of the dead who turned up in his lab. He'd call when he had something lining his stomach.

"I rang that tailor on Deansgate, described the suit and sent an image of the label," Stuart began, putting cup and sandwich on Hedley's desk and taking the page from his mouth. "They've just emailed me this. I've also spoken to Rawlins' solicitor, who says he's heard nothing from him this last year."

Hedley wasn't listening. Carefully, he peeled open the sandwich and examined the contents. It was some sort of cooked meat and didn't look too fresh. He bit into it tentatively. "What's this? Tastes like nothing I'd like to describe."

Stuart smiled. "Tongue, with a generous dollop of mustard. It was all they had left."

Hedley tossed the concoction back into the packet. "Brings back weird memories, that does. When I was a child, I used to visit a great aunt of mine. It was her that first gave me tongue sandwiches. Bought them in special, she did, as a treat. I had to sit on a straight-backed chair at the table while she watched me swallow every bite. Leave any and I got me legs slapped and the silent treatment." He pulled a face. "She lived in a little terrace in Longsight — you know the sort, one back yard between four houses, with the lavvies stuck in the corner. I never did go upstairs in that house, not once. When she died, she left me the two pot dogs she kept on the mantlepiece."

"I bet you don't go a bundle on tripe either," Stuart said with a grin.

Hedley was about to utter a witty reply when his mobile rang. It was Millicent Austin from the *Recorder*. If she was after information about this morning's murder, she was out of luck. But that wasn't it at all.

"I thought you should know, Hedley," she said. "Cowboy's dead. He was found thirty minutes ago in the cellar next to where the other body was discovered. Your lot were unable to get in there until now because the door had a load of concrete rubble dumped in front of it. My source told me he'd been shot once in the head, poor man."

Cowboy was a well-known homeless man who hung around Piccadilly, so named because he always wore a black and gold cowboy hat. In his sixties, he was one of the longstanding homeless, and took a lot of the younger ones under his wing. Cowboy was unusual in that he was dead set against drugs. He had no problem with drink, but drug taking of any sort, particularly the new fashion for spice, sent him into a rage.

"You're sure it's him?" Hedley asked Millicent. "Who'd take against Cowboy?"

"It's definitely him. My source knows him well. Your uniformed lot are at the scene. Want to give me a quote now, Hedley? Go on. The public are getting restless. City centre Manchester is fast becoming murder central."

Hedley hung up on her. Millicent would have to wait. He'd deal with the press later. He swallowed some coffee and contemplated what this news meant. Was Cowboy's death connected to that of their other victim? If so, what possible part did a penniless, homeless man have to play? Probably none, he concluded. More likely the poor old man was in the wrong place at the wrong time, saw too much.

He picked up the phone and called Gabriel again. "You know the duvet brought in from the tram shelter? Check it for any DNA belonging to a homeless man known around the city as Cowboy. He's been busted for drunk and disorderly in the past, so his details will be on the database."

"Cowboy, you say? I know of him — Albert Roberts. I'll check of course, it's part of the process, but we've found a number of items hidden inside the duvet. An engraved watch and a silver cigarette case, both bearing the name Cowboy."

So he did know something about the man in the other cellar, and had paid the ultimate price.

"There is something else," Gabriel added. "The duvet was thrown over the first victim within the last couple of days and, like I said, not when he was killed."

"How d'you know?" Hedley asked.

"To put it bluntly, the duvet wasn't stuck to the body, nor was it soiled with the fluids from the decaying corpse."

Hedley pulled a face, the images forming in his head turning his stomach. "So, someone went back there after the murder, saw the body and decided to cover it. Possibly Cowboy, given that it's his duvet. But what did he do to get himself shot, I wonder?"

"That's your problem, I'm afraid. All I can give you are the forensic facts," Gabriel said.

Call over, Hedley looked up at Stuart. "We've got another body. Shape yourself — we need to go."

But Stuart had his eyes on the printout. "Hang on, Hedley. That suit the victim was wearing — the tailors have only made three from that fabric in the last two years, and one of them was for Dean Rawlins."

CHAPTER TWELVE

Though Chloe had told Brenda she'd be fine on her own, her neighbour insisted on staying. She made them both a cup of tea and put away the few kitchen items that Chloe had left on a packing case.

"You should ring Simon, tell him what's happened," she said. "That detective definitely wants a word and he's not going to just let it drop."

Chloe shook her head. "Simon doesn't like me ringing him when he's at work."

"I think you should make an exception today," Brenda said. "I'm sure he'll understand."

Why wouldn't this woman be told? Even if she told Brenda the truth, she still wouldn't get it How could she? "I think I'll have that lie down now," she said to get rid of her. "D'you mind?"

Brenda pulled a face. "You want me to go. Fair enough, but this won't just go away. Be sure to tell him when he comes home. Delay, and those detectives will be back."

Given the way she felt about her husband, she hoped he wouldn't be home too soon. Chloe was fast coming to realise that life with Simon wasn't what she needed. She wanted out. But that required some thought.

She accompanied Brenda to the front door. "Thank you for being here, and for the advice. I will take it on board, I promise." Easily said. Simon was one thing, but where to find the information the police wanted? She had no idea.

Brenda gave her a hug. "It's okay, love. I'm happy to help. I just want you to be less stressed, that's all."

Chloe watched her cross the road and disappear into her house. Then she locked and bolted the door. She needed to be alone, to think, to gather her thoughts. Things could get tricky and she had to work out what to do, what answers to give the police. Despite all her offers of help, there was no way she could discuss her problems with Brenda.

Chloe was halfway up the stairs when the doorbell rang. She swore under her breath. Brenda must have forgotten something. But when she opened the front door, it wasn't her neighbour standing on the doorstep. It was Selina Harris.

"You look like shit," Selina said at once. "Sorry, Chloe, but you do. What's the problem — all the fresh air round here not suiting?" Pushing past her, Selina strode down the hallway and into the sitting room. "Got any booze? A large glass of bubbly would go down nicely. We should celebrate the two of us meeting up again after all this time."

Chloe shook her head. A visit from Selina was the last thing she wanted. Didn't she realise how much Chloe hated her? "Bubbly? How dare you. We've got nothing to celebrate. I want you to leave." Her tone was cold, hard, and she was pleased to see Selina wince. In all the time she'd known her, Chloe had rarely had this effect on Selina.

"I'm trying to be nice, Chloe. New house, new people. I thought you'd like having an old friend around. Besides, we need to talk."

"We've nothing to talk about," Chloe said flatly.

"That's where you're wrong. There's this house for a start. I bet you didn't know it belongs to me."

Chloe was stunned. This was some sick joke, surely. There was no way that could be true. She stared at Selina, looking for a trace of humour, with a growing feeling that she could be speaking the truth. Why else would she bother coming here? "You're lying. Simon found this house for us. It's to be our forever home." True, Simon had found the house, but he had never explained how, or what the arrangements were for paying for it. Chloe had been suspicious about it from the start, and now it seemed the police were too. As for it being their 'forever home', nothing was further from the truth.

Selina laughed. "Ooh, how romantic. Not like the Simon I know. He doesn't do 'forever'." She gave Chloe a sly look. "But you know that. You know very well that Simon doesn't have a romantic bone in his body. This marriage of yours is nothing but a sham. I bet you're both being paid to do the loving couple thing. Want to tell me about it? Who's paying you?"

How had she stumbled on the truth? First the police and now Selina. Chloe's life was fast spiralling into a nightmare. "My relationship with Simon is none of your business."

"Fair enough," Selina said. "But tell me, how did you find this place?"

"Simon found it. He searched the property market for weeks before settling on this one."

"Bullshit. It's a good choice, I grant you that, but he didn't find it on the property market." Selina plonked herself down on the sofa and crossed her long legs. "You see, this house was never on the market. I can appreciate why he'd like it — you too. But you can't stay here. Believe me, Chloe, this house has not been sold or rented to anyone. In effect, you're squatters."

"Why should I believe you?" Chloe said. "You're a liar, always have been. Simon knows what he's doing."

"Do you know who the previous owner was? Didn't Simon tell you?"

Chloe sniffed. "I don't know what you're talking about. The purchase was above board. Simon will have made sure of that."

"That's where you're wrong," Selina said. "For starters, he never told me he was moving in. Thus, as I said, you're squatting."

"Why should he tell you? You've nothing to do with it."

"You're not listening, Chloe. I *own* this house. And I want you out."

Chloe stared at her. Selina had to be playing some elaborate joke.

"I can see from your face that you don't believe me. I used to live here. I quite liked the place, actually. The neighbours are a great crowd, particularly Brenda."

Chloe was hearing warning bells. Selina knew Brenda. Perhaps she wasn't lying after all, and she had lived here. "I'm just happy to be wherever Simon is," she said lamely.

"Don't come with the good little wife act. It doesn't suit you." Selina flashed those perfect teeth of hers. "If you still refuse to believe me, fine. Check the deeds."

Having this woman in her home unnerved Chloe. Selina had always had the power to make her feel inadequate. A weakness she'd never been able to shake. Somehow, Selina sapped her strength, her ability to both act and think straight. Chloe had always known that sooner or later their paths would have to cross once more, but she'd hoped it would be on her terms. Now Selina was in her face, and threatening the very foundation of everything she was struggling to do.

"You do know that this property was once owned by Dean Rawlins?"

Chloe nodded, Brenda had told her as much. But so what? Simon worked with the man. "In that case, Simon and Dean will have come to some arrangement."

"No, they didn't."

Selina sounded so positive that Chloe was thrown into doubt. She shook her head. "I don't believe you. And why would I need to look at the deeds? The solicitors would have dealt with all the legal stuff."

Selina smiled again. "What solicitors? Like I said, this house wasn't actually sold, Chloe. At best, Dean and Simon came up with some vague agreement between them. But that should not have happened because this house hasn't belonged to Dean for some considerable time."

Chloe stared at her. Selina had to be wrong, there had to be a mistake. "You're lying. Of course Dean owns it. Otherwise, how could he and Simon have arranged the transfer between them?"

"That's where you're wrong. Dean doesn't own it. Just over a year ago, the house was transferred into my name. I'm Dean's wife so it was all perfectly legal. And take my word for it, I haven't let it or sold it to anyone."

Now Chloe really was thrown. As far as she knew, Dean Rawlins didn't have a wife. But suppose Selina was telling the truth? "No, you're wrong. Simon and me have every right to live in this house. He signed all the relevant documents. He . . . he must have done."

Selina handed her a large buff envelope. "The deeds. Go on. Take a good look."

Chloe was confused. Acquiring this property was supposed to have been so simple — Simon had promised. Taking the paperwork from the envelope, she sat down opposite Selina and stared at it. She felt dazed; the words were written in legalese and made no sense. Finally, she looked up. "I don't understand, what does all this mean?"

"Obviously there are things about me, Simon and this house that you're unaware of," Selina said. "As the deeds plainly state, I'm the owner. I'm not trying to trick you."

This was one bombshell Chloe hadn't expected. She said nothing but simply stared at the woman. She knew about Rawlins and his reputation, of course she did. Simon had worked with him. She also knew that at one time there had been something between Rawlins and Selina, but she had no idea they'd actually married. The niggles were starting, building inside her head.

"Simon told me he bought this house in the usual way. Or maybe he's renting it?" Chloe was beginning to flounder. "But I'm sure he mentioned a mortgage."

"He's lying. Didn't you wonder how things could move so quick?" Selina said.

"I didn't think."

"Take my word for it, he does not own this house. He doesn't even have a legal rental agreement," Selina said.

"No, Simon wouldn't do something like that, not just move in. He and Dean must have come to some agreement between them."

"It's not up to Dean though, is it?" Selina retorted. "This is my house and I want it back."

"Dean won't like it."

"Probably not, but there's not a lot he can do, and if he tries to intimidate me, I'll have the police on him. I was married to him for eight months before I threw in the towel. I left him two years ago but we never actually got divorced. He took up with that Della woman and moved her in here. But when things got tough and he had the police on his tail and believed that he might have to do a runner, he wanted to make his assets safe, and that's when I suddenly became useful. As you will see from the document in your hand, Dean transferred ownership of this house into my name."

"But why didn't Simon say something?" Chloe wailed.

"You'll have to ask him. Simon worked for Dean. When Dean disappeared, I think Simon knew the house was empty and, being the sort of man he is, simply moved the pair of you in."

"He wouldn't do that."

"But that's exactly what he did do, Chloe. Your husband saw an opportunity and took it." Selina paused, giving Chloe time to consider her words. "You do know that no one has seen Dean for months now? Simon probably thought he was reasonably safe. Particularly if he had something to do with Dean's disappearance."

"Now you're the one who's stupid," Chloe said. "You're making out that Simon took advantage."

Selina shrugged. "If that's how you see it, fair enough."

"We can't leave this house. We love the place." It was a lie, but moving again so soon was not part of Chloe's plans.

"You're dreaming, Chloe. I own this house and I intend to sell it as soon as I can."

CHAPTER THIRTEEN

Chloe had heard enough. "I want you to leave now." Her voice was shaking. Why did this woman always reduce her to a trembling wreck? It had been the same at school. Selina was always there dripping poison into her ear.

"Sorry, no can do. Haven't you been listening to a word I've said, Chloe? This house belongs to me. I spoke to Simon about the situation on the day of Graham's funeral. He knows about my plans. Make no mistake, I'm serious about this. I want to sell it. I need to recoup some of the cash Rawlins owes me."

"Simon won't let you get away with it."

"What can he do? I'm still Dean Rawlins' wife, and as such I can call on all the help I need, legal and otherwise, to make it happen."

Chloe knew that 'otherwise' meant Dean Rawlins' heavy mob. "We will contact our solicitor, take advice."

"Take as much advice as you wish. Personally, if I was you, I wouldn't waste my money. You can keep those deeds, they're copies. The originals are locked away in the safe at my solicitor's office."

"How do we contact Dean Rawlins?" Chloe had found some firmness from somewhere. She stood straight, hands on hips, facing her old enemy. "We need to speak to him. Get his take on what's happened. I ask because there are all sorts of rumours circulating, some even have him dead."

Chloe fully expected that mouthful to get a reaction, and it did.

Selina, too, got to her feet, her eyes glinting as they faced each other. With anger, she said, "I hope that isn't true or we're all lost. Or have you forgotten?"

"Forgotten what?"

"Don't get coy with me. You know very well. Dean and Simon each hold part of the solution that will make us all rich."

Chloe shook her head. "I've no idea what you're talking about."

"Don't give me that," Selina spat.

"You're wrong. Simon doesn't discuss much with me."

"I think he'll have discussed this," Selina said. "The diamond robbery."

"Oh, that." Chloe shook her head. "I never really believed in that. Not the amount of money that was involved anyway."

"Well you should. I will need your help to get the combination out of Simon. Dean and he hold four digits each. Remember that? Stupid idea of Dean's, but he reckoned it was the only way they could stop one of them cheating the other."

Chloe shook her head. "I can't. Simon will never give those numbers to anyone, certainly not me."

"You'll just have to try harder, won't you?" Selina moved closer. "Once I catch up with Dean, I will do my part. He's careless and his memory is abysmal. He often writes things down. He will have done the same with his half of the combination. It'll be on a scrap of paper somewhere, either stuffed in one of his pockets or in that office of his. Either way I will get my hands on it."

"It can't be that simple," Chloe said. "Honestly, there's no way we can cheat them. It's just not worth it. Dean would kill us both."

"You're not thinking straight." Chloe watched Selina's body stiffen and her eyes grow narrow. A shiver slid down her spine. "You will do as you're told or suffer the consequences. I will get hold of the numbers Dean holds and you will get Simon's out of him, even if you have to threaten or drug him to do it."

"I can't," Chloe pleaded. "It won't matter what I do, he won't tell me."

"If he doesn't, if you fail me, you'll suffer," Selina warned.

"I don't care."

Selina took hold of Chloe's arm and dragged her into the kitchen. "Nice layout, isn't it? I designed it myself. I particularly like the cooker. It was state of the art when I lived here."

It took her just a moment to turn on one of the ceramic plates on the hob. "These get good and hot in no time, you'll know that." Selina smiled evilly. "But I wonder if you know what a mess they can make of human flesh."

Chloe heard the words but took several seconds to interpret them as a threat.

Selina pulled her closer to the cooker. "You're smaller and lighter than me, Chloe." She ran her fingers through Chloe's hair. "I turned it up full. Another few seconds and the hob will be as hot as it gets. I grab a handful of those long locks of yours and slam your pretty face hard into that glowing circle of pain. How long would it take to do real damage, d'you reckon? A few seconds? A minute? Not long before you're begging to help me. But it'll be too late then, because you, Chloe, will never be the same again." Selina's eyes gleamed and she continued to stroke Chloe's hair.

Seeing those eyes, Chloe realised the threat was real. She began to shake with sheer terror.

"I don't think you want that, do you? You're such a pretty little thing. It would be a shame to spoil those looks. Think of the pain, the dreadful disfiguration. Burns are easily infected, I'm told, and that makes them hard to treat. If you want to avoid all that, you know what to do. It's simple. Persuade Simon to give you those numbers."

Chloe knew there was no use arguing with her. But she also knew that there was no way Simon would just give her those numbers.

"Come on, help me. We could be rich," Selina whispered, still stroking Chloe's hair. "Think of that. You would be free to go anywhere. You wouldn't need to be tied to Simon anymore."

Chloe summoned all her strength and shook herself free of Selina's grip. She took a step back, her eyes on the hob, which was now glowing. Selina was staring at her, a strange look on her face. "We'll have no more questions about Dean's whereabouts. And you will do as I say."

"It's not going to happen, Selina. Neither Simon nor I will tell you what we know. Besides, I blab to you and Simon will kill me anyway."

"Your choice. It's either him or me. One of us will have that pleasure."

Chloe took a few more steps back. She had to do something, calm Selina down before things got completely out of hand.

"You don't use your married name, do you? Why not?" The words tumbled out of Chloe's mouth before she'd had time to think.

"What? Would you take his name if you were in my position and with Dean's reputation? Set yourself up as a target? I think not. I decided that keeping my own name was the safest option."

"What d'you intend to do now?" Chloe asked.

"Nothing. Yet." Selina flashed her another smile, turned off the hob and moved back into the sitting room. "Sorry about the threats, Chloe. But I'm not giving up. For a start, I want this house, so you and Simon must get out. And never forget that the diamond robbery was down to Dean. He was the brains and he provided the brawn. As his wife, I deserve my share."

"You're wrong," Chloe said. "Simon helped too. Dean isn't the only one with a brain, you know."

" Simon is an idiot. He's easily intimidated and he certainly isn't able to stand up to Dean and his thugs."

Chloe said nothing. Selina was right. Whenever Simon had come back from a meeting with Dean, he was a nervous wreck.

"We've only just moved in here. Where will we go?"

"I've no idea, and frankly I don't care. That's your problem. You need to wake up and see how things really are. Simon tried to get one over on Dean. He won't take kindly to that." She aimed a kick at one of the boxes lying about the room. "And I wouldn't bother unpacking that little lot. It'll be a complete waste of time." Selina gave her a smile. "Well, I've had my say. I'll leave you in peace now. I'm sure you've plenty to think about."

As soon as Selina closed the door behind her, Chloe started to shake. She'd just had one of the most frightening experiences of her life. Selina was insane. But mad or not, Chloe knew this wouldn't be the end of it. Whatever it took, Selina was determined to get her hands on the diamonds.

Chloe needed help. She went to the shelves by the window, looking for the card the fat detective with the nice eyes had given her. If she played this right, Selina could be behind bars before the end of the day.

CHAPTER FOURTEEN

Hedley was on the office phone when his mobile rang. "Get that, would you?"

Stuart Vasey picked up the mobile, which had been lying on the desk, and found himself speaking to a frantic Chloe Todd.

"She tried to kill me!" she screamed at him. "And she's promised to come back and finish the job. You have to help me."

He took the phone from his ear and muttered in Hedley's direction, "Trouble. Chloe Todd has had a visitor.

"Calm down," he said to Chloe. "We'll be with you shortly. Lock the doors and don't let anyone in until we get there."

"Don't leave me on my own, I'm frightened. I can't cope with it."

"What sort of trouble? What's she been up to now?" Hedley asked.

"Chloe Todd has been threatened by some woman. She's terrified out of her wits."

"Can't she get the husband to protect her — still missing, I suppose."

"The woman threatened to kill her. This is a police matter, Hedley."

Hedley saw the look on Stuart's face. "Why so worried?"

"She needs help. Surely you can see how the woman's fixed. We've not seen hide nor hair of the husband for days. And I'm *concerned*, not worried."

"Try telling your face that. You look as if some relative of yours has just died."

"It's putting up with you does that," Stuart retorted. "You're not the easiest person to work with, you know."

"I'm a realist. You want to try it sometime."

"What? And turn out like you? I prefer dealing out a bit of compassion. You should try *that* sometime."

"Cheeky bugger. Don't forget who's the superintendent in this relationship."

After a display of reckless driving with Stuart at the wheel, they were finally at the Todds' front door. Stuart bent and called out through the letterbox, "It's us."

Hedley stood behind him, shaking his head. "You're a right soft touch. This will be a fall-out over bugger all, you mark my words."

Chloe opened the door and, on seeing the detectives, heaved a sigh of relief. "I need protection," she screamed at them. "You have to help me. That woman meant what she said about killing me."

Hedley looked doubtful. "People get overwrought and say all sorts. Anyway, first things first. Do you know this woman?"

Chloe hung her head, unwilling to admit to knowing Selina. Better to tell them she was someone Simon knew. "I think Simon knows her. He works with her husband."

"Are your husband and this woman having an affair?"

As far as Hedley was concerned, this was a perfectly reasonable question but it annoyed Chloe Todd.

"Of course not. Simon wouldn't do such a thing."

"Can we come in, Mrs Todd?" Stuart asked. "We can hardly discuss this on the doorstep."

She stood aside for them to enter and locked the door behind them.

"You should ring your husband," Stuart told her. "Get him to come home. I'm sure he'll want to know what's happened so he can look after you."

Without answering, Chloe led the way into the kitchen, where she pointed to the cooker. "She turned on the hob and threatened to push my face onto it."

She began to cry, which made Hedley nervous. Weeping women weren't his thing. "When was this?"

"About an hour ago," Chloe said. "Just before I called you. She forced her way in. Bold as brass, she was."

"She must have wanted something to threaten you like that," Hedley said.

"This house," Chloe said. "That's what she wants. She told me she and her husband used to live here."

That got Hedley's interest. Rawlins had owned this place. "I know who owned this place, and a right piece of work he was."

"I know," Chloe admitted. "She told me he's a gangster and I wouldn't like having him or his wife on my back."

"We'll make sure that doesn't happen," Stuart said, getting himself a filthy look from Hedley for his trouble.

"You can't. Rawlins wants to get his hands on someone and no one can stop him."

Hedley noted the tears, the nervous shaking of her hands, but he still wasn't sure he believed her. There was something about Chloe Todd he didn't trust. "Does this woman have a name?"

"Selina Harris is what she said. At one time her and her husband both lived here, but then she left him."

"You seem to know a lot about her," Hedley said, raising an eyebrow.

"That's what she told me."

"D'you know where either of them live now?"

"I think Selina lives with a friend of Simon's called Gerald Jacks in Openshaw."

"We'll check it out and warn her off," Stuart said.

That got an immediate reaction from Chloe. "She needs more than warning off. You have to stop her, make sure she can't do anything like this again."

"Why did she come here and attack you?" Stuart asked.

"She wants the house back, simple as that."

Stuart nodded. It fitted with what they'd found out. "We can't leave you alone," he said. "We need to speak to your husband urgently."

Chloe shook her head. "He's at work. I've tried ringing him," she lied, "but I was told he was in a meeting."

"D'you have his mobile number? He has to know what's happened to you. This is one incident you have to tell him about," Stuart said.

Chloe's stomach was turning somersaults. So much for her lies. She was beginning to wish she hadn't called them. "I told you before, Simon doesn't like me disturbing him at work."

"Surely he wouldn't mind, given the circumstances. You need someone with you. Would you ring him, please?" Stuart asked firmly. "A quick chat and we'll leave you in peace. But I will arrange for a patrol car to watch the house."

"He'll be angry. I have strict instructions never to contact him at work."

"Please, Mrs Todd." Hedley's voice cut through the air like a knife. By now, irritation didn't begin to describe what he was feeling. "Stop messing us about and ring your husband. We need to speak to him and that's what we're going to do, whether you like it or not."

They both watched as Chloe took her phone from the coffee table and made the call. "See? He's not picking up. Like I said, he'll be busy."

"Can I have that?" Stuart Vasey asked.

Chloe passed the mobile over and he copied down Simon's number.

"When did you last see him?" he asked.

Chloe knew the expected response was 'this morning at breakfast', but the truth was she couldn't remember. "Look, the medication I take knocks me out. A couple of pills and I can sleep for hours. I think he was here earlier but I really can't be sure." More lies.

Hedley watched her closely, trying to weigh up her behaviour. She looked like a frightened kitten but that could just be for their benefit.

"I wasn't well yesterday. The pills are sometimes a necessity, I'm afraid."

Hedley shook his head. "I'd have a word with your doctor if I was you. Strikes me you could do with some different medication."

"If your husband doesn't come home soon, you should ask a neighbour to sit with you. Perhaps the woman who lives across the road?" Stuart suggested.

"Not a bad idea," Chloe said. "If that woman tries again, Brenda is just the person to stop her."

"This house," Hedley said, changing the subject. "Do you have any solicitors' letters, or better still, a sales or rental contract we can look at?"

Chloe shook her head. "I think Simon keeps things like that in his safe at work."

"You should know that if he doesn't phone me soon, I intend to issue a warrant for his arrest," Hedley said. "It's in your interests to speak to him and get him to ring me."

"What d'you intend to do about Selina Harris?" she asked.

"Any more nonsense and we'll issue a restraining order. That should clip her wings," Hedley said.

CHAPTER FIFTEEN

As soon as they were outside the house, Stuart tried the number Chloe had given him. "Unavailable, sir. I reckon he's turned the thing off."

"Or it was never turned on, or it wasn't working in the first place. All that guff about being attacked, I didn't see a mark on her, did you? If you ask me, that woman is taking the piss." Hedley's face was hard, his expression the one that said 'don't try my patience'. He got enough of such treatment from proper villains. Mind you, the Todd woman was doing a good impression of being one. "Dealing with Chloe Todd is like patting fog," he grumbled. "Did you contact the land registry?"

"Yes, they're going to email me the information later today."

"Seller and buyer? Copy of the deeds? We need the lot."

Stuart nodded. "Have you considered that Chloe might be telling the truth? That house did belong to Rawlins. If there was no proper agreement, his wife might well want it back."

Hedley pulled a face. "Too bloody reasonable, that's your trouble. Okay, I'll go with that — for now — but I still think the Todd woman is keeping something from us."

"What about the attack?" Stuart asked.

"The jury's out on that one. Then again, no woman can be wed to Rawlins and not pick up some of his ways. We'll take her to task over it, get her side of this sorry tale."

"We've got to find her first," Stuart said.

"The Todd woman gave us a lead on that one. About the only favour she's done us."

"D'you think Rawlins' ex will know what her husband was up to?"

Hedley climbed heavily into the car and threw Stuart the keys. "We'll be sure to ask her, but in my opinion, if those two men had anything to do with each other, then she had to have known about it."

"What about Simon Todd? He's got some cheek, moving into Rawlins' house like that," Stuart said.

"If he hasn't got the villain's permission. He must have thought it a safe move, that there was no chance of having Rawlins on his tail. Rawlins is missing, so it was convenient, cheap, and there was no flak to contend with. Even so, who d'you know who'd take advantage of Rawlins in such a way? But just in case there is some sort of agreement, when we catch up with him we ask him what he knows about Rawlins' whereabouts. That villain is number one on our most wanted list. Two outstanding murders, a missing man, two battered coppers and a diamond robbery."

"*Alleged* murders, and as for the diamond robbery, we were never one hundred percent sure that was down to Rawlins and his mob. What we need is facts not theories," Stuart said.

"What we need, laddie, is to get our mitts on Todd and shake the bloody truth out of him. If Todd has been in communication with Rawlins at any time in the last year, then I want to know about it," Hedley said. "There's something not right here. If, as I suspect, Todd got that house off Rawlins, and on the off chance that there are documents, knowing when they were signed could give us a clue as to when that piece of work Rawlins was last seen."

"And Cowboy?" Stuart asked, switching on the engine. "We mustn't forget about him."

"I think we can take a reasonable guess about what happened there. He found the body, possibly told someone and got killed for his trouble. The poor bugger wouldn't have stood a chance."

Hedley was on his mobile again, speaking to Rufus Kane. "We've been delayed. It'll be about an hour before we can get there."

"We've already moved the latest victim to the morgue," Rufus said. "There were too many people at the crime scene and forensics needed space to work. We took plenty of photos and your young detective constable Ogden was in attendance."

"Okay, well, the day's rolling on so we'll meet you at the morgue in the morning," Hedley said.

"Millicent Austin wants a word later, too. Apparently, Cowboy and she were friends."

Millicent was friends with most people who hung around the city centre. She'd been writing an article about the drug-runners and regularly tapped Cowboy for information. "He passed on stuff to her about what was going down in the drug world. Not that Cowboy was the big expert or anything, but Millie did get the odd whiff of something interesting off him."

"Which in turn she passed on to you."

Hedley chuckled. "What're friends in the press for?"

"A bit of good news," Rufus said. "We found the bullet from our mystery victim embedded in the plaster of the cellar wall. I reckon the one that killed Cowboy is still in his head. When we find it, we'll do a comparison, see if they match."

"They will, you can be bloody certain of that," Hedley said. "Cowboy saw something and got his head blasted for his trouble." The thought of the poor man's fate made Hedley angry. Cowboy might've been trouble on occasions, but he didn't deserve this. The most he was guilty of was being a tad eccentric.

"Does he have family?" Rufus asked.

"I'm not aware of any. Millicent might know. I'll ask her."

"There is something else," Rufus told him. "A bloodstain on the toe of one of the shoes the unknown victim was wearing. His blood would have been splattered on the wall and around his head. Given the state of the body, it's hard to tell, but there is only one small patch so I suspect it might belong to someone else. I'm testing it for DNA. If I'm right, I'll let you know."

Hedley gave a small smile. A break of sorts and, if it panned out right, a much-needed one.

"Millicent is on my mobile," Stuart told him.

Hedley finished the call to Rufus and took Stuart's phone from him.

"It's been a bad day, Hedley," she began. "Cowboy rang me two nights ago wanting to meet up. He said he had info about a shooting and other stuff too. He said it was a murder that had happened a while ago and that I'd definitely be interested. I was at the hospital with Fred so I had to put him off until this morning. Had I met him when he wanted, well . . ."

"You can't blame yourself, Millie. Fred is a sick man, what're you supposed to do? What other stuff? Did he say owt about that?"

"Yes, he did, and it's big. Cowboy reckoned that he knew where Rawlins was. He also mentioned a man called Todd. Said he'd seen the two together a while ago going into some fancy office. He had a word with a girl who worked in the restaurant on the ground floor and she told him Todd was a friend of Rawlins'. You know what Cowboy was like, always poking around trying to get the lowdown on these big villains."

Hedley's face set like stone. Why hadn't Cowboy come to him with this? He'd have made sure he was kept safe. "Thanks, Millie. When we have something we can release, you'll get the story. Meanwhile, I'd appreciate it if you didn't make too much of it for now. If Todd was involved, we don't want to give Rawlins or his associates the heads-up. We also don't want them knowing that Cowboy ever spoke to you. You get my meaning?"

"You've made yourself crystal clear, Hedley. But Cowboy did say that the sighting was ages ago. It must've been just before you lot arrested him, I reckon."

"Even so, better it doesn't get out that you've been blabbing about Rawlins to us, not until we've found him and have him under lock and key. I'll come to your office tomorrow when I'm done with the morgue."

"No, don't do that," she said. "I'm off to the hospital to sit with Fred. I'll ring you in the morning. Am I in danger, Hedley?" There was real fear in Millicent's voice. "I don't do the wimp thing as a rule, but Rawlins' mob are the real deal. He's got some nasty specimens working for him. One of them gets the idea I can do real damage to their organisation and I'm toast."

"If we consider that to be a possibility we'll protect you, Millie. But for now, don't you be worrying," he said. "How is Fred anyway?"

"He's likely to be in hospital for a while. They're going to do yet more tests and another scan tomorrow. Hopefully, then we'll know what's going on."

Hedley nodded. For as long as he'd known her, Millicent's husband, Fred, had been ailing. It had been one thing after the other — some real, some imagined. This time, however, it looked like he'd hit the jackpot. "I'll give you a ring before I turn up. Might be an idea to keep a low profile until we know for sure what's going on."

Call over, Stuart checked his phone. "I've had an email from the land registry. They'll send over what we want tomorrow. There's a strike going down apparently, and they've no office staff."

Hedley checked his watch, it was getting late. "In that case, I'll ring and fix a time for tomorrow."

CHAPTER SIXTEEN

Day three

Whacked after her encounter with Selina and the interview with the police, Chloe had gone to bed early. But as soon as her head hit the pillow, she was wide awake, plagued by worries. Maybe she should have rung Brenda. She hadn't reckoned with Selina being so dangerous. The realisation of what the woman was capable of was terrifying. One way or another, Chloe had to be free of her.

She got up, feeling tired and listless. She had things to do, a heavy day lay in front of her. There was the problem of Selina for a start. She'd spent the night thinking it over but still hadn't come up with a solution.

Chloe showered, made herself a pot of tea and picked up the buff envelope that Selina had left. Sipping her tea, she spent a good half hour scrutinising the contents.

Selina had been telling the truth. She did own this house — Rawlins had signed it over to her. Chloe spent the next hour searching through Simon's desk, but she could find no evidence of a mortgage, rental agreement or correspondence from the solicitor. What was he playing at? More importantly, what was she supposed to do now?

Whatever she decided, she had to get it right from the outset. Selina was no fool and a formidable enemy. But Chloe did have one card that she could play: the diamonds. Selina needed her in order to get her hands on them. And that wasn't going to happen.

The front doorbell rang. It was Brenda. For a moment, Chloe wondered if the detectives had had a word with her, but they hadn't.

"A few of us are getting together for coffee and a gossip later. I thought you might like to come." Brenda smiled.

Gossip. Normally that wasn't something Chloe went in for, but the way things were, it could prove useful. She nodded. "I'd like that. Whose house?"

Brenda smiled. "Mine. The neighbours can't wait to meet you properly. They're a friendly bunch. They're not all middle-aged like me, either," she added with a laugh. "We have a fair number of young couples on the avenue. Come across at about half eleven."

Chloe locked the door behind her. This was an opportunity not to be missed. She could glean important information from the people who lived round here. Particularly if their memories stretched as far back as when Selina had lived here with Dean Rawlins.

The prospect of a morning spent chatting with a bunch of total strangers cheered her up. Chloe was good at making up stories. She could be whoever she liked. There was no need to drag up her past, her upbringing or the problem of Simon. No need to mention that he was difficult and treated ber badly either. That could be dealt with later, after she had decided what to do about Selina.

Chloe dressed casually in jeans and a T-shirt and made herself look human again with a dab of make-up. She smiled at her reflection in the mirror as she applied her lipstick. Some of the old fight was back. Coffee with the neighbours and then she'd ring Selina, invite her over for a chat. But this time it would be on her terms.

You can do this.

At eleven thirty on the dot, Chloe went over the road to the house with the red door and rang the bell. Brenda greeted her with a warm smile.

"Come in, lovely. I'm so pleased you came. We're in the conservatory."

Not sure what to expect, Chloe was pleasantly surprised. There were eight women sitting there, chatting and drinking coffee. All of them turned to look at her as she walked in.

Brenda introduced her to the expectant faces. "Chloe from across the road. She's new to the avenue and I'm sure she'll be a great addition to our little group."

"I'm Karen," one woman said. "This lot call me Kaz for short. I live further up the hill." She winked. "We don't just do coffee mornings, we're not averse to a few of what we call 'wet Wednesdays'. That's a little evening gathering in one of our houses, a gossip to put the world to rights while we hit the gin."

Chloe smiled back and sat on a free chair. "It's nice to meet you all. In the last place I lived, hardly anyone talked to each other and I felt really isolated."

"No chance of that here," Kaz said. "We're really into our socialising, and you look as if you'll fit in just fine."

"I never met the people who sold us the house, so I'd no idea what to expect."

"Della was great, that fella of hers not so much." Kaz leaned forward and lowered her voice. "Rumour has it that he was a gangster, a drug dealer from Manchester and worth a mint."

"You'd never have known it though," Brenda said. "He came across as your regular law-abiding citizen. He was kind-hearted and jolly. Look at the money he helped us raise for the church."

"Give over, that was nothing but show. There had to be something going on. You just had to look at the way they lived," Kaz said. "The cars, the holidays, and how they behaved. Dean had money all right, and no way that I could see of earning it."

"Sounds fascinating," Chloe said. "D'you still see the pair of them?"

"No, love," Brenda said. "Haven't set eyes on them for at least twelve months."

"And the rumours are rife, believe me," Kaz said. "The builder they had working on the summer house just before they disappeared reckoned they'd both been murdered and are buried underneath it."

Chloe looked round at the faces, all watching for her reaction. They no doubt expected her to be shocked at what she'd been told. Well, she wouldn't disappoint them. She made her eyes wide. "Surely that can't be true. If they're missing, someone must have reported it to the police. There must have been a search. Are you sure it isn't just gossip?"

"Very wise of you not to believe a word of it, Chloe." The voice, all too familiar, rang out from the doorway. "Of course there's no truth in it. This lot thrive on drama, that's all it is."

Chloe could scarcely believe it. Brenda must have invited Selina to come along to meet the new neighbour.

CHAPTER SEVENTEEN

With the group behind her, Chloe felt safe enough to face her enemy. She smiled at Selina. "Come on then, tell all. You're married to the guy, what *did* happen to him?"

Selina looked discomfited. She obviously hadn't considered Chloe brave enough to speak out.

She had a lot to learn.

Chloe sat back, relishing the way Selina prickled under the eyes of the watching women.

"You lot never change," Selina said. "Get hold of an interesting snippet and you're like a pack of hounds after some poor fox. But you're forgetting I left the weasel long before he went missing. And who says he's missing anyway? Most likely he's simply sunning his idle backside somewhere on the Costa del Sunshine. If I was you, I wouldn't give the likes of Dean Rawlins a second thought."

"Fair enough," Brenda said, sitting down next to Chloe. "I didn't realise that you two knew each other."

Chloe waited with interest to hear Selina's response.

"We were at school together," Selina said at last. "You won't be surprised to learn that I was the school bully, and I'm afraid I really put poor Chloe through it. She was everything I hated — clever, pretty, petite, just the type of little girl that everyone loves. It got so that I couldn't stand the sight of her."

Thinking back to those days made Chloe feel sick. School had been torture. Selina and her cronies had always had the upper hand — nothing they could inflict on her was too nasty, too cruel. Once Selina had a group of girls hold Chloe down while she cut her hair. She watched the dark curls hit the floor and could do nothing to help herself. By the time they'd finished, Chloe was almost bald. She cried all the way home. Not that Dora was much use. One glance, a shake of the head, then she bunged her a few shillings to get chips for her tea. No kind words, no taking her to the hairdressers, nothing. It took her friend Abby to at least attempt to put things right.

"You always were a spiteful bitch," Brenda said, shaking her head. "Had I known you were connected in that way, I wouldn't have invited you."

"It's okay," Chloe said. "All that was years ago. Fortunately, the pair of us have grown up since then."

Watching Selina, Chloe knew that was a long way from the truth. Selina was every bit as evil as she'd always been. If Chloe was to get her own way this time, she'd just have to go one better.

"Are you liking it on the avenue?" Kaz asked, attempting to lighten the mood.

"I reckon I'll settle in before long," Chloe said, grateful to her. "Everyone seems so friendly and welcoming."

Kaz nodded. "Any problems, or you fancy some company and a chat, just come and find one of us. Your husband Simon works a lot, so Brenda says. So don't go spending all day, every day, on your own."

Simon. At the mention of his name, Chloe felt the world crashing in on her once again. What to tell them? Not the truth, or even anything approaching it. "He has a time-consuming job in the city and he often works late."

"D'you work?" Kaz asked.

Chloe shook her head.

"D'you think you might? It's a good way of meeting new people in the area. I volunteer at the charity shop in the village and I meet loads of folk, all local."

"I'll see," Chloe said without much enthusiasm. Work wasn't what she had in mind.

"Okay, everyone. Coffee and cake in the kitchen," Brenda announced.

Everyone got to their feet, leaving Chloe and Selina on their own.

"Can we have a word later," Chloe asked, moving to sit next to her. Then, leaning in close, she whispered, "I've got a proposition for you."

Selina shook her head. She wasn't giving it a second's thought. "If it has anything to do with the house, the answer is no, so think again." She patted Chloe's knee, just a bit too hard. "I want you out as soon as possible. That valuable pile across the road is going back on the market."

"It could be in both our interests for you to let me stay."

"You're wrong, it's not in my interest, Chloe. Refuse to leave and I'll send in the bailiffs and have you and Simon thrown out." Now it was her turn, she leaned in close and hissed, "And don't think I haven't got the contacts to make that happen."

One of the women, Julia, returned with a mug of coffee in her hand. "There's a bring and buy in the church hall most Friday afternoons," she told Chloe. "I go to a craft group and we make stuff to donate — you know, crochet toys, small knitted items, that sort of thing. Feel free to come along and see what we get up to if you like."

Selina tapped her knee again. "Go on, knock yourself out. This lot would bore the pants off a saint. Is this really what you want, Chloe? Church halls and coffee mornings, a life of idle chit-chat? It's not for me, I'm afraid, never was, none of it." Selina got to her feet and handed Chloe her card. "My number is on there. Ring me within the hour. I'll agree to that chat but not at the house. We'll meet somewhere on neutral ground." At the door, she turned and looked at Chloe. "Don't forget what I said. I meant every word, and I won't wait much longer."

CHAPTER EIGHTEEN

"I never did like her much," Brenda said after Selina had gone. "Her and Dean used to argue a lot. Proper screaming in the street affairs, complete with her hurling anything she could get her hands on at him. It didn't surprise me when they split. And I must say, the avenue's a much quieter place without them."

"If you weren't particularly friendly, why invite her today?" Chloe asked.

"Because she rang me and asked if I was having any get-togethers. She said she was missing the old crowd. I didn't see any harm in asking her to join us, but I didn't know about your history then, did I?" Brenda tutted. "Bullied by Selina Harris. Poor you. I can't think of anything worse."

"Like I said, we're both grown up now," Chloe said, thinking about the cooker hob. The truth was, Selina hadn't changed at all. She was every bit as vicious today as she'd been as a young schoolgirl. "I'd better get going. Simon has promised to come home early and take me out for a meal. He fancies one of the village pubs he's seen on his travels."

"That's nice. About time he treated you." Brenda smiled. "But don't forget what I said, we're all here for you."

She meant well and, in another world, Chloe would have been grateful. But in her current circumstances she found Brenda's almost constant presence stifling.

As she crossed the avenue back to her own house, she took her mobile from her jeans pocket and rang Selina. "Where d'you want to meet? And make it simple — I don't know this area, remember."

"The park in the village, that simple enough for you? Twenty minutes, and don't keep me waiting."

Selina had that edge in her voice again. It cut like a knife — no, an arrow, barbed and poisonous. Chloe went indoors, put on her leather jacket, grabbed her bag and left. She checked a map of the village on her phone and thought she knew more or less where the park was. She wanted to get there first, find an empty bench and sit and wait.

Selina had to be persuaded to let her stay. It meant using the lure of the diamonds. Not that she wanted to but what choice did she have? Chloe bit her lip. If her little plan worked out, she'd get to stay in the house for a while longer. Selina would get her comeuppance in time.

* * *

The park was small, bounded on one side by the High Street and on the other by the river. There were a number of mums watching their small children running around.

Chloe closed her eyes for a moment. This was what she could have been doing with Lily if things had been different. A couple of years down the road she could have brought her daughter to a place like this, fed the ducks bobbing on the river and watched her play on the swings.

"What've you got to dream about? Or perhaps it's a nightmare you're having. Yes, that's it, a nightmare, with me in the starring role." Selina spoke sharply, obviously intending to startle Chloe, put her on the wrong foot.

"You rate your power to intimidate me too highly," Chloe said, opening her eyes. "You don't scare me, Selina. I'm a different person now. It was the shock of having you suddenly back in my life that made me nervous. But I've had time to think and I'm over that now."

Selina merely laughed and sat down beside her. "I hate this place — this village and the people in it. It's full of noise and messy kids. I can't imagine why you'd want to stay here. Anyway, I don't have a lot of time, so out with it, what's this proposition you've got for me?"

This was it. Once Chloe had said her piece, there would be no going back. The fate of both women would be sealed. She took a deep breath and began.

"I need to stay in the house a little longer, a month should do it." Chloe had things to do, and being seen to do a runner would not help her cause. If her plans worked out there'd be questions, and she must be around to answer them.

Selina's lip curled. "No. I want you out, Chloe. You have no right to live there."

Unless she applied pressure, this was a battle she couldn't win. Pleading her case, saying she had nowhere to go, wouldn't wash with Selina. She needed to give a reason to stay that Selina could not argue with.

"Anyway, why should I do you any favours?" Selina continued. "I want my property back pronto. I've arranged for an estate agent to visit the day after next. He will put it on the market, I'll accept the first reasonable offer, and then me and Gerald will move somewhere warm."

"Gerald's not your type and you damn well know it. You're only with him because of his money. You're being a right bitch about this."

"Come on, Chloe, get real. I owe you nothing. Get that husband of yours to sort something. I'm sure it's not beyond him."

Chloe took a second or two, inhaled, and said, "We have to stay because he's under orders from Dean."

"Why would Dean give a stuff where you live?"

"You know very well that Simon has an ongoing project with Dean. You spoke about it yourself."

"You're talking about the diamond robbery," Selina said. "That's sorted. The diamonds are in Dean's safe."

"But they haven't been sold and that's why Dean isn't around," Chloe said.

The lie got Selina's interest. "How d'you know that? Knowing Dean like I do, he'd have arranged all that before he did the robbery."

"That's where you're wrong. The buyer Dean had lined up has backed out," Chloe said.

Selina began to play nervously with the rings on her fingers. After a while, she said, "Is the safe still where Dean left it?"

"Of course," Chloe said. "It's much too large and heavy to even try moving it."

"We need that combination," Selina said. "That means both of us doing our bit."

"I'm working on that," Chloe lied.

"Good girl. You're finally coming round to my way of thinking. We get this right and we won't need either Simon or Dean."

"But we still need to sell them," Chloe said. "We should wait for Dean to find a buyer and take it from there."

Selina smiled. "I like it. You sound like me, Chloe."

Heaven forbid! Chloe turned and looked Selina in the eye. "Where is Dean? There's a rumour doing the rounds that he's dead. I don't believe it for a minute. It's the people Dean and Simon mix with — they have vivid imaginations."

The words had an instant effect. For a moment Selina turned pale. "That's twice you've said that. But you're joking, I take it. There is nothing to the rumour?"

"Nothing at all," Chloe said with a smile. "He's in hiding. The rumours are geared to take the heat off him. Only a few days ago he was on the phone to Simon. Simon wouldn't go into any detail but he seemed a lot happier after they'd spoken. Things go well and Dean will break cover soon enough. It's then that the pair will want to retrieve the diamonds, and if we're not careful, you and I will miss our chance."

"You're serious about double-crossing the pair of them? I'm sorry, Chloe, I didn't think you had it in you. But I can go along with that."

"Good. I thought you would."

"But I don't see what my house has to do with it. Why should I let you stay?"

"The last thing we want is for Dean to get suspicious. When he spoke to Simon he gave him explicit instructions to stay in the house for the time being. Why that is, I've no idea. I ask questions but Simon won't get into a discussion about what he's thinking, or where Dean is. All Simon told me was that Dean wants us to stay put and await further instructions."

"You're lying," Selina said. "If Dean was able, he'd contact me, not Simon. He's well aware that I know his plans. Take me for a fool and he'll not like the consequences. And don't forget, he put that house in my name. He must have had a good reason for doing that."

"It was part of his plan. After the first buyer for the diamonds pulled out, Dean had to disappear so that he could arrange for another buyer without having the police or his rivals coming after him. Putting the house in your name ensured that Simon could move in and be exactly where Dean wanted him."

Chloe was really winging it now. She could see from the look on Selina's face that she was in two minds about whether or not to believe her. Time to up the pressure. "You turf us out and Dean won't like it. He'll come after you. Us, too. You might feel confident about where you stand with him but he scares the life out of me. He's a thug. He shoots first and asks questions afterwards. There's a lot of money at stake, which means he could well kill us all without giving it a second thought."

"I see you've got the measure of the man," Selina said sarcastically. "As for me, I've always been able to handle him."

"Two million in diamonds changes the equation, Selina. Simon is his right-hand man. Dean's relying on him to look after things this end. And don't forget, Simon knows the other half of the combination to the safe. They need each other. That's a good enough reason for Dean to want Simon where he can find him. But if you want to explain your side of things to Dean, I'll speak to Simon, tell him to pass your wishes on. He'll tell him you intend to sell and that you won't even give us another month."

"You swear it was Dean who rang Simon?"

"Yes. Simon said it was him. When that call ended, he was a lot calmer, as if a weight had been taken off. He told me that things were moving forward. I overheard part of the conversation. Dean is in Amsterdam and has spoken to his associates, notably a potential buyer from Dubai. They're close to agreeing a sale. All we have to do is keep our nerve."

Selina got to her feet. "A month then, and no more. Dean gets in contact with Simon again, tell him to ring me. And get Simon to remind him that he can't do anything without his half of the combination."

"I'm not stupid. I know what's at stake."

"Just get this right, Chloe. Tell Simon to warn Dean not to even try double-crossing me. He's not the only one who can get nasty."

That was rich coming from her. Chloe watched her walk away. A month, Selina had said. Fine. She wouldn't need that long but it suited her to have the house a little longer. There were things she had to do, things she didn't want anyone to know about.

Chloe stood up. House sorted, she now had to ring someone to take the stuff she didn't need and put it in storage. There would be a number in Simon's notebook. He was a lot of things but for all his faults he was one of the best organisers she'd ever met. Now she would pick up where he had left off. Apart from the hiccup of Selina, everything was falling into place. Get the next bit right and her life could change forever.

CHAPTER NINETEEN

The body of Albert Roberts, alias Cowboy, was lying on the slab when the two detectives arrived at the morgue.

"His head's a mess," Rufus said. "But the man had several tattoos which his nearest and dearest were able to identify him by."

"Who was that?" Stuart asked.

"A lad who lived on the streets with him. Apparently, Albert had no family."

That sounded about right. Hedley took a look, pulled a face and stepped back. "Poor bugger. A case of wrong place, wrong time. Mind you, Cowboy saw a ruck and he couldn't help but join in."

"I have some news that might please you." Rufus gave him a rare smile. "I can confirm that your other victim is Dean Rawlins. The DNA confirms it."

Rufus could not have given Hedley a better piece of news. He clapped Rufus on the back and gave him a beaming smile. "That's the best thing I've heard in months. And unlike poor Cowboy here, Rawlins' is a death well deserved. I hope he suffered. That man has been the bane of my life for years, I can hardly believe he's gone. Anything else you can tell me?"

Rufus gave him a disapproving look. "Given the length of time Rawlins had been dead it was almost impossible to find any clues as to who killed him. There's nothing I can use. There are no fingernails — in fact there's barely any hands at all, so there's no way I can tell if he put up a fight. What I can tell you, though, is that prior to death he had been drugged. There's quite a cocktail lurking in what's left of that body. He was a long-time user too, his hair tells me that much."

Hedley turned to Stuart. "You know what this means? We'll have to find Rawlins' next of kin. That means a chat with Selina Harris, the woman who attacked Chloe." He was silent for a moment or two. "Interesting that. Makes you wonder what the ruck between those two was really about."

"Don't forget Rawlins and his wife weren't living together," Stuart said.

"Can you blame her? Who'd want to be wed to that," Hedley huffed. "We should check the details. Make doubly sure there wasn't a divorce. If there was, it would make things a lot easier."

"Back to the station?" Stuart asked.

"Okay, and you can check if we've got that info about the house through as well. It might help us with the timeline."

"Gabe is taking another look at everything we got from the Rawlins crime scene. He gets anything and we'll be in touch," Rufus said.

* * *

Back in the incident room, Stuart looked at the records and confirmed that Rawlins and Selina had never divorced. The email from the land registry was finally in his inbox. "Rawlins was a canny sod. He was married, no record of divorce, and about a year ago he transferred ownership of the house to his wife, Selina Harris. Looks like she told Chloe the truth."

"Is this Selina known to us?" Hedley asked.

"She was done for speeding three years ago. She got violent and was arrested. But the brief she hired got her off.

Interestingly, the address given here for her is the house in Saddleworth. No mention of her moving to Openshaw."

Hedley sighed. The irritation this case was causing him was growing by the minute. "Bloody Rawlins. He's still giving us trouble, even after his death. I'll lay odds the Todd woman knows the pair better than she made out."

"Not necessarily, if all the arrangements were made by Simon Todd. The aggro she's getting from his wife could be as Chloe says — she wants her house back."

"Either way, we'll have to find this Harris woman and tell her her husband is dead."

"Where do we start?" Stuart asked.

"We find her address in Openshaw and pay her a visit. That man the Todd woman spoke of, this Gerald Jacks, apparently Selina Harris is living with him." He looked round at the team, all busy at their desks. "A job for you, Ogden. Find me Jacks' address. Shouldn't be too difficult, try the electoral register. No divorce, house in her name, and if there's no rental agreement, she has every right to ask Chloe Todd to leave."

"Ask, Hedley? Not coerce, like Chloe told us. It sounded like a pretty frightening attack to me," Stuart said.

Hedley stuck his hands in his pockets. "That's if she's telling the truth. You're too easily taken in, d'you know that?"

"She's a vulnerable woman who spends most of her time alone," Stuart said. "She doesn't even know where her husband works."

"And whose fault is that?" Hedley said. "Anyway, I bet she does. Chloe Todd is a practised liar and you'd do well to look beyond the pretty face."

"I've found it, sir," an enthusiastic Ryan Ogden said. "Gerald Jacks lives in Foundry Street."

Hedley nodded to Stuart. "Get your stuff, we'll go and have that word."

CHAPTER TWENTY

The house in Longsight was a red-brick terrace lining a backstreet.

"A world away from the house in Saddleworth," Stuart remarked. "You can see why she wants it back."

Hedley just grunted. Rawlins' old lady could live in the gutter for all he cared. He banged on the front door. "On your guard, laddie. Don't be taken in. Remember she was wed to that evil bastard and what he was responsible for."

"Evil done by Rawlins, Hedley, not her."

"Don't split hairs. She must have known what he was like. In my book, that makes her as bad as him."

The woman who opened the door was tall, elegant, blonde. "You're police," she said at once. Then smiled. "Over time one gets a nose for them."

After a brief appraisal of Hedley's bulk, the creases in his coat, she turned her attention to Stuart.

"Can we come in, Ms Harris?" Stuart asked.

"Why? What can you possibly want from me?"

"Answers to a few questions," Hedley said sharply. He'd had enough of women giving him the runaround.

"It's important," Stuart added, "and best not discussed on the doorstep."

With a sigh, Selina Harris moved aside and waved the pair inside. "You'll have to be quick, I've got an appointment."

The tiny sitting room was littered with women's clothing. It looked to Hedley as if she'd been trying to decide what to wear. "Important this appointment, is it?"

"None of your business," she retorted.

"We have news of your husband," he said. "And it isn't good."

Selina shrugged. "It never is with him. Go on then, spit it out."

"I'm afraid he's dead," Stuart told her.

For several seconds, Selina Harris stared at them both, her face blank. If she was upset by the news, she hid it well. Hedley couldn't weigh her up at all.

"What did you expect? Tears?" she said. "Me and Dean were long since over. There was just no living with him."

"Well, you're still his next of kin," Stuart reminded her.

"More's the pity. Doesn't he have someone else who can deal with burying him and all that?"

"I've no idea," Hedley said. "That's something you're more likely to know than us."

"I was never that interested in Dean's family," she said, and smiled wickedly. "The lifestyle is what attracted me. All that money he splashed around. He could be generous to a fault, but back then I didn't know he was a gangster." She checked her watch, went to the front door and opened it. "You've kept me long enough. Like I told you, I have to go out."

She didn't appear to be in the least bit upset Hard-hearted perhaps, but Hedley found her honesty refreshing.

"You don't want me to identify him, do you?" she asked. "Only I'd have to draw the line at that."

"He's too far gone," Hedley said. "He's been dead a long time."

She pulled a face. "Well, that's a relief."

"When did you last see him?" Stuart asked.

"A while ago — sorry, but I can't be precise. We were married for eight months and then I left. As I said, Dean wasn't easy to live with. I haven't even seen him socially since we split."

At the door, Hedley turned back to face her. "One more thing. Chloe Todd. We've had a complaint from her about your behaviour. She told us you attacked her."

Selina made a gesture of impatience. "Rubbish," she retorted. "Can she prove that? What injuries does she have? Is she covered in bruises? Did I cut her? No, of course I didn't. The woman is a fantasist and a fool."

"Okay, I put it wrong," Hedley said. "I should have made myself clearer. You *threatened* her, threatened to slam her head onto a red-hot cooker hob."

"Never. No way would I do a thing like that."

Selina appeared genuinely shocked. Or was she simply a good actress? Another woman Hedley couldn't make his mind up about.

"She's nothing but a lying bitch." She stepped closer to Hedley and, looking him in the eyes, said, "That's what she does. Chloe isn't right. The reason she behaves like she does is because she can't accept what happened to the baby. If you'd spoken to her a bit longer you'd know that."

Hedley nodded as if he understood.

"What happened changed her," Selina said. "You can barely talk to her these days without her taking offence."

"Nevertheless, I want you to leave her alone from now on," Hedley said. "D'you understand?" he said firmly. "No phone calls, no visits, and no bumping into her accidentally. Any more complaints from Mrs Todd and I'll arrest you."

"She's got some cheek accusing me like this. Do I look like the kind of woman who'd do something like that?"

Hedley didn't reply. As far as he was concerned, Selina Harris looked as if she was capable of anything.

* * *

Selina watched from her window as the two detectives drove away. She could kill Chloe for dropping her in it like that. Well, she wasn't getting away with it.

She picked up her mobile and punched in Chloe's number. "Dean's dead," she barked at her. "You know what that means?"

Chloe said nothing.

"What's up? Cat got your tongue? You swore that Dean was alive. In Amsterdam, you said, arranging a sale. You're a lying bitch, Chloe, and I don't appreciate you running to the police either. Grassing me up was not on the agenda. I can forgive you a lot of things but not that."

"I'm sorry about Dean, but it doesn't change anything. When Simon took that call, I really did think it was him. I could only go from what Simon told me."

"Doesn't change things! Are you stupid? Of course it does. How will I get Dean's half of the combination now?"

"Perhaps you should look at his stuff, like you said you were going to."

"I don't actually have much of his stuff. I meant to get close to him again, get it out of him that way."

"That's that then. We can't get at the diamonds," Chloe said.

"No, that's not it, stupid. I'll get a safe-breaker on the case straight away. I know just the man. There's not a safe in the land that he can't crack — at least that's what he maintains."

"A bit risky, isn't it, sharing what we know with someone else?"

"You've got a better idea? I've had just about all I'm prepared to take. Those diamonds belong to me and I'm not waiting any longer to get my hands on them."

"What about me?" Chloe asked.

"You are no longer part of this." Selina's voice was cold, hard, and Chloe knew she meant it. "You can tell Simon that when he turns up — and you can get out of my house."

CHAPTER TWENTY-ONE

Visit to Selina Harris over, Hedley and Stuart were on their way back to the station when Hedley received a call from Gabriel Stubbs, head of forensic science.

"It's about your body," he began, "the Rawlins fellow. Well, we did a fingertip search of the immediate scene and found nothing, so we went a bit wider. Good job we did, because this time we had more luck. We found something lodged in a crack in the concrete floor about ten metres from the body. If we hadn't been so meticulous, it could easily have been missed."

This sounded better. At last, something to work with. "Go on then, don't keep me in suspense," Hedley said. "What did you find, Gabe?"

"A gold sovereign medallion that most likely came off a chain," Gabriel said.

"So, what's so good about it?" Hedley asked, thinking it probably got there years ago.

"It has a name engraved on it — one Connor Murray. Sounds familiar to me. Isn't he a long-time rival of Rawlins?"

Of course. What a fool. He should have realised. The way Rawlins was killed — a bullet to the head and the body dumped where it was unlikely to be found — was typical of Murray.

"Murray's DNA is on record," Gabe added. "And what's more, apart from his name, the pendant has a spot of Rawlins' blood on it. Also, those leather shoes Rawlins was wearing? If you recall, I said we'd found a spot of blood on them. Well, that turned out to be Murray's too."

"I've spent the whole of this last year trying to piece together what happened to that bastard," Hedley said. "This could be it." Hearing his jubilant tone, Stuart, who was driving, raised an eyebrow. Hedley gave him a big grin.

"I reckon there was a scuffle," Gabe said, "and both of them were injured. Hence the blood. And that would be when the pendant came off."

"I wonder what brought the two of them together in the first place?" Hedley mused. "Like you said, Gabe, the two are sworn enemies, always have been."

"I'll leave you with that one," Gabriel said. "Anything else comes to light, I'll be in touch."

This was beginning to look as if it was all about gang warfare after all. Hedley shook his head. "And there was me putting the whole thing down to a domestic."

"What did I tell you?" Stuart looked smug. "I said this had nothing to do with Chloe. She's a delicate little thing, she doesn't have the resources to take on a man like Rawlins and win."

"The jury's still out on that one," Hedley said. "Mark my words, Chloe Todd's no dainty little flower. There's more to that woman than you think."

"You're wrong," Stuart said. "All my instincts tell me you are. I mean, you've just got to look at her circumstances. Chloe is bullied by her husband and now she's being bullied by Selina Harris as well. She can't tell us where Simon Todd works because either she doesn't know or he's forbidden her to say."

Hedley rolled his eyes. "There you go again. Are you sure you're not soft on the woman?"

The look Stuart gave him said he was pushing things too far.

"You know what this means, don't you?" Hedley said. "We'll have to reappraise everything we've gathered on Rawlins over this last year, make sure we've not missed anything. Gabe has done us proud. We now have solid evidence that puts Murray at the scene of Rawlins' murder."

Stuart didn't look impressed. "We'll have to bring him in. I, for one, am not looking forward to that."

"We'll be fine. We'll go in mob-handed, plenty of back-up," Hedley said. "It'd help if we knew where he was hanging out these days. Last I heard he was shacked up with some woman in Stockport."

"We're going to need his address," Stuart said.

"I'm sure it'll be on record somewhere."

Back at the station, this was the first thing Stuart checked. "According to the record, Murray is living in a flat above a club in Stockport's shopping precinct."

Hedley wasn't surprised. Murray never did have Rawlins' ostentation. "We'll pick him up right away. Get the troops organised and we'll get it over with."

"Charging him with murder, are we?" Stuart asked.

"We certainly want to know what his pendant is doing within a spit of Rawlins' body, with the gangster's blood on it. I wonder what they were arguing about that brought them to fisticuffs?" Hedley said. "And why there, in that dump of a cellar? It's hardly the style of either of them."

"They didn't end up there by chance. They must have arranged to meet," Stuart said.

"Imagine those two in a *meeting.*" Hedley laughed. "Having a *discussion.* I tell you, laddie, I'd love to have been a fly on the wall."

"Perhaps they were cooking up something big, something that needed them to pool their resources. Like the diamond robbery," Stuart said. "It's not so far-fetched."

This pulled Hedley up short. Could Stuart be right? If he was, it could also be the reason they had the ruck and Rawlins got killed.

CHAPTER TWENTY-TWO

Chloe Todd heard the key turn in the front door lock. Simon was back. Her stomach turning somersaults, she wondered what mood he was in. Did he know about the visits from the police. Or — worse — had he heard about Rawlins? If so, he'd know that was the end of the diamonds and he'd be in a foul mood.

She attempted a smile. "I haven't cooked, I'm afraid," she greeted him. "I didn't know when you'd be back."

"Shut it," he barked. "I can do without you wittering in my ear. And before you get any bright ideas, I'm not stopping."

This was the Simon only she knew. The one he kept hidden from friends and neighbours. He wasn't usually this bad, however. Something was wrong.

"Did you hear? Dean Rawlins is dead." Not the best way to start a conversation, but the words were out before she could think.

He turned to look at her, a weird expression on his face. "What's that got to do with you?"

"Well, nothing, but the police have been here looking for you." For a moment, Chloe thought he was going to hit her. "Something to do with the house and how come we're living here. They told me that it used to belong to Rawlins."

"It's nothing," he said shortly. "I'll fix it."

There was no way he could do that with Rawlins dead and Selina insisting they leave. "They wanted to see evidence of a rental or sales agreement."

"Shut up, bitch!" he shouted. "Stop going on. The police come back, you know nothing. Got it? You haven't seen me and you don't know where I am."

Chloe cowered, fearing a blow. "I . . . I also had a visit from Selina," she stammered. "She said I was to ask you about some numbers."

"Drop it, Chloe. I'll deal with her, too."

"She threatened me," Chloe whimpered. "I was frightened. I don't think she'll be fobbed off that easily."

"Ignore her. The woman is all talk."

Chloe realised that Simon wasn't going to help. He was in a bad mood, worse than usual. She sensed an element of fear behind the angry bluster, which wasn't like him. He certainly wasn't up for answering her questions.

Instead he was rooting through the drawers of the bureau. "I need a few things."

"Tell me what you're looking for, maybe I can help."

"You can keep out of my business."

"I met the neighbours," Chloe said, changing the subject. "They're nice. Very welcoming."

"As long as you didn't talk about me. I'll meet them in my own time."

"What do I do if Selina comes back? We can't just ignore her. She wants the house, she said we have to get out."

"Not going to happen," he said. "Don't worry, I'll sort Selina. She's no longer your problem, all right?"

It was all very well for Simon to say he'd sort it, but was he going to stop Selina being a constant thorn in her side?

"I need some clean clothes," he said, thrusting a holdall at her. "Shirts and that, and my good shoes."

Chloe went upstairs to get him what he wanted. Back in the sitting room, she asked him where he was going. "At least you can tell me that."

"There's no need for you to know," he said.

"The police are suspicious," she said. "They think our marriage is a sham because I know nothing about you."

"And that's how I want it to stay." He gave her an odd look. "Things turn out, I'll be back soon and then I'll answer all your questions. If they don't, you may never see me again."

More bewildered than ever by this statement, Chloe wasn't sure how to respond. "Why? What's going on? You have to tell me something, at least where you can be reached. I won't tell anyone else. It's just in case something happens that you need to know about. I am your wife, Simon. You can trust me."

"I'm going to disappear for a while, that's all I'm saying."

"The last time you ran away, you stayed in a caravan belonging to Rawlins, the one on that building site in Audenshaw that Rawlins used for meetings with his dealers. Is that where you're going?"

His only response was a scowl. She'd guessed right. "Can I call you on your mobile?"

"I've ditched it. When I say disappear, that's just what I mean. I'm not to be found."

"Who are you scared of, Simon? Someone close to Rawlins? The police?"

"The police, of course. Rawlins' people don't have any argument with me."

"But if the police come calling, they're sure to ask where you are."

"Stall them. Surely that's not beyond even you."

Minutes later, he was out the front door and gone. Within minutes of his departure, the front doorbell rang. Her mind still on Simon, she nearly jumped out of her skin. Who was this now? Please, not Selina again.

Thankfully, it wasn't. There on her doorstep was Brenda.

"I saw Simon drive off and was worried about you," she said. "You've been crying. What's he said? Why did he race off like that?"

"It's okay, he's busy with work, that's all," Chloe said. "He'll be back soon."

"So why the tears? Has he hurt you?" Brenda asked.

Chloe shook her head. "No. It's just that I'd been hoping he'd be staying. But all he wanted was a change of clothes. He's up to his eyes in it."

"He's a selfish git, leaving you on your own. He knows how you've been." Brenda gave a sigh and asked, "Why d'you stay with him, Chloe? You're an attractive woman. You could do so much better for yourself than him. I don't know why you put up with the likes of Simon Todd."

Chloe gave her a half-hearted smile. "We sort of drifted into marriage, I suppose I didn't give it much thought. Simon said we should get wed and that was that."

Brenda gave her a hug. "You really need to start thinking for yourself, Chloe. A marriage like this is what happens when you don't."

Brenda insisted on making Chloe a sandwich and a pot of tea. Chloe just wished she'd go and leave her alone. It was late and she needed to sleep. When Brenda finally left, Chloe switched off her phone, locked all the doors and went upstairs to bed. Selina had said she'd ring tonight but no way could she face that. She would deal with her tomorrow.

CHAPTER TWENTY-THREE

Day four

Connor Murray had been arrested and brought to the station late the previous day. Having languished all night in the cells, he was in a foul mood, shouting abuse and hurling the food he'd been given at the cell door.

"I want my solicitor," he screamed at the officer who took him his breakfast. "I know my rights."

"You'll be interviewed soon enough, and your solicitor will be present," the officer said.

This was no good. He had important business to attend to. He had no idea why he'd been arrested. He'd been told he was to be charged with the murder of Dean Rawlins, but that couldn't be right. He'd heard the rumours of Rawlins' death, but what evidence could they have that incriminated him?

The officer was just locking the cell when he bumped into Hedley.

"How's our guest? Had a good night, has he?"

"He says he wants his solicitor, sir."

Hedley went up to the cell door and peered in through the observation window. Murray saw him and snarled. "You wait, Sharpe. Soon as I get out of here, I'll have you. Your life won't be worth living."

Hedley gave him a grin. "Tut tut, that's no way to behave. Didn't your mother teach you any manners?"

"You've no right locking me up. I've done nowt."

Hedley shook his head. "We both know that's not true, Connor. Your best bet is to stop pissing me about and tell me the truth about Rawlins."

"What truth? I haven't seen him in months," Murray bellowed.

Hedley grinned at him again. "That I can believe. Nevertheless, the last time the pair of you met was eventful, to say the least, so much so that only one of you walked away alive. That's what we're going to talk about."

"I don't know what you mean."

"Don't worry, all will be explained during the interview." Hands in his trouser pockets, Hedley strolled back to the incident room. Murray could lie all he wanted, but they had the evidence. It was irrefutable, strong enough to put Murray away for good.

"What time's the off?" Stuart asked.

"Give that fancy solicitor of his a ring and we'll start as soon as he gets here. I don't want any delays with this one. I'm not letting him go, so the sooner we get him charged, the better."

Hedley went to his office and took another look at the evidence they had against Murray. It was compelling. Murray's pendant, his blood on Rawlins' shoe. The two had to have met in that cellar and for some reason had a fight. He picked up the office phone and rang Gabe at the lab. "Got owt else for me on the Rawlins murder?"

"I have, as it happens. I've found Murray's blood on that pricey suit of Rawlins', a smear on one of the pockets. The pair had a set-to all right, and Rawlins came off worst."

That was all to the good but, for some reason, Hedley couldn't rid himself of a feeling of doubt. Despite all that

Gabe had given them, he had a premonition that Murray was about to slip through his fingers.

Stuart stuck his head round the office door. "Murray's solicitor, William Bagley, is here. He's already going on about wrongful arrest and that Murray will sue."

Hedley snorted. "Rubbish, Murray's going down. He has to, or there's no justice in the world." He looked up at his partner. "You up for this? Only, despite all the evidence, the whole thing's upsetting my digestion."

"That gut of yours, Hedley. Come on, the evidence is irrefutable," Stuart said.

"That's as may be, but something's niggling me. I still don't feel confident about this one."

"Well, you should," Stuart said. "We go into that interview room all guns blazing, so to speak, and we nail the bastard. No other outcome is possible, given what we have."

Hedley wished he could believe him. "Murray's like Rawlins, a slippery bugger. But I take your point. If there's any justice, the day is ours."

With the file tucked under his arm and Stuart at his side, Hedley made his way along the corridor to the interview room. Once the formalities were over, the verbal fisticuffs began.

"What's this all about, Sharpe? Like I told you, I've done nowt. This is nothing but a miscarriage of justice." Murray shook his head. "I'm fast getting seriously pissed off, so if you value your health, I'd release me pronto."

"In your dreams, Murray," Hedley retorted.

Bagley gave his client a warning look. "Calm down, Connor. We'll hear Superintendent Sharpe out and then we'll decide how to proceed. We will certainly not issue any threats."

Hedley shook his head. "The evidence we've got is simple but damning. We can place Murray at the scene of a murder. His DNA is on the victim and on an item belonging to Mr Murray that was found at the scene." He looked at Bagley. "So, Mr Solicitor, how much more do I need?"

Bagley whispered something in Murray's ear. "Do you intend to charge my client?"

"Too bloody right I do. He'll be charged with the murder of Dean Rawlins and possibly that of Albert Roberts, aka Cowboy." Hedley looked Murray in the eye. "What was the fight about? Rawlins double cross you, did he?"

"I don't know what you mean."

"You certainly fell out about something. The diamond robbery, perhaps? Want to tell me about it?"

"That had nothing to do with me."

For the moment, Hedley let that go. "I can understand why you'd kill Rawlins, but why Cowboy? What had he done to upset you?"

"I never touched him. I never touched either of them," Murray insisted. "I'm serious now. Why would I want to get rid of Rawlins? We helped each other in many ways."

"Oh, sure," Hedley said. "Come on, Murray, the pair of you had no time for each other."

"All that was for show, to keep you lot on your toes. The reality was we often met up and swapped information. He'd give me something and I'd give him something in return. Information can be highly profitable, so why would I want to get rid of the source?"

More whispering. Then Bagley said, "Are you interested in a deal?"

Hedley didn't believe a word about the pair of villains being in cahoots, but he cocked his ear at this one. Murray had more knowledge about the drug dealing in this city than the police had amassed in years. He knew the dealers, but what was more important, he knew the suppliers too.

"What's he prepared to give me? Worthwhile, is it?"

"The lowdown on who's running drugs in this city. Who brings it in. Who is instrumental in distribution. The lot, in fact."

Hedley was sorely tempted. With information like that, they'd be able to clear up dozens of cases in one fell swoop. But could Murray be trusted? If they approached the CPS with the evidence they had, the gangster would be tried for murder and wouldn't see the light of day for years. And then there'd be less crime.

Hedley thought about it. "Sorry, Murray. Not interested. You'll be charged, and when it goes to court, I have no doubt you'll be found guilty."

CHAPTER TWENTY-FOUR

As Hedley entered the incident room, a hearty cheer went up. Giving the team a huge grin, he strode to the front of the room.

"We did it," he boomed. "The Rawlins and Murray saga is well and truly over. And about bloody time too. This city is now rid of two ruthless villains who've been a right pain in the arse for as long as I can remember. You all did your part and you all deserve to take a slice of the praise." Another cheer went up. "I'll put some money behind the bar at the Old Soldier across the road. Get your backsides over there and take advantage. I don't do this often — as you might have noticed."

"That's right," Stuart piped up. "Bit of a tight-wad is our super."

Hedley laughed. "As a rule, but this is the exception. I've long dreamed that this day would arrive, but I was never sure it would really happen. Well, it has, and we should all celebrate it."

Speech over, Hedley retired to his office to start work on his report. It wasn't long before Stuart came to join him.

"You can get off if you want. Make the most of the lull in our workload. Things will change soon enough," Hedley said.

"It's you who needs the down time, Hedley. You look done in."

"Don't worry about me, laddie. I'll finish up here, go home and get some of my special scotch down me. An early night and then I'll be as right as rain."

Stuart was on his way out when a uniformed PC knocked on the door.

"There's been an incident, sir," he said to Hedley. "A body found in a burning caravan in Audenshaw."

Hedley groaned. What now? Wouldn't he ever get a moment's peace? "A fire, you say. Accident, was it?"

"Doubt it, sir. The body has a bullet in his head."

With a sigh, Hedley asked, "Owt else known, lad? Victim's name, for instance?"

"Sorry, sir, that's all I was told. As soon as the death was deemed suspicious, Dr Kane was called to the scene."

Hedley dismissed him with a wave of his hand and called Rufus on his mobile.

"The Audenshaw job. What've we got?" he asked.

"A body."

"The fire did for him?" Hedley asked.

"The fire didn't kill him. As for smoke inhalation, that'll have to wait for the PM. What did for him was a bullet in the head. I imagine the killer thought the fire would cover his tracks, but a local called the fire brigade and they responded pretty quick. So, with luck we should be able to get some forensic evidence."

"Audenshaw, you say?"

"That building site off Ashton Road."

"We'll be with you soon," Hedley told him. He turned to Stuart. "So much for an early night. We've got a stiff with a bullet in his head."

"I'll drive," Stuart said. "I'll drop you off at yours once we've finished."

"You're not my bloody mother. I'm quite capable of getting home by myself, you know."

"You're knackered, Hedley. I don't know. When will you be told?"

"At least we know that this has nowt to do with Rawlins or Murray. That fact alone gladdens my heart."

"A bullet is still a bullet. Maybe someone is trying to jump into Murray's shoes."

"I doubt anyone would dare. Knowing Murray, he'll have someone ready and waiting." Hedley put a hand on his back. "Bloody chair doesn't do my lumbar region any good at all. I can sit on all the cushions I want but it damn kills me at the end of the day."

* * *

The traffic was heavy, so it took half an hour to reach the site. Hedley got out of the car and lumbered over to Rufus, followed, more nimbly, by Stuart. "What's this all about then?"

"Some poor beggar got shot and the killer tried to cover his tracks by setting the place alight. He would have succeeded too, if it hadn't been for the quick action of that bloke stood over there."

"Have we got a statement off him?" Hedley asked.

Rufus nodded. "That young constable did the honours."

"Killed here, was he?"

"Yes, there's blood splatter on the walls around him. He was in bed at the time. Whether he was awake or not, I couldn't say until I've run tests."

"Do we have a name?" If not, it would need a deal of research.

"Luckily for us, his wallet and mobile were still in his pocket," Rufus said. "His name was Simon Todd."

"What?" Hedley could barely believe what he was hearing. What could this mean? He turned to Stuart. "Well, well. Our elusive Mr Todd seems to have got himself murdered. You know what this means, don't you?"

Stuart shook his head. "Only that poor Chloe is going to have her day ruined."

"Todd was an associate of Rawlins', had to be — he was living in his wife's house. Wife threatens your precious Chloe, and now this."

"The Rawlins case isn't quite as over as we thought, then," Stuart said. "But where do we even start?"

Hedley turned to Rufus. "We'll be relying heavily on forensics with this one. Let me know the second you have owt."

CHAPTER TWENTY-FIVE

Hedley checked his watch, it was gone seven in the evening. "By the time we get to Saddleworth and back, it'll be time for bed," he grumbled. "I had a quiet drink and an early night planned too." He thought for a moment then added. "But given that don't sleep that well I might have gone for slap-up meal at the local Indian place down the road."

"You should eat properly," Stuart said. "How often d'you eat fast food?"

"I live on it, laddie. The curry mile is only down the road and Mrs Chandani makes a lovely beef madras. There's nothing to touch it."

Stuart shook his head. "You're a fool to yourself. One of these days your unhealthy lifestyle will catch up with you."

"Perhaps, but not today. Too much to do, thanks to Simon Todd."

It took them an hour to reach the Todd house, by which time both detectives were done in. Stuart had done the driving, and listening to Hedley complaining hadn't done his mood much good. Nonetheless, they had to get this next bit right. Having to tell Chloe that her husband was dead was not a task he relished. He couldn't work out how she'd take it — probably badly, he decided in the end. Whatever their relationship, she depended on her husband and he doubted her ability to go it alone.

"Can I ask that we err on the sympathetic side," Stuart said as they pulled up outside. "Try not to forget that the poor woman did lose a child only twelve weeks ago, and we're just about to tell her that her husband is dead."

"I don't think the soft touch has any effect on this one. Despite the muddled, know-nothing impression, the lovely Mrs Todd is as hard as granite. I doubt she's told us the truth once throughout this whole investigation. You can stuff the sympathy, laddie. Any more lies and we'll see how she likes a night in the cells."

Stuart winced. He could only hope that Hedley might see sense when he actually had Chloe in front of him. "Go easy. That's all I ask."

* * *

The moment Chloe answered the door, she knew it was bad news. It was the look on the tall detective's face, the concern in those nice eyes. "What do you want? Has something happened?"

"You tell us, love," Hedley said.

She noticed the tall one nudge his colleague. He was on her side. Chloe gave him a small smile and asked them to come inside.

"We're here about your husband," Stuart began.

"He's not here," she said.

"We know that," Hedley said. "The poor bugger's lying in the morgue with a—"

The tall one shoved him aside and said, "I'm afraid your husband is dead, Mrs Todd. He was found in a caravan on a building site."

Chloe had no idea how to react. What would they expect of her? "I . . . I don't understand."

"That makes three of us," Hedley said. "Where did you think he was?"

"At work, like he is most days. What building site? He works in insurance, I don't know — finance or something like that. He has nothing to do with construction."

"I'm afraid he's been stringing you along, love," Hedley said. "Your husband has been working for a villain called Dean Rawlins. Name ring any bells, does it? It should. It was his wife who came round here and threatened you."

"Of course I know who he is." Chloe put on a defiant front. She'd had enough of this pair. The fat one in particular seemed to think he could walk all over her. "The neighbours speak highly of him. I very much doubt that he's a villain — he can't be if he was an associate of Simon's."

"Just goes to show," Hedley said coolly, "you never can tell with folk, and you certainly can't go on face value or tittle tattle."

"When did you last see him?" Stuart asked.

"He popped home yesterday to pick up a change of clothes. He didn't stop long, less than an hour. He told me he had an important meeting away somewhere and said he'd ring me."

"And did he?" Hedley asked.

"Well, no actually, he didn't."

"Weren't you worried?" Stuart asked.

"No. Simon was always working, so why should I have been worried?" She looked from one man to the other. "Am I supposed to identify him or something? I'm not sure I could face it."

"You are his next of kin," Stuart said. "He's not well known around here so it's down to you, I'm afraid. We'll make it as easy as we can, don't worry."

The superintendent glanced at his colleague and shook his head. He wasn't impressed. "Is there anything you want to ask us?" he said.

"You've made yourselves clear enough," Chloe said.

"I don't think so, Mrs Todd. We've told you where he was found and you've asked a couple of questions but you haven't mentioned the big one."

Chloe stared at him. What did he mean? He'd made it obvious he didn't like her and was looking for anything suspicious in what she said.

"You haven't asked us how your husband died."

Chloe met his eyes and began to weep.

"He was shot in the head," Hedley told her. "If it's any comfort, it would have been quick."

CHAPTER TWENTY-SIX

As soon as they were outside the house, Stuart turned on Hedley. "You were rather hard on her back there, Hedley. You'll be lucky if she doesn't make a complaint."

"She won't dare," he retorted. "She's up to something, I damn well know it. Her dodgy ways set my teeth on edge. The bloody woman gives me the creeps. I've had enough of her mucking us about. Much more of it and she'll find herself in the cells."

"What for? Chloe Todd is guilty of nothing except not fitting some idea you have of a victim's wife. She's probably one of those women who suffers in silence. She doesn't want to show her feelings to the likes of us. And who can blame her with you firing questions at her right, left and centre. You had no right to go for her like you did. She's had a hard time. Living with that husband of hers was no picnic, from all accounts. She deserves our sympathy and help."

Hedley slapped him across the back. "Just listen to yourself. She's well and truly got to you, hasn't she? You're not thinking with your brain, laddie. She's an expert at playing the ill-done-to little woman. She's a sham, I tell you. Don't be taken in."

"That's not how I see it," Stuart said. "She had a stillborn baby just weeks ago. She's living in a new environment. She doesn't really know anyone on that Avenue. You only have to look at her to see she's telling the truth. Chloe Todd is a deeply troubled woman. It's written all over her face and in the way she speaks. I'd say she needs our sympathy, not our suspicions, and a deal of help. Personally, I'd recommend counselling."

"She flashes you a pretty smile and you're taken in like a love-struck teenager. Bloody hell, Stuart, wake up and see the truth! Chloe Todd is not only clever but she's an expert liar as well." He shook his head. "You've a lot to learn. A woman like that could do you and your career serious damage. Come on, back to the station," he said with annoyance. "I want to know what Lou has turned up about the needy Mrs Todd and her dead husband. And you, laddie, can get your head straightened out."

Hedley was in a bad mood. For starters, he'd thought better of Stuart. He couldn't understand why his colleague refused to see things the way he did. Then there was the case. It looked as if they'd cracked the Rawlins murder, but Cowboy's death still had a question mark over it. There was no evidence to put Murray in the frame for that one, and he was denying it like everything else. On top of that, they now had the murder of Simon Todd to deal with. Was it connected to the other two in some way? His instincts told him it was, but he couldn't figure out how.

They were halfway back to the station when Hedley received a call from Rufus.

"I've got the bullet that killed Todd. The striation marks match the bullet that killed Rawlins but not the one that hit Cowboy."

Hedley tried to get his head round that one. What Gabe had told him meant that the same person had probably shot Rawlins and Todd. Given that they were partners of some sort, it did make a certain sense. But who had done for Cowboy?

"Any other interesting little nuggets to confuse us?" Hedley asked, putting the phone on loudspeaker.

"I've done the PM. It was fairly straightforward. Todd was a fit man in his mid-forties, there's no sign of heart disease and he was a non-smoker. Like Rawlins, he had been drugged prior to being shot, and at some time in the past he'd had a vasectomy. Apart from that, there's not a lot to report."

That piqued Hedley's attention. "The snip, eh. Are you sure? It's not that I doubt your expertise, Rufus, it's just that he's supposed to have fathered a child within the last year or so."

"Impossible. There are no sperm present and the scars are well healed."

"How long ago then, d'you reckon?" Hedley asked.

"Several years, perhaps five or six."

Hedley looked at Stuart and nodded. "You know what this means, don't you? Chloe Todd was playing away, so we'll have to speak to her about it. We need to ask how she managed to get pregnant when her husband was infertile."

"There could be any number of explanations, Hedley," Stuart said. "A sperm donor, fertility treatment, who knows?"

"Of course, a much simpler explanation is that she cheated on him, which was why he behaved like he did towards her. If she was unfaithful, he probably felt like wringing her bloody neck. Anyway, we'll ask her when she comes in to do the identification."

"He didn't wring her neck though, did he? It was him who got it, not her," Stuart said.

"From what little we know, he was giving her a hard time. If that got too much for the fragile Mrs Todd to take, she could well have done him in herself."

"Now you're being ridiculous, Hedley. I don't see that at all."

Hedley sighed and shook his head. He didn't understand how Stuart could be so convinced of her innocence. Given her relationship with her husband and now this, Chloe Todd had motive. There was no getting away from that. But what about opportunity? The timescale meant that if she did kill him, it would have to have been late yesterday.

"I wonder if Mrs Todd ever goes out on her own? And more to the point, was she missing late yesterday?"

"I know what you're thinking but you're wrong. I doubt the woman even drives. I've never seen a second car. Think about it, Hedley. If he takes his car to work, where's she keeping hers?"

CHAPTER TWENTY-SEVEN

Was that the worst over? Chloe doubted it. There was still Simon's identity to confirm and then yet more questions. Not to mention the neighbours. What would she tell them? For once, she would be grateful for Brenda's input. Brenda would be more than happy to take on the task of telling everyone. It had been a hard few days. All Chloe wanted to do now was put the whole awful business behind her and rest.

She was debating whether to ring Brenda and give her the bad news when her mobile rang. It was Selina Harris.

"I've been trying to get hold of Simon. Is he there?"

"No," Chloe said.

"Well, when he surfaces, tell him I want to talk. Tell him to make it quick. I need those numbers off him after all. The safe-breaker I've found reckons having half the combination will help."

Chloe couldn't help but smile. It gladdened her heart to spoil Selina's plans. She gave a sob. "I can't."

"Don't give me that crap. You'll do as you're told and so will Simon."

"I'm afraid this time I'll have to disappoint you. You see, Simon's dead. Murdered. The police came to tell me the news. They've just left."

"Dead?" The line went quiet for a few seconds. "Are you weeping? Don't bother putting on an act for my benefit, Chloe. They're false tears. You don't give a toss about Simon, never did. Trust him to get himself killed just when I need him. I don't suppose he gave you the numbers, or you've found where he might have written them down?"

"No, Selina. Simon didn't operate like that. Those numbers will have been in his head, so they've died with him. Sorry, but your safe-cracker will have to continue without them."

"You're really enjoying this, aren't you? Positively lapping it up. Well not for long, Chloe. With both Dean and Simon dead, there's no longer any reason for you to stay in my house. I want you out, and quick. You've got until the end of the week, and don't even bother asking for an extension. That's not going to happen."

The line went dead. No goodbyes, no condolences for her loss, nothing. Selina was spiteful to the last. Chloe hadn't expected anything else. She looked around her. She'd stacked most of the cases against a wall, keeping the one holding her most treasured possessions apart. Later, she'd transfer them into a holdall, ready for the off.

Selina could rant and rave all she wanted but she would not win this one. Chloe smiled to herself. Selina's stint as top dog was almost over. And when her reign ended, she'd find herself in the worst trouble she'd ever been in, and she'd have no evidence to prove herself innocent. No way could she worm her way out of this one. Chloe hadn't an ounce of sympathy for Selina Harris. She deserved everything that was coming to her.

Chloe made the call to Brenda. She needed a friend and, more importantly, she needed someone to tell the police just how cut up she was about her husband's death. Her neighbour would be only too glad to fill the role.

"It's Simon," she sobbed. "He's been killed. Murdered somewhere in Manchester. Those detectives have been here. Oh, Brenda, I don't know what to do."

There was a long moment of silence. This was big. Brenda would be taking it in, the most excitement the avenue had known since Rawlins' disappearance.

"Stay put, love. I'll be right with you."

Chloe dabbed her eyes and sighed with relief. She knew she could rely on Brenda — she was that type of woman. In seconds, she was at Chloe's front door.

"You'll be in shock," she said at once. "I know you had your problems but he was your husband, a constant in your life."

Chloe nodded. She let Brenda wrap her comforting arms around her. "I can't believe it. How could this happen? What could he have been mixed up in to get him killed like that?"

"How did he die?" Brenda asked.

Chloe gulped. "It's so awful I can barely take it in. I don't understand, Brenda. He was shot in the head." She looked up at her neighbour. "What sort of people do that? I had no idea he knew anyone capable of such a thing. And why would anyone want to kill him anyway? None of it makes any sense. All this time I thought he was working. I now realise I didn't know him at all."

"Are you sure the police haven't made a mistake?" Brenda said. "How do they know it was Simon?"

"His belongings, found in his pockets — his mobile phone and his wallet. They've asked me to identify him. I can't, I just can't," Chloe wailed. "I've never seen a dead body before."

Brenda tightened her arms around her. "If it would help, I can come with you, hold your hand. If it is Simon, we'll speak to those detectives and find out what they know. One way or another, we'll get to the bottom of it."

CHAPTER TWENTY-EIGHT

Day five

Chloe got the call to go to the morgue early the following morning. This was it then. The end of her life with Simon. Chloe felt slightly guilty at being so elated. From this point forward the bully, the man she'd hated more than anyone, was out of her life. It was finally over. The battle was won.

She rang Brenda and told her she had to go and identify the body.

"I'll be with you in ten minutes," Brenda promised. "Don't worry, I promise I won't leave your side. You won't be doing any of it on your own."

Thank God for nosey neighbours, Chloe thought, when the call was ended. Over the next few days, Brenda's help would be invaluable. More invaluable still would be what she told the others about the marriage.

Chloe put on a jacket, grabbed her bag and went outside to wait for Brenda. The morning was going to call on all her resources. Despite how she appeared when first told Chloe would have to act the distraught wife, a woman whose husband had been killed in the most dreadful way. She had to put on the performance of her life.

Brenda's car pulled up at the gate. "Hop in," she said. "And don't worry, it won't be as bad as you fear. He will look just as you remember him. Years ago, I had to identify my father. My mother wasn't up to it. I must admit he looked quite good in death, certainly a lot better than when he was alive and drinking — which he usually was."

Chloe gave her a wan smile. "It's very good of you to do this, Brenda. There's no way I could have faced it on my own."

"How d'you feel? Be honest now, there's no need to hold back with me. Relieved to have him out of your life? I wouldn't blame you."

Chloe hung her head. Brenda knew some of what had gone on between her and Simon, so there wasn't much use denying it. "Him dying like that is a tragedy, but it does mean that I can lead my own life now. I can do what I want, go anywhere, without having to answer to Simon." She made big eyes at Brenda. "Does that make me a bad person? Am I wrong to be thankful that he's dead?"

Brenda shook her head. "From what I know of your relationship, no, you're not. That man was no good for you and he deserved all he got. Given where he was found, it looks like he might have been mixing with the wrong crowd. Dean Rawlins might be missing but his gang is still active."

Missing is that what people thought? Well, let them. For now, it suited Chloe to keep quiet.

It wasn't far to the morgue, and soon Brenda was pulling into an empty parking spot. She grabbed hold of Chloe's hand. "Don't worry, you'll be fine. I'm with you."

* * *

Hedley had been in his office since early that morning, trawling through everything they had, and he'd identified some gaps.

As soon as Lou arrived, he marched into the incident room. "Background on the Todds, what've you got?"

Stuart turned up and came over to join them. Her reply stopped both detectives in their tracks. "Simon Todd doesn't exist, sir. Not until three years ago, anyway. Who he was before that is anyone's guess."

Hedley had half expected something like this. It had always been a distinct possibility, given that the man worked closely with a gangster. "Do more digging. We have his DNA, so see if there's a match on the database. What about the wife?"

"She checks out. Her name was Chloe Harrop prior to marrying Todd. Her mother is one Dora Harrop. Dora was charged with being drunk and disorderly on one occasion, so she has a record."

"And Chloe?" Hedley asked.

"We've got nothing on her, sir. She doesn't have much of a work record — couple of pub jobs and a stint at a holiday park on the east coast. She married Todd nine months ago — a civil ceremony in Manchester. The witnesses were two individuals who worked on the premises."

"That means she was pregnant when she wed," Hedley said. "Whoever was responsible had to have been fairly recent on the scene. So why not wed him? Why settle for a charlatan like Todd?"

Hedley told Lou and Ryan Ogden to carry on with the search. "The pair of you, get me some answers. I didn't care much for the mysterious Chloe Todd before, and I care even less for her now. This entire marriage thing looks like one of convenience to me. I want to know why she thought it necessary to wed the likes of Simon Todd."

"You think she's on the make?" Stuart asked.

"Remember who he was, Stuart, Rawlins' man, no less. Of course she's on the make."

Hedley went up to the whiteboard and added a few notes. "Chloe Todd is coming in this morning. After she's done the identification I'd like to know how much she knew about her husband's antics. Don't let her go until I've had a word with her. I think we'd better speak to Ms Harris too. See how she really feels about the news of her husband's death."

CHAPTER TWENTY-NINE

With Brenda holding her hand and Stuart hovering in the background, Chloe moved closer to the viewing window.

"Take a good look, Chloe," Stuart said, as the technician pulled the sheet away from Simon's face.

Grasping Brenda's hand even tighter, Chloe looked at the body. Tears streaming down her face, she turned to him and nodded. "Yes, that's Simon."

"Come on, love, we'll go and get a cup of tea," Brenda said.

"Actually, we'd like a word," Stuart said. "It won't take long, just a few questions."

"Have you no heart!" Brenda shouted at him. "Can't you see she's in shock?"

"Like I said, it'll be quick," Stuart said.

Chloe let go of Brenda's hand. "I don't mind. I'll answer their questions."

"I'll wait for you in the canteen," Brenda said.

Chloe followed Stuart down the corridor. What were they going to ask her? And more to the point, what answers would she give?

Stuart showed her into an interview room. "Want a cup of tea?"

"No, I just want to get this over."

As soon as Hedley entered the room, Chloe was on her guard. If anyone was able to see through her, it was this man.

Hedley sat down opposite her. "Were you aware that Simon Todd was not your husband's real name?"

Chloe was gripped with a sudden rush of panic. How to answer that one? Of course she'd known, but dare she admit it? "I had no idea. Why would I? He's always been Simon Todd to me, and I never had any reason to question it. There's a birth certificate, driving licence and passport at home in that name."

She dabbed her eyes with a tissue. Hedley had no idea if the tears were real.

"There has to be some mistake. You have him confused with someone else."

"No, it's the truth," Hedley confirmed. "D'you know if your husband had any enemies?"

"I know very little about what went on in Simon's world."

Hedley raised his eyebrows. This was the first time she'd been that candid with them. "I'm afraid we do have a couple more questions, and you might find them difficult."

"Just spit it out, whatever it is," she said through her tears.

"How come you got pregnant when Simon had had a vasectomy?"

This was news to her. Simon had never mentioned it. She said nothing.

"I suppose Simon didn't want children but you did," Hedley said. "Did you and he discuss it?"

"Yes, but mostly we argued about it. At one point it nearly caused us to split. It was then, when I was at rock bottom, that I met up with an old boyfriend and we had an affair."

"Very convenient," Hedley remarked. He was finding her as difficult to believe as ever, and was beginning to get angry. She was playing them again. "An old boyfriend just happens along, and bingo. Didn't you feel guilty about cheating on your husband?"

"Of course I did," Chloe said. "I was distraught. I didn't think Simon would want to know me or the baby."

"Does this old boyfriend have a name?" Hedley asked.

"I'd prefer not to say. He's happily married now and I don't want him or his wife upsetting."

"Convenient that," said Hedley.

"Simon was okay with it," she protested. "He said he understood and that I wasn't to worry. He wasn't happy but he didn't want to lose me, so we decided to give the marriage another go."

She's hoping the sharp-eyed detectives won't see through her, Hedley thought. Well, this one does. "That's a blatant lie, isn't it, Mrs Todd?" he said. "I can't see a man like your husband taking something like that so casually. I think the truth is more likely that your husband didn't care what you did. Yours was a relationship built on convenience and not much else."

"Hedley!" Stuart exclaimed.

Chloe gave him a small smile. "It's okay. He's right to be dubious. Our marriage wasn't perfect in many respects."

"It was far from it. What I can't work out is why you married him at all. It's obvious to me that you had no feelings for each other." Hedley stared at her. "Meaning you wanted something from him. Maybe what you wanted was revenge. Well?"

"You're mad. I loved Simon and he loved me."

Hedley didn't believe a word of it.

Suddenly, he shot at her, "Do you have Simon's work address? We could do with talking to his colleagues."

Chloe shook her head. "All I know is that it was in an office block on the Quays. Look, Detective, not everything in our marriage was perfect. The bottom line — Simon didn't trust me. He tended to keep a lot of his life secret. He never said much about his work, we just talked about the home stuff. His work was important to him and he didn't want me spoiling it. I never even got to meet the people he worked with."

More lies. Hedley's gut told him that this woman was up to something — something he wouldn't like at all. "Okay, we'll leave it for now, but we'll talk again. And you might need to give us the name of whoever it was you had the affair with."

This seemed to rile her. "I don't see why," she snapped. "It's over, and anyway, we don't move in the same world."

"Nonetheless, bear it in mind. It depends where our investigations take us." Hedley got to his feet.

"I may have to go away," she said. "A close friend is ill and I've promised to go and stay with her for a few days."

"Well, before you disappear, make sure you give me an address where you can be contacted," Hedley said.

CHAPTER THIRTY

"She doesn't know anything," Stuart insisted once Chloe had left.

Hedley shook his head. "Wake up, lad." He could understand why a young man like Stuart would be taken in. Chloe Todd was attractive and told a good tale. Yet something about her wasn't right. "She knows something, I'm certain of it, and I intend to find out what that is."

"Fair enough, Hedley, but don't go stomping all over her like a charging bull."

Ignoring his words, Hedley said, "She said she was going away. Where to, d'you reckon?"

"Like she said, to look after a sick friend. We've no reason to doubt her. Look, if it helps, I'll ring her, get the address of where she'll be."

"Fine. You do that." But Hedley wasn't reassured. He couldn't shift the notion that Chloe Todd was playing games with them. "We'll have her watched, see what she gets up to."

"No, Hedley. The woman has just lost her husband. She must be devastated. All this stuff about her not being on the level is in your head."

* * *

As soon as Hedley entered the incident room, Lou handed him the phone. "Gabe. He's got news."

"What you got?" he said, hoping the news was good.

"Forensics from that caravan where Todd was found," Gabriel said. "They found a bracelet that must have dropped off someone's wrist. Plus, a used coffee mug with prints on it."

"But what do they tell us? Come on, Gabe, I'm way beyond riddles, I'm desperate here. I want this little lot wrapped up and then we can all go home."

"Calm down, Hedley. Think of your blood pressure. The good news is I've matched the prints and also found a match for the DNA on the bracelet."

Hedley recognised that smug tone only too well. "Okay, you're good and we'd struggle without you."

"I had to test a great deal of stuff in that caravan, everything that wasn't burned or smoke-damaged. Mostly I found Todd's prints and DNA. The interesting items were found close to the body, and as you know, the fire didn't reach that far."

"Well done. So, who is the match?" Impatiently, Hedley tapped the desktop.

"They match one Selina Harris," Gabriel said.

Hedley hadn't expected this. He'd been half hoping that any forensics would lead back to Chloe Todd.

"Selina Harris was nicked for a speeding offence three years ago and got shirty with the officer who stopped her. Blacked one of his eyes, in fact. Hence, she was arrested."

"Yes, we know about that. Thanks, Gabe, good work. We'll be in touch."

Conversation over, Hedley turned to face his team. "Selina Harris. I want her bringing in, and quick. Lou. Do a full background check. We know about her previous arrest but see if there's owt else."

"Try the house in Longsight," Stuart told them. "That's where she appears to be living."

"You know the address. Take a couple of uniforms and check it out. And don't forget, she's as slippery as that husband of hers was, so don't give her an inch." Hedley looked over at Stuart. "I can't wait to get her take on this."

Stuart smiled back. "So much for suspecting Chloe. I told you all along that she's got nothing to do with this. She hasn't hurt anyone and is as much in the dark as we were until now."

Hedley still wasn't convinced. "We'll see. There's a lot more to this entire case than meets the eye. Trust me, laddie, my instincts are never wrong."

Stuart shook his head. "Old-fashioned thinking. We have to go with what the evidence tells us and it does not implicate Chloe Todd."

Hedley turned to Lou. "I want to know Simon Todd's real identity. See what you can do with what we've got."

"We have his DNA, so I'm having it checked against known crims in the hope that we get a match."

Hedley went back into his office and sat at his desk, head in hands. He still couldn't rid himself of the notion that Chloe Todd had something to do with all this. He didn't enjoy being so at odds with Stuart, it was a rare occurrence. The pair were usually so in sync. He'd asked Stuart to speak to Chloe's neighbours but now decided it was something he should do himself.

Back in the incident room, he found Stuart at his desk. "I've waited long enough," Hedley said irritably. "I want to know a great deal more about Chloe Todd. We'll take a ride out to Saddleworth and speak to the neighbours. See what their take is on Chloe."

"It'll be the same as mine," Stuart insisted. "Anything else is in your head."

The truth was, the woman annoyed Hedley. He was convinced that she was putting on an act. He just couldn't prove it.

CHAPTER THIRTY-ONE

Stuart sighed. "You do realise this is a waste of time."

"We'll see. A word with the neighbours might set my mind at rest." Hedley sat back in the passenger seat and tried to relax. Was Stuart right? Was he obsessed with Chloe Todd? Was her guilt all in his head? If so, it was a sign that he was losing his touch and should seriously consider ending his time as a detective.

"The neighbours will all back me up," Stuart said. "They'll have seen Chloe for what she is, a downtrodden, bullied wife with a husband who mixed with villains. Why she ever married him is beyond me."

"That's a question we should ask her, and keep on asking until she gives us a straight answer. If we see her today, I'll put that right."

"It's time to let this drop, Hedley. We speak to the neighbours. We get the gist of what Chloe is like and then we leave it. We've got Selina Harris to deal with, remember her? Now there's someone who is guilty and we've got evidence to prove it."

After an hour's journey, they finally pulled into the avenue. Across the road in the house Chloe was living in, the curtains were pulled tight.

Stuart knocked on Brenda Howells' door first. "Could we have a few words?"

"Is this about the shenanigans across the road?" she asked.

"In a way, but it's more about Chloe herself. May we come inside?"

Brenda led the way into the sitting room. "You have to understand that I have only recently met Chloe, but I recognised right away the type of woman she is and the problems she's having."

"We'd value your opinion," Hedley said.

"It's simple really. Chloe was the victim of coercive control. That husband of hers gave her so little freedom that she was almost afraid to breathe unless he said so."

Stuart looked at Hedley. "See, it's like I said."

"Did you at any time get the impression that she could be acting?" Hedley asked.

Brenda shook her head emphatically. "No way! I witnessed the tears. I saw the marks on her arms where she'd cut herself. I saw for myself the way he treated her. No. Take my word for it, Simon Todd was an evil man who took pleasure in making his wife's life as miserable as possible, and I, for one, am pleased that he can't trouble her any more. She deserves better, poor woman."

"Did anyone ever come to visit her?" Hedley asked. "Anyone you didn't know?"

Brenda pursed her lips as she shook her head. "Have you not been listening, Superintendent? Chloe wasn't allowed to have friends or visitors. She wasn't even allowed to mix with the neighbours." Brenda gave a sigh. "But I'm a pushy sod. I was determined that she should meet us all, have a bit of fun. I had a coffee morning and introduced her to a group of the other women who live on the avenue. Unfortunately, Selina chose that very day to turn up. I had no idea that they knew each other. Apparently, apart from the fact that their husbands were in cahoots, Selina and Chloe had known each other at school."

Hedley nodded. "So, in your opinion, with Chloe Todd, what you see is what you get."

"Exactly. And I'm going to do everything I can to see that she recovers from all this."

"Thanks, Mrs Howells, you've helped ease my mind. It seems I'm the only one out of sync where that woman is concerned."

"Hopefully you're not anymore. All Chloe needs is time to recover. She's damaged, but with the counselling I'm hoping to arrange for her, she will get better. What she doesn't need is you lot hounding her."

Hedley took a second to think. This woman seemed like a sensible soul, and he'd trust Stuart with his life. Was it time to let the Chloe Todd thing drop and sort the case with what they'd got? He made the decision not to speak to the others on the avenue. Given they'd hardly interacted with Chloe it would be a waste of time.

They were close to solving two murders, but what about Cowboy? As for the diamond robbery, there was never any real evidence that Rawlins was involved, so why would Simon Todd have been?

They got back in the car. "The station?" Stuart asked. "And are you satisfied now?"

Hedley gave a reluctant nod. "Seems I have no reason not to be."

"D'you want a word with her before we go?"

"No, we'll leave the woman in peace. Put your foot down, laddie. Young Ogden should have found Selina Harris by now, and I can't wait to see what she's got to say for herself."

CHAPTER THIRTY-TWO

Selina never got tired of hurting Chloe. The young woman was everything she hated, and being able to cause her yet more grief was the icing on the cake.

Number one on her list was to get her out of that house. Selina had given her long enough, she'd listened to excuses until her head hurt. No more Simon meant no reason for Chloe to stay. So she made her mind up to go and give it to her straight.

Getting out of this dump would be no hardship either. Up until now, it had suited her to be here. No one but the police and Chloe knew where to find her, and that was just how Selina liked it.

She was putting a few things into a suitcase when there was a knock at the front door. Not the police again, surely? Didn't they have anyone else to bother? But it wasn't the police. It was Chloe.

"What now? Haven't you got a funeral to organise or something?"

"You're a cruel woman, Selina. You've no heart at all. But no matter, you'll get yours."

"You wish," Selina said. "But as you're here, you might as well know that I want my house back. Me and Gerald intend to live in it for a while. So, if you wouldn't mind, do the honours and make yourself scarce."

"Don't you care? Doesn't it mean anything to you that Simon is dead?" Chloe asked.

"I don't give a damn. I never did like the fool. Dean only put up with him because he was good with figures. He did his accounts, remember?"

"He was also part of the diamond scam. He helped Dean and they trusted each other. They even shared the combination. That must mean something."

Selina stepped up to Chloe and poked her in the belly. "All it means is that Dean was as big a fool as Simon. It doesn't matter now anyway. What they knew has gone to the grave with them."

Selina turned away and carried on with her packing. "Now, if you don't mind, I'm about to go out."

"You're all dressed up," Chloe said. "Lunch date?"

"Mind your own business." Selina picked up a white silk blouse from the sofa. "This or the lace, d'you reckon?"

"The lace. Much classier."

Selina nodded. "Normally, I'd agree, but I wore that last night, so the silk it is. I'll go and find my pearl necklace to go with it."

Selina disappeared from the room, leaving Chloe on her own. She picked up the blouse, noting the designer label.

"Leave my stuff alone." Selina was back in the room. "I don't want your grimy finger-marks all over it."

"Can't you give me another week?" Chloe asked. "Give me a chance to arrange something."

"Nope. A couple of days, tops. Don't disappoint me, Chloe. You will not appreciate the consequences."

"Is that a threat?"

"It's anything you want it to be. I owe you nothing. I was never your friend and I only put up with you these last days because I thought you could be useful. But with Simon dead, that's no longer the case. Cut your losses, Chloe, and find someone else to foist yourself on."

"You really are a bitch, Selina."

"Yes, I am. It's what gets me through."

* * *

With Chloe gone, Selina continued to get herself ready for her lunch date. A few minutes later, there was another knock on the door. If this was Chloe whining on again, she was ready for her.

But it wasn't. It was DC Ryan Ogden with a warrant for her arrest. Selina was shocked and outraged, protesting her innocence all the way to the car.

"You are going to regret this. I'm suing you for wrongful arrest," she spat. "Do I look as if I'm capable of killing someone?"

"I'm sorry, ma'am. The constable here will take you in while we do a thorough search of the premises." He held up a warrant. "I also want the clothing you were wearing yesterday evening."

The look she gave him was glacial. "Bloody cheek. That's designer gear, I'll have you know. You'd better not damage anything or your career is finished."

Ryan was finding it hard not to feel intimidated. He'd never met anyone with such a temper. The woman was practically spitting fire.

"I want to speak to your superior," she demanded, "and I want my solicitor. Do you understand?" She spoke to him as if he was a half-wit. "It's difficult to tell if you even understand. Look at you, standing there with your mouth hanging open."

"Detective Superintendent Sharpe will interview you, and your solicitor will be present. That's your right."

Selina was seething. Who did these people think they were, coming to her home and charging her with murder? What did they have to go on? Was this some sort of joke? Unlikely. As Dean always said, he'd never met one yet who had a sense of humour.

"I've been set up," she said, her temper finally under control. "Someone wants to finish me and has decided that prison is as good a way as any. Well, they won't get away with it. I will fight every inch of the way."

"It's unlikely that you've been set up, miss, if you don't mind me saying. It's a lot of effort to go to and they would have had to get everything exactly right. Our forensic people are very good at their jobs."

"There are some clever people out there, Detective. Knowing how to cover your tracks is only a matter of research."

Her words fell on deaf ears. This young detective was no longer interested. She had to think, and quick. Who did she know who would do this, and exactly what did they have on her? Whatever it was must be damning to bring the police to her door.

Selina suddenly felt something that had not troubled her for years. Fear.

* * *

"Has her solicitor arrived?" Hedley asked.

"Not yet, he says he's stuck on the motorway. She asked for a Douglas Montfort, and when Ryan Ogden told him he jumped at the chance. Apparently, he used to work for her husband."

Anyone who'd worked for Rawlins was more than likely a rogue. "Montfort, eh? Not a name I know," Hedley said. "See what you can find out. But first, put Ms Harris in interview room one and give me a knock when this lawyer arrives."

Hedley went into his office and went through the file on Todd's murder. The evidence was cut and dried. They had her bracelet as well as her prints on a coffee mug found in the caravan where Todd had been killed. Since then, Gabe's team had also found strands of her hair on Todd's jacket. There was no way she was going to wriggle out of this one, though Hedley didn't doubt she'd try.

Ryan Ogden stuck his head around the door. "Montfort is here, sir. He's not a happy bunny either. Reckons we've made a huge mistake."

"He'll change his mind when he hears the evidence." Tucking the file under his arm, Hedley collected Stuart from the incident room and the pair made for the interview room. "She's going to be every bit as slippery as her old man. She'll have an answer for everything, mark my words. But remember, we hold all the aces. She's guilty, and we are going to make sure she's sent down."

The two detectives went into the room. At once, Selina got to her feet. Her expression told them she was in no mood to stand any nonsense. "Enough is enough. You've had your bit of fun, now it's time I went home."

Stuart got on with the preliminaries and took a seat next to Hedley. "You're hereby charged with the murder of Simon Todd," he announced.

Selina leaned forward and wagged a finger at him. "That's a ridiculous idea. Apart from a brief hello at a relative of Gerald's funeral, I haven't seen Simon in months. And anyway, why would I want to kill him?"

She did have a point there. Hedley had been wondering what her motive was. But evidence was evidence, and they had plenty of that. "You're lying," he said. "You drugged Todd, shot him in the head and tried to destroy the evidence by setting the caravan he was staying in alight. Had that worked, you might have got away with it, but thanks to the quick action of a passerby, the caravan was saved."

Hedley watched her face turn pale. "Where has all this rubbish come from? I haven't killed anyone. You can't pin this on me. And what caravan? Where was this, and why wasn't Simon at home?"

"You can deny it all you like," Hedley told her. "But we have evidence that puts you in that caravan with Todd."

"Never! If I wanted to see Simon, I'd ask him to my place, or meet him in a pub. Not some caravan."

"We believe Todd might have been trying to hide from someone," Hedley said. "Perhaps that was you, Ms Harris."

The bewilderment on her face puzzled Hedley. It looked genuine. She was either a good actress or she was telling the truth. But what about the evidence? "You were in that caravan with Todd. That's a fact you can't deny, given what we've found."

Selina shook her head. "What have you found? Whatever it is, it has nothing to do with me."

"That's where you're wrong," Stuart told her. "As my colleague said, we have evidence that puts you in that caravan."

"No, no, you're not listening. You're not seeing this for what it is, a set-up. What evidence are you talking about? Is there anything there that could not have been planted?"

Thinking about it for a moment, Hedley had to admit to himself that she was right. But why should he believe her? She was known to be violent. She'd threatened Chloe Todd, scared the life out of her, in fact.

"Okay, I get it," she allowed. "You've got some items that make it look as if I'm guilty of the murder, but I'm not. Someone is trying to make it look that way. And I can only think of one person who would do that. Have you spoken to Chloe Todd? Does she know that you've arrested me?"

"Why, what's it got to do with her?" Stuart asked.

"I suspect it might have a lot to do with her." Selina looked at Hedley. "Have you looked into her background? You haven't, have you?"

"We, er, know her mother wasn't much cop," Stuart said.

"No, she wasn't. Chloe had a hard time of it. She even had a spell living on the streets, dossing down with the druggies in Piccadilly and the rest. Not a nice way to live, but it was a matter of survival, I suppose. Then she met a bloke who helped her."

"Does this bloke have a name?" Stuart asked.

"Sorry, but I never knew who he was, just that he was a reporter looking into Manchester's drug problems."

Like Millicent Austin, Hedley realised. "Are you sure you don't know who he is? Didn't Chloe ever say?"

"No. I'm sorry I can't be more help. But the drug problem is popular with journalists, they all have a go at it at some point."

That was true. Drugs was about all Millicent went on about. Hedley checked his watch. It was late, too late to speak to her now, she'd be sitting with her husband in the hospital. He'd give her a ring in the morning and ask if she could tell him anything about this man Chloe knew. He was a journalist like her and looking into the same issue, so it was feasible.

Meanwhile, a chat with the bloke himself might help. "Where is he now, this journalist?"

"I've no idea," Selina said. "I only got in touch with Chloe again recently, before that we hadn't spoken in years. And what I do know about her life is just hearsay and can't be taken as gospel."

CHAPTER THIRTY-THREE

Day six

The following day, Hedley was at his desk good and early. The case was getting to him. Something was wrong. It all looked just fine on paper — murders solved, killers apprehended, but it had been too easy. Hedley tossed the file to one side and picked up the phone. He wanted a word with Gabe. What Selina had said about the evidence having been planted had played on his mind all night.

"Fear not, my friend," Gabe said. "I've found Todd's blood on the clothing Ms Harris was wearing the night he was killed."

Hedley was relieved. Ogden had done his job right. "What clothing? Where?"

"Her blouse. When she shot Todd, the blood splattered, as we know. A drop landed on the cuff of her sleeve."

"Gabe, you've made my day. That puts paid to something she said to me when we spoke to her yesterday. I owe you."

Call to Gabe over, Hedley rang Millicent Austin. "Hope I haven't caught you at a tricky moment."

"No, Hedley, I've got time before I leave for the office. What can I do for you?"

"D'you recall a reporter who was researching the drugs problem?"

"There have been any number of us. Does he have a name?" she asked.

"I don't know it. All I know is that while he was carrying out his research, he took up with Chloe Todd. Rescued her from the streets, so I'm told."

"Nice chap, but it could be anyone. You know what Manchester's drug problem is like. We all think we can put a new slant on it but it still ends up as the same old story. Why d'you ask?"

"I'd like a word with him, that's all. The person who told me about him didn't know his name."

"Why not ask Chloe Todd herself? She must know who he was."

"I will, but the more I know, the better prepared I'll be for the crap she'll spout."

"Things getting tricky? Come on, Hedley. Chin up. I'm sure you'll get there in the end."

Hedley wished he had the same faith in his abilities. "Have you heard any rumours about a reporter who spoke to either Rawlins or Murray perhaps?"

"Most of us do eventually, even me. They were the experts after all. Rawlins was scary. I didn't take to him at all. And I couldn't take Murray seriously. Far too flippant for me."

What Millie had just told him was useful but sadly lacking in facts he could use.

"I wonder why she left the reporter and married Todd," Millie mused. "He was a shadowy figure. Yes, he was part of Rawlins' gang but he always maintained a certain distance. That distance allowed him a freedom that Rawlins didn't have. No one was more surprised than me when I heard that he'd married. I saw her once and I didn't think she was his type. I imagine he was totally different from the kind soul who'd rescued her from the streets."

"Thanks, Millie, that's useful information. If I get anything I think you can use, I'll be in touch."

Millicent's information threw up even more questions. If she had someone who was prepared to look after her, why had Chloe taken up with Simon Todd? And how had she met him? Surely a fragile woman like her wouldn't fall for a bully like Todd. Yet that's what appeared to have happened. Ordinarily, he'd have discussed this with Stuart, but against his better judgement, he decided to go it alone.

Hedley needed to face Chloe Todd with his questions and watch her reaction. But not yet. First, he wanted to know who Simon Todd really was. That might help him work out the answer to this little conundrum.

He went into the incident room and bellowed at Lou. "Simon Todd, who the hell was the bugger? You must know by now, his DNA is on record, for pity's sake."

"Sorry, sir, the database was having an update these last couple of days but it's back to normal now."

"Good. Get me that information and bring it to me."

"Dr Stubbs was on the phone earlier, asking for you. He says would you ring him."

Hedley picked up the office phone and called Gabe. "You got something for me?"

"Yes, Hedley. I can now confirm that it was most likely Murray who killed the man known as Cowboy. We found fibres from the coat Murray was wearing when he was arrested on Cowboy's clothing. He also has bruises on his body that suggest a fight. Unless Murray enlightens us, we can only surmise what went on in that cellar, but it looks like Cowboy stumbled on Rawlins' body. Perhaps he told the wrong person and got himself shot for it."

Another neat solution. Hedley was getting tired of them. "Thanks, Gabe, that's wound that one up."

Hedley put the phone down just as Stuart entered the room. "Good news?"

"Of sorts," Hedley said.

"Selina Harris is asking to see you."

She was the last person Hedley felt like talking to but he had no choice. She still had information, and right now he needed all the information he could get.

"I'll get round to her shortly. First, I'd like another chat with Murray."

"Want me along?"

"No, you go over the Selina Harris file. Make sure we've got all we need."

* * *

Hedley had Murray brought to an interview room. He'd asked the duty solicitor to be present as this could get tricky.

"Treating you well, are we?" he greeted the man.

"This place is a bloody shambles. You've got this all wrong. I did not kill Rawlins, although I admit I wish I had. And I certainly didn't kill that tramp."

"So you say."

"I've been set up," Murray said.

Someone else who was screaming that he'd been set up. Wasn't that what everyone said? Or was the feeling that he was missing something a warning he should heed?

"Why not just tell me what happened," Hedley said wearily. "Answer my questions and we can wind this up."

"I'm not admitting to anything," Murray said.

"Why did you kill Cowboy?"

"I didn't. Why would I?" Murray said. "I'm not interested in the homeless."

"The problem is we have evidence, Connor, and evidence doesn't lie."

"What evidence? You're trying to trick me."

"Not our style," Hedley said.

"I've never even seen this Cowboy, so go and question someone else."

"Then why are there fibres from your coat on his clothing?" Hedley said.

He watched the colour drain from Murray's face. "There can't be. They've been put there. Like I said, I've been set up."

"You don't believe that any more than I do. Tell me what happened, Connor. It'll go better for you in the end."

"I'm admitting nothing," Murray said.

"Okay, tell me about the diamonds," Hedley said.

"Why should I? I say anything and you'll twist it to suit," said Murray.

"I'm curious. There's some think that robbery is nothing but a myth, but I reckon Rawlins was responsible."

Murray smiled. "Rawlins and his gang robbed that armoured van all right. You might not believe this but the whole thing was supposed to be a joint effort. Me and Rawlins called a truce in order to carry it out. We were supposed to split the proceeds but Rawlins went ahead on his own. Cheating bastard."

Hedley thought for a moment. "You're saying Rawlins stole the diamonds?"

"Yes, and he hid them. I was told that only him and Todd knew where."

"Did you believe that?" Hedley asked. "Why Todd? What did he have to do with it?"

"I don't know. Perhaps Rawlins threatened him. No reason not to. Well, they've never turned up, and to this day no one seems to know where they are," Murray said.

"Was that why you killed Rawlins?"

Murray looked him in the eye. "How many times do I have to say it? I did not kill Rawlins."

"We have plenty of forensic evidence says you did, Connor. You see, my problem is that both Rawlins and Todd are dead. You say you're not guilty, but you've just given me the perfect motive. Rawlins cheated you."

"That's as may be, but it wasn't down to me," Murray said. "And why would I kill that Cowboy bloke? I didn't even know him."

"Cowboy was in the wrong place at the wrong time. I think you were searching for Rawlins, in his druggie hangouts, saw Cowboy and was afraid he would talk. You shot him and dragged the body into the cellar next door. That was when the fibres we found were transferred."

"That's nothing but a fantasy," Murray said.

"We'll see what the CPS have to say about it."

Chat over and with lots to think about, Hedley made his way back to the incident room.

"Selina's solicitor's here," Ryan told him. "The pair of them are in the interview room, heads together, plotting."

Hedley nodded to Stuart. "Want to come along?"

Stuart grinned. "I'm not missing the chance to see her make mincemeat out of you. That's one feisty lady. She's not eaten a bite of food and she's complaining about everything."

"We'll interview her formally. I want her brief to know the strength of the evidence we have against her."

As they walked along the corridor, Hedley told Stuart what he'd learned from Gabe and Millie, and that he'd tackled Murray about Cowboy's murder. "Gabe has made our case against Selina a lot stronger. Todd's blood on her clothing seals her fate, I reckon."

"Good old Gabe. Selina for Todd. Murray killed Rawlins and Cowboy. A neat ending to a complex case."

"Too bloody neat, if you ask me."

"Give it up, Hedley. We've all worked hard on this one. We deserve the odd break now and again."

"I agree, but now we've got ourselves another puzzle to solve. Without a name it's damn near impossible, but I'd give my eye teeth to know who the bloke was who helped Chloe get off the streets. We don't know that he's not connected in some way."

"I don't see how he can be," Stuart said. "Why hasn't he come forward? Granted it was months ago but Rawlins' murder has been in all the papers. I doubt there's anyone round here particularly who hasn't heard. Plus, Chloe has never said anything about him."

"Weird that, don't you think?" Hedley said.

Stuart said nothing.

Hedley was mulling over the information about the reporter. It had thrown them something of a curve ball. But what did it mean?

CHAPTER THIRTY-FOUR

Just as Hedley was on his way out of the incident room, Lou called to him. "Sir, I've got a DNA match and a name for Simon Todd."

Hedley went over to her desk. "Anything interesting, or was he just an everyday thug?"

"His real name was Terry Blake. He had a record, small-time robbery, late-night shops mostly. On one occasion he assaulted the owner and was arrested. But interestingly, he comes from the same part of Manchester as Chloe. In fact, they both lived on the same street while she was still living at home."

Why didn't that surprise him? Hedley wasn't sure what it meant yet but it had to be significant in some way. "If she knew him from her old life, she must have known he was bad news."

"That means nothing." Stuart came across and joined them. "Sorry, but I overheard the conversation. Chloe is a victim, not a killer."

"A victim who knew damn well what she was getting into," Hedley said. "So why all the melodramatics about being kept in the dark? Insisting she knew nothing about Todd or what he did for a living? Eh? We all know now that he was a bloody crook, and if she knew him in the past, she must have known too."

"Calm down, Hedley," Stuart said. "This new information is interesting but think about it, it takes us nowhere. We have all the answers we need as to what happened to those three men."

He was right but Hedley couldn't accept that it was that cut and dried. "You might have, but I've still got questions."

"Not that again," Stuart groaned. "I wish you'd let it drop."

"I can't, and I intend to speak to Chloe Todd about it. She withheld information in a murder enquiry and I want to know why."

"Ask yourself, is the information that important?" Stuart said. "So, she knew Todd in another life. Give her a break, Hedley, she must be sick to the back teeth of you by now. Either that, or she's scared stiff you'll find something to blame her for after all."

Hedley pulled a face. "Don't get cocky with me, laddie. And you're right, I may yet find something to throw at her."

Stuart turned away and went back to his desk.

"That's it, run off and sulk." Hedley returned to his office and slammed the door shut. He logged onto the system and looked up Terry Blake. It was as Lou had said. A few misdemeanours that got more serious over time until, finally, the assault happened. What Hedley was looking for was any connection to Rawlins in the early days. But as far as he could see, there was nothing obvious. But the two had known each other, they'd worked together these last couple of years at least. The question that was eating Hedley now was what had they been working on. Was it the diamond robbery, like Murray said? Neither of them was around to answer the question, but Selina Harris might know. If she didn't, or wouldn't say, he'd ask Chloe. Although what she'd tell him was anyone's guess. She'd likely deny all knowledge and turn on the tears.

Terry Blake and Chloe had both lived in Ardwick and gone to the same school. On a hunch, he checked where

Selina had been educated. He wasn't surprised to see she had also attended that same school. That meant all of them had known each other. Rawlins and Selina, Blake and Chloe — what had they been planning together that had got two of them killed?

* * *

Now in a better mood, Hedley nodded at Stuart on his way through the incident room. "With me. I want Selina Harris to talk to us. If she plays the game, it might be possible to offer her some sort of deal."

"I thought that went against your sensibilities, Hedley. What's changed?"

Hedley just shook his head. The fact was, despite all the evidence, he was beginning to think that Selina was right, she had indeed been set up.

* * *

They found Selina huddled at the table with her solicitor. "You should try eating something," Hedley said. "I'm told you haven't touched a bite since you joined us."

"No way am I eating that muck. I'll starve first." She folded her arms and glared at him. "I want out. Mr Montfort here thinks like me that your evidence won't stand up in court, and that anyone could have planted it."

Hedley merely smiled at the pair and took his seat. Montfort had a sheaf of notes in front of him and a self-satisfied look on his face. A look that suggested he was right and they were all fools.

"I might have agreed with Mr Montfort if we hadn't found Todd's blood on your blouse. Any idea how it got there?"

Hedley waited for a response. Montfort cleared his throat and scribbled something on his notes. Selina's eyes narrowed. She appeared to be considering his words. "You can't have," she said eventually. "Because I was never in that caravan and I didn't kill him. I haven't been anywhere near Simon Todd for ages."

"Well, that blood got on your sleeve somehow," Hedley said.

"And it's definitely Simon's?"

"Absolutely. There's no mistake."

The news appeared to deflate Selina, which was a first. She looked anxiously at Montfort for guidance.

"What do I do?" she asked quietly.

"You tell the truth," he said.

At this, she slammed her hand on the table top. "But it is the truth! Why won't anyone listen to me?"

"You don't make it easy," Hedley said. "But supposing for a moment we do believe what you're telling us and we go with your theory that you've been set up. Why would someone go to all that trouble?"

"I've been thinking about that too," she said. "I can think of only two reasons. One is revenge, someone wants to teach me a lesson of some sort. And the other," she looked at Hedley, "has to do with the diamonds. As for the revenge angle, I'm not a nice person. I upset people. I know that. I've never been any different. I also know that some of those people are in a position to get their own back."

"Can you name names?" Stuart asked.

"I'll think about it, though at the moment top of the list is Chloe Todd."

That got Hedley's interest. "Are you sure? She's such a delicate little thing according to my colleague here. Is she up to planning such a thing?"

Selina shrugged. "Who knows? But she does have a motive. Anyway, if we discount her there are plenty of others. Look who I was married to."

"What about the diamonds?" Hedley asked. With both Rawlins and Todd dead, Selina was the only one left who might offer some insight as to where they were being hidden. "Do you know where they are?"

"Yes, I do. But I doubt that anyone will be able to get their hands on them."

"Let me be the judge of that," Hedley said.

"After the robbery, Dean stashed the diamonds in a safe. He and Simon shared the combination, they each created their own half."

"D'you know where this safe is?"

"It's the one in Dean's office on the Quays."

"And Chloe is not involved at all," Stuart reiterated, much to Hedley's annoyance.

"Simon used her as window dressing, that's all. They were supposed to play the happily married suburban couple. Dean didn't want Simon drawing attention to himself."

For the first time since he'd been dealing with this woman, Hedley believed she was telling the truth. The look on her face said it all. At one point he thought she might even burst into tears. No doubt the prospect of years in prison was catching up with her.

"Tell me about the robbery," he said.

"It was about a year ago, masterminded by Dean."

Now they were finally getting somewhere.

"The jewels were being transported from a strongroom to various high-class jewellers in the North West when the vehicle was attacked. Two of the guards were badly injured and a third was killed. The company who owned the diamonds were afraid of losing business. Fearing that their customers would lose trust in their ability to look after their costly stock, they played it down."

"They certainly did that," Hedley said. "There was a rumour going round that there never was any robbery."

"It took place all right. The company who were distributing the jewels greased a few palms and managed to get a media blackout imposed for a while, until someone leaked the story. It became headline news and the insurance company paid out."

"Did you ever see the diamonds yourself?" Stuart asked.

"No. As far as I know, the only people to have had that pleasure were Dean and Simon. Dean may have shown images of them to potential customers. He had someone in Dubai in mind. He'd sold stuff to him before."

"Name?" Hedley said.

"You must be joking. Dean would never confide something like that to me. I spent months waiting for him to return and claim them. When he didn't, I began to get suspicious. At first I thought Simon might have double-crossed him, but even he wouldn't have been that stupid."

"And now you can't get at them because you don't know the combination to the safe," Hedley said.

Selina gave him a wry smile. "A bugger, isn't it? All that wealth and no way of accessing it."

"Poetic justice in a way," Hedley remarked. "Tell me about these enemies. Anyone in particular?"

"Too many to mention," she said. "Thugs who worked for Dean and helped with the robbery and reckon they're owed. The latest being Simon Todd. Not that I saw much of him but me and Chloe did wonder what he was up to. Then there is Chloe herself. As you know, her and Simon have been living in my house, so I got a taste of what that relationship was really like. Chloe hated Simon. Despite the impression they tried to give the neighbours, they were not a happy couple."

"You think Chloe had a hand in Todd's murder?" Hedley asked.

Selina considered this for a moment or two. "Well, I certainly didn't kill him — despite the evidence you say you have — so it has to be someone else." She shrugged. "I reckon Chloe could kill if pushed."

"Did Chloe have anything to do with the diamonds?" Hedley asked.

"She was never involved. I doubt Simon trusted her enough, and Dean rarely saw her."

CHAPTER THIRTY-FIVE

"Where exactly is this safe?" Hedley asked. "That block of offices is several storeys high."

"Dean's office is on the second floor," Selina said. "The safe is in the first office on the left-hand side as you go into the corridor. It's a fairly average-looking thing but heavy. There's no way it can be moved."

Hedley smiled. "I wasn't thinking of moving it. But I would like to get it open."

He saw the look Selina gave him, a mix of anger and despair. "So would I."

Hedley looked at Montfort. "I'll give you some time with your client but you must know that we have solid evidence, and now it appears we have motive as well."

"Don't be stupid," Selina said. "Why would I kill the only person who could help me get at the diamonds? He did have half the combination."

"There are other ways of opening a safe, Selina. Don't tell me you haven't already given that one some thought," Hedley said.

"It would have been easier with the combination," she admitted.

"But you did intend to try?" Hedley levelled at her. "Okay, tell me what your plan was."

Selina turned away from them. "I've got a safe-breaker on the job. Apparently, he's the best in the north."

"Jack Langley," Hedley said at once. "And you're right, he was good in his day but he's getting on and pretty much past it by now. How's he doing anyway?"

"How should I know? I've been incarcerated in here all night and haven't been able to contact him." She looked at Hedley, then Stuart. "But if he does get that safe open, he won't be able to resist. Who could? He will help himself and be richer than he ever dreamed possible."

"Okay. Address of this office," Hedley demanded. He passed Selina a pad and pencil. "Write it down."

* * *

"I know where that is, the new business part of the city," Stuart said when he saw the address.

"Is back-up arranged?" Hedley asked. "This is a fortune in diamonds we're hoping to find."

"Everything's in place," Stuart told him. "Selina is under lock and key and it looks as if Chloe is innocent. Not what you want to hear but it's looking highly likely. So put your face straight. You look as if you've been sucking on a lemon."

"Cheeky bugger. D'you reckon Selina told us the truth?" Hedley asked. "I still have my doubts. What d'you think we'll find when we open that safe?"

"Diamonds, according to Selina. But I don't see it being that simple," Stuart said.

Hedley shook his head. "Me neither, too many variables. We've been led to believe that after the robbery, those diamonds went from the armoured vehicle to Rawlins' mob and then to the safe. No detours. Allegedly, they have been there ever since. So what was Rawlins doing in that cellar? That's the part I don't get."

"It has to have something to do with Murray. It was Murray that killed him, after all," Stuart said.

Hedley shook his head. "I don't go with that. If Murray had got hold of those diamonds, he'd be long gone. If they are stashed in that safe, Murray must have known he wasn't going to get his hands on them. No, there's something else. Like I said, the theory that Murray killed Rawlins for those diamonds is too convenient. Think about it. Murray and Rawlins plan the robbery together. Rawlins cuts Murray out, he feels cheated and they fight. Murray uses a gun and Rawlins ends up dead. But there is a glaring hole in that theory. If we presume the robbery had already taken place, there's no way Rawlins would have met Murray on his own in a place as isolated as that cellar."

"You could be right," Stuart said. "But if you are, it means the diamonds have to be in that safe. Getting it open could be tricky."

"Jack Langley is good," Hedley said. "But not as good as that new firm we've got. They'll have it open before you can blink."

"I've never seen that amount of wealth before. I must admit I'm having difficulty believing it," Stuart said.

"Me too, laddie. But if they aren't where Rawlins put them, we're stuffed. We'll never recover them."

Stuart gave a deep sigh. "If those stones are not where they're supposed to be, I'm at a loss."

"You and me both."

* * *

What with the traffic and the one-way system it took them nearly an hour to get to Rawlins' office. A handful of uniformed officers were waiting for them when they arrived.

"There's people inside," one of them said. "Rawlins had the suite of offices on the second floor. PC Bannister has been up and told Langley to stop what he's doing."

Hedley nodded. "Bet he loved that. And no fee off Selina to look forward to. Have our own people turned up?"

"Lancaster Safe-Breakers, yes sir. The boss, Martin Adams, reckons a few hours tops and he should have it open."

This was music to Hedley's ears. He'd been chasing these diamonds for over a year. Now, finally, he might get his hands on them. 'Might'. Where Dean Rawlins was concerned, he couldn't be sure of anything. Even in death, the man was giving him the runaround.

Stuart smiled. "I'm getting quite excited. Are you coming up? See the booty first hand?"

Hedley gave him a reluctant smile. "Wouldn't miss it for the world."

CHAPTER THIRTY-SIX

While they waited for the safe to be opened, Hedley wandered around Rawlins' former domain. He couldn't work out what the villain had actually done here. There was no paperwork, nothing in the filing cabinets — in fact, the place was empty.

"An expensive place to house a safe," he said to Stuart. "Because that's all these offices appear to have been used for."

"I've had a word with the people who work upstairs," Stuart said. "They say the place was hardly ever used. Occasionally mail was delivered, and a man fitting Todd's description came in once a week to check the place and pick it up. The receptionist downstairs remembered Rawlins too. Said he was pleasant enough, always had a kind word."

That was just like the villain. He had always worn a veneer of respectability. Not that it had ever fooled Hedley. The two had engaged in enough verbal fisticuffs over the years for Hedley to know the truth behind the façade. Hedley had had the pleasure of arresting Rawlins on any number of occasions; the problem was making anything stick. The one he recalled most vividly was when Rawlins was up on a charge of armed robbery. He should have gone down for it — as far as Hedley was concerned, they had a cast-iron case — but a clever lawyer got him off. It didn't do the solicitor much good though. Rawlins must have been afraid he'd talk, because two days later he ended up dead at the wheel of his posh sports car. The steering had been interfered with but no one could prove who had done it. Naturally, Hedley had his own ideas but the powers that be made him drop it.

"Want to find a coffee?" Stuart asked. "The noise that bloody drill is making is doing my head in."

"He's drilling out the lock," Hedley said.

"I know that. I'm not stupid. I just wish he could do it more quietly."

Hedley gestured to one of the uniformed officers. "Keep your eyes peeled. If and when they get that door open, send someone to find me."

Hedley wanted to be there at the moment the door swung open. He wouldn't admit it but he was as nervous as a kitten.

"We find those diamonds and it will wrap this case up nicely," Stuart said. "No more Rawlins, and his right-hand man, Todd, is out of the way too. Murray is under lock and key, things couldn't be better."

"D'you mean that, or are you just being sarcastic?"

"I mean it, Hedley. It's a year since Rawlins went missing. Remember the day he didn't turn up at court? A lot has happened in the interim and it's taken a lot of work to get to where we are."

"Sorted now though, isn't it? And if the diamonds are in that safe, it will top things off." Despite what he'd just said, Hedley was reserving his judgement. There were too many possibilities and all involved Rawlins. And what about Chloe Todd? What part had she played in it all? He still couldn't shift the feeling that she was mixed up in it somewhere. Hedley had made up his mind to have another word with her, and this time he'd go it alone. Stuart would only complicate matters. The sooner he forgot all about her, the better.

Coffee finished, Hedley was fed up with waiting. "Nip upstairs and see how far they've got," he told Stuart. "Your legs are younger than mine."

Without arguing, Stuart got up from the table and left. As soon as he'd gone, Hedley took a scrap of paper from his pocket. On it was the number for Brenda Howells, Chloe's neighbour.

"It's Hedley Sharpe," he said. "Sorry to trouble you, but could you tell me if Chloe is at home?"

"Yes, but I believe she plans to go and see a friend, perhaps stay over for a few days. Why? You're not going to bother her again, are you?"

"Not at all. We're wrapping up the case. I just thought she might be able to help with a couple of things to do with that husband of hers."

"That husband of hers was a monster. Chloe was terrified of him, and with good reason. Please be careful what you say to her, won't you? Chloe is still fragile. She's not left the house since we identified his body. I have been taking meals across for her but she has no appetite. The last thing she needs is you on her back."

"It's nothing heavy, Mrs Howells, I assure you. But there is no one else we can ask."

"D'you want me to tell her you're coming?" Brenda asked.

"No. As you say, we don't want to upset her. I'd appreciate you being on hand in case she finds my presence worrying."

"Shall we say later today then?"

"Perfect," Hedley said.

Just as he ended the call, Stuart returned. He shook his head despondently. "Not today, I'm afraid. The drilling is taking longer than anticipated. Something to do with the hardness of the metal. He reckons he should have it open tomorrow."

Not ideal but it would have to do. "In that case, we might as well wind up for today. We've put in the hours this last week, so I reckon we deserve some down time."

"Sounds good to me," Stuart said. "I'll drop you at the station."

CHAPTER THIRTY-SEVEN

Chloe had been keeping a low profile since Simon's death. Brenda had told her the neighbours were keen to rally round but she'd asked her to keep them away; she wasn't yet ready to face people. They were kind and sympathetic but she knew they'd have questions she'd prefer not to answer.

Brenda had done a great job. She'd done exactly as asked. Chloe had met no one like her, except perhaps for Abby. Thinking of Brenda cheered her up. If all went well, she'd ring her soon, say that last goodbye. Chloe couldn't wait for this to be over so she could relax and pick up some of the threads of her old life.

Relax? Was she kidding herself? Over the last day or so she'd worn herself out going over the recent events in her head, checking that she'd made no mistakes. Everything the police have must point to Selina killing Simon. She prayed that things would stay as they were and Selina remained the chief suspect. Selina deserved everything that was coming her way. The last thing Chloe wanted was for the police to believe they'd made a mistake and release her. If that were to happen, Selina would come straight after her.

Chloe was about to go upstairs and have a bath when the front doorbell rang. She went to answer it, assuming the caller to be Brenda. But it wasn't. Standing on the doorstep was none other than that fat detective, Hedley Sharpe. What now? Surely not more torment from this man that she'd come to detest.

"I wasn't sure you'd still be here," he said. "I thought you might have moved out or gone to see that poorly friend of yours."

"Visiting my friend will take a couple of days at best. Other than that, I've nowhere to go." They were both lying. "Selina wants me out and refuses to give me any leeway. But I'm afraid she'll have to wait. I'm doing my best but finding somewhere isn't easy."

"Selina is under lock and key," Hedley said. "She's in no position to bother you about the house or anything else."

"She has solicitors to do her dirty work." Chloe picked up a bundle of letters from the hall table. "All these are threatening to have me evicted."

As Hedley well knew, Selina was used to getting her own way. And Chloe was right. If she didn't go willingly, it would only be a matter of time before Selina arranged for some of Rawlins' thugs to throw her out.

"If you're that desperate, I'm sure your friend Brenda would help. Perhaps she'll take you in. She seems like a kind person to me. In fact, if you want her to be here with you now, I'm sure she'll oblige."

"No, I'll be okay. I've put on her enough recently. I think it's about time I fended for myself. It's just that I'm at a loss as to how to go about it."

Chloe wasn't lying about that one. For two or three years now, there had always been someone to lean on. This last year it had been Simon, and as much as she hated him, he had provided a home and money for the pair of them. Being on her own scared Chloe but she had to look at the positives. If all went well, a new life beckoned, one in which she'd want for nothing.

Hedley followed her into the sitting room. He couldn't fail to notice the packing cases stacked high against the wall and the fact that the furniture consisted of a single sofa. But Chloe didn't care. Let him think what he wanted.

"I might have to leave in a hurry," Chloe explained, gesturing at the mess. "Selina has threatened to send in the bailiffs. Better to be ready." She narrowed her eyes. "Why are you here anyway?"

"Oh, nothing heavy, don't worry," he said airily. "We've more or less sorted the case now, but there are still one or two things I want to clear up. Tell me about the man you met when you were living on the streets. You know, the man who got you straightened out. The man before Simon."

This was unexpected. Talk of him was like a blow to the guts. It would take Chloe every ounce of self-control she could muster to keep from breaking down. Did the detective have any idea what 'the man before Simon', as he'd referred to him, had meant to her, the depth of feeling they'd shared? No, he couldn't. It would have taken a deal of research and why would he be interested anyway?

She swallowed. "Who d'you mean?"

"I don't know his name, just that he was a reporter researching the Manchester drug problem. You knew him well, so I'm told."

"Well, you were told wrong," she said. "I never met anyone like that. I did live on the streets for a while but then I went home, and shortly afterwards I met Simon." The words almost choked her. How could she deny the existence of the love of her life? But it was too soon to tell anyone about him. If her plan was to succeed, she had no choice but to keep quiet.

"Are you sure you didn't know him? Only, the person who told me about you and him was so sure of it."

"Who was that?" Chloe demanded.

"Actually, it was two people. One of them was Selina Harris."

Chloe gave a little smile. A way out had just presented itself. "That explains it then. I don't know what her game is but she's lying. Where I'm concerned, she always lies."

"I said two people, Chloe. Selina might well lie but I have absolute trust in the second person. No way would she lie to me." He wasn't lying either, Millie was totally trustworthy.

Chloe tried to stop herself squirming under his gaze. No doubt he was waiting for her to trip herself up.

"Come on, Chloe, why not tell me the truth."

"You're trying to trick me," she wailed. "I've had enough. I want you to leave now."

Hedley raised his hands. "Okay, but it would be easier if you were honest with me. I will find out the truth eventually. I'm told you loved this man, so I can't imagine why you would deny knowing him."

Chloe had no choice if she was to succeed. Unbeknownst to the detective, the case he was working on had everything to do with the man he was asking about. Had he guessed as much? Put the pieces of the puzzle together? Chloe didn't like the way he was staring at her. "You said Selina was under lock and key. Why is that?"

"I shouldn't discuss this with you, but we're holding her on a charge of murder."

"Simon?" she asked.

"Why d'you ask that?"

Chloe smiled. "Rawlins is dead, so that only leaves Simon. Selina made no secret of the fact that she hated him."

"Selina has known Simon a long time. I'm surprised the pair of them weren't more friendly," Hedley said.

"What d'you mean by that?" Chloe asked.

"She knew him when he went under the name of Terry Blake. You knew him too, I believe."

He had been digging. Chloe didn't like that. "The three of us all went to the same school. So what? As for Terry, I met him again when he was doing well for himself and we started seeing each other."

Had he swallowed her explanation? She couldn't read his expression.

"Now if you don't mind, I'd like to get on."

"Of course. Sorry to disturb you." He was almost at the front door when he stopped and turned back. "Do you know anything about the diamond robbery?"

Why bring that up? "What? Do you think Selina's responsible for that too?" She laughed, but it sounded false even to her. "I've always believed that if the robbery took place at all, it would've been down to Rawlins."

"We believe that too," Hedley said. "Did you know that his gang got away with two million pounds worth of stones?"

Chloe nodded. "Do you know what happened to them?"

"We think we do," he said. "We also think that Dean kept that information to a couple of close associates — his wife, your husband, and that was it. But I wondered about you. Did Simon tell you where they were hidden, Chloe?"

She shook her head. "All I know is that Rawlins was keeping them hidden until it was safe for him to retrieve them. Now that he's dead, there's not much chance of that happening."

"You and Simon were together at the time. Are you sure you don't know where Rawlins hid them? That Simon didn't let it slip?"

"I said no, didn't I? Plus, if I knew where he'd stashed a fortune in diamonds, d'you imagine I'd still be here worrying about where I'll be living next week?"

Did he believe her? His face said not but he had no proof. All she had to do now was keep her nerve.

"I'm surprised you were kept in the dark," Hedley said. "Selina knew, and she's had the sense to tell us. All goes well and we should have retrieved them by this time tomorrow."

Chloe smiled. "Well, I wish you luck. That'll be quite a coup. You'll have rid the world of two crooks and found the diamonds. You should get promoted."

What a joke. The man was a fool if he believed he was going to find them so easily. There had only ever been one person who knew where those diamonds were, and it wasn't Simon, or Dean Rawlins.

CHAPTER THIRTY-EIGHT

Day seven

Hedley was in a good mood. Two cups of coffee, a large fry-up and he was ready for whatever the day threw at him. Fingers crossed, it would be two million pounds' worth of diamonds.

Stuart picked him up and they made their way to Rawlins' office on the Quays. "We're on a promise this morning." He winked at Hedley. "What d'you think? Are those stones in that safe or not?"

In truth, Hedley didn't know what to think. Knowing the way Rawlins operated, he would be surprised if they were. Nothing to do with that gangster was simple. But if they weren't there, what the hell had Rawlins done with them?

Stuart glanced at him. "You don't look too happy. What's up, nervous?"

"Of course I'm bloody nervous. We're hoping to find a fortune in diamonds, aren't we? To be honest, I can't help feeling that even from the grave, Rawlins is laughing at us."

"Don't be daft. He robbed that armoured truck and stashed the stones in his safe until he could sell them. After that, Murray shot him. Therefore they're still where Rawlins left them — in that safe. Have faith, Hedley, and curb the imagination."

Hedley wished he had Stuart's confidence. A dozen scenarios played out in his head. What if Rawlins hadn't had time to stash the stones in the safe? What if he'd been intercepted first? But if that was what had happened, surely Murray would have them? After all, he was the last person to see Rawlins alive. Given that Murray appeared to be living on the breadline when they'd found him in Stockport, that was obviously not the case.

Hedley decided it was no good trying to second guess what they'd find. Better to wait until the safe was opened and then all would be revealed.

When they arrived, the police guard was still in place, and had been there all night. If anyone had had any bright ideas, they wouldn't have got very far.

The pair parked up and made their way to Rawlins' office. More uniforms were positioned around the room.

"Another ten minutes and I'll be in," Adams, the safe-breaker, told them. "It's been bloody hard. Thank goodness they don't make them like this anymore."

Hedley peered over his shoulder. If the stones really were there, he wanted to be the first to see them.

"Ready?" With a flourish, Adams pulled on the handle and the door swung open. "I hope you find what you want. I worked hard on that safe, so it had better be worth it."

Without answering, Hedley bent down and squinted. Stuart stood behind him, holding his breath. The atmosphere was electric. Both men had different expectations, different theories. Hedley remained bent over for a few seconds, and then he straightened up. His face said it all. He hadn't really expected anything else. The interior of the safe was tiny, with only enough room for a few papers or a small box. But it was empty.

"There's nothing here." Despite himself, he was disappointed. Once again, Rawlins had got the better of him. "What's that crafty bugger done with them?"

"Calm down, Hedley. After all, you half expected this," Stuart reminded him.

"That doesn't help." Hedley felt the anticlimax keenly. "This gives us a right problem. There's two million in diamonds lurking somewhere, and we haven't a clue. What's worse, there's no one left to ask."

"There's always Selina," Stuart reminded him.

"Even if she knows, she won't help us. You know what she's like. Anyway, why should she?"

"I thought we'd spoken about a deal. You were all for it at one point."

"Not anymore," Hedley said firmly. "I doubt we'd get the truth out of her. Like everyone else, she'll simply conspire against us. Whoever has got those stones is one clever crook. They've led us a right merry dance and now we're back where we started."

The trouble was, Hedley couldn't think of anyone who was that clever. Someone new perhaps, someone who up until now had been keeping their head down. But who could that be? All the suspects were known to them.

"I doubt there's anyone else involved," Stuart said. "Rawlins had them, we know that. He brought them here and is believed to have put them in that safe. The way I see it is that only one of three things could have happened. Someone took them from him in that cellar. Someone as yet unknown to us opened the safe and took them. Or Rawlins hid them somewhere else."

Hedley knew there was a lot of sense in what Stuart was saying but it didn't help. And which option were they supposed to go for? "No one would dare take anything from Rawlins. Remember how he was. He could have taken on the very devil himself and won." He nodded at the safe. "As for opening that bugger, there was no damage to the lock so whoever took them must have known the combination."

"Perhaps Simon Todd knew it."

"In that case, why hang around? Why all the pretence?"

"Then Rawlins hid them somewhere else," Stuart said.

"Where they'll never be found unless our luck changes. What I can't understand is why."

"Perhaps he thought the safe was too obvious," Stuart said.

"I could go for that except that no one knew for sure that Rawlins was behind that robbery. It was an urban myth until recently. Todd kept quiet and so did Selina. I doubt anyone else had any idea. Hence, there was no reason for anyone besides the two of them to suspect that they weren't here." Hedley thought for a moment. "Of course, that's what Rawlins could have wanted folk to think — that he'd locked them in the safe — while the truth was very different."

"He was bluffing, in other words," Stuart said.

"Leading us all up the bloody garden path more like." Hedley glanced over his shoulder at Adams, who was hovering in the background. "You might as well call it a day, mate. There's nothing to be had here."

"So, where do we look next?" Stuart said.

"What about that big house of his?" Hedley said.

"Okay, we'll mount a search."

CHAPTER THIRTY-NINE

"How are our guests?" Hedley asked Ryan Ogden when they were back at the station.

Ryan rolled his eyes. "Still sounding off. Yelling that she's innocent to anyone who'll listen. And she wants to see you. Reckons she's remembered something that will prove she didn't do it."

This Hedley had to hear. No doubt it would be good. Selina had had plenty of time to make up a good tale. "Want to join me?" he asked Stuart.

"I really don't fancy another run-in with her. The woman is poison, hasn't a good word to say about anyone."

"Come on, laddie. We have no choice. If Selina thinks she can prove she's innocent, as far-fetched as we think it is, we have to listen to her."

Ten minutes later, they walked into the interview room to find a very different Selina. Her voice was silky smooth. "I can't believe I forgot about Desmond," she purred. "And we had such a good time too."

"Desmond?" Hedley echoed. "Who the hell is he?"

She smirked. "The man I was with when Simon Todd was getting himself killed."

"And you've only just remembered him," Hedley said. "Come on, Selina. Giving a false alibi is a criminal offence, and it won't just be you who'll be charged. This Desmond, whoever he is, will be in serious trouble too."

She smiled. "You're trying to frighten me, Superintendent."

"I can't just take your word for it. I do need some proof."

"Of course," she said. "Go and ask him. Let me have something to write on and I'll give you his address."

The uniformed officer handed her a pad and pen. She scribbled it down and handed it to Hedley. "Speak to Desmond and he'll confirm that I was with him that night." She winked. "And I mean all night. I stayed at his till morning."

Hedley didn't know what to think. If she was right, it blew this case wide open.

"Something else for you to think about," she added. "If I didn't kill Simon, you should ask yourselves who did. I know who my money is on."

"Exactly who are you talking about?" Hedley asked wearily.

"Isn't it obvious? Chloe, of course. I admit I'm surprised. At first I didn't believe she was up to it, but languishing in here I've had plenty of time to think. She hated Simon and she hates me. Killing him and framing me was the perfect way for her to get her own back for all the ills of the past." She pulled a face. "And believe me, there have been a fair few. I've not been very nice to Chloe over the years."

"And this Desmond person will back you up?" Stuart asked.

"You bet your life he will. Desmond is a good friend and as honest as the day is long."

That remained to be seen. As far as Hedley was concerned, this was far too neat. "Did he take you out?"

"No, we fancied a quiet night in. We got a box of chocolates, a bottle of wine and had a catch-up."

"Okay then, we'll go and speak to him."

Hedley left the interview room with more questions than answers. Why hadn't she mentioned this man before? And more to the point, if this was a fabrication, they must have spoken. Perhaps that dodgy solicitor of hers had helped out there.

"What d'you think?" Stuart asked. "Is she on the level, or is she playing us?"

"We'll have to speak to this Desmond bloke first." Hedley checked his watch. "Given he lives out Bolton way, we'll pay him a visit and then call it a day."

"What about the search of Rawlins' house?" Stuart asked.

"It's not going anywhere, tomorrow will do."

* * *

Desmond Potter was not the type of man Hedley thought Selina would go for. Like his house, his style of dress was old fashioned, and he was considerably older than her. Hedley put him in his late sixties.

Stuart made the introductions and Desmond invited them inside.

"We're here to talk about Selina Harris," Hedley said. "You're a friend of hers, I believe."

"Indeed. I've known Selina since she was in her teens. I knew her parents, and since their demise I've kept an eye on her." He gave a little smile. "Which isn't easy because Selina is somewhat wild."

"Have you seen her recently?" Stuart asked.

Desmond nodded. "I took her out a few days ago. It was a lovely evening so we went for a stroll in a park near here and then I took her out for dinner."

Hedley took note of that one. Selina had told them that the pair had stayed in.

"How long was she with you?"

"From about five thirty until I dropped her off at home at about eleven."

Another inconsistency. Selina had said that she'd been at Desmond's house all night.

"And you're sure about that?" Stuart asked. "There's no mistake."

"Look, I'm not yet in my dotage. I have an excellent memory and I know exactly when I last saw Selina and how we spent our time."

"Would you be prepared to make a statement to that effect?" Hedley asked him.

"Of course."

"What you say will be used as evidence in court," Hedley warned him. "You may not be aware of this but Selina is up on a murder charge and has named you as her alibi. If you lie to us, I'll charge you with obstruction."

"Yes, yes, I know all that, but it's as I said, she was with me."

The man sounded so positive.

"We went here for supper." He handed Stuart a leaflet. "The Chinese restaurant on the High Street."

Stuart looked at it. "And they will vouch for you? Confirm you were there?"

Desmond looked confused. "You intend to ask them?"

"Naturally," Stuart said.

"On second thoughts, perhaps it was the Indian restaurant." He shook his head. "You've got me all mixed up now. I'm really not sure which one it was."

"She said you gave her chocolates," Hedley said. "Where did they come from?"

"The newsagent's on the corner," Desmond said.

"And you're prepared to give a statement that includes everything you've just told us?" Hedley repeated.

Desmond nodded. "I want to do all I can to help Selina. She's not capable of killing anyone."

How wrong he was. "I'll send an officer round later to take your statement," Hedley said. "Thank you for seeing us, sir."

Out in the car, Hedley said, "That man has no idea what a serious matter giving a false statement is. What he told us is very different from Selina's story."

"It smacks of them not having enough time to get their stories in sync. Anyway, it's easily checked out," Stuart said.

“I’ll get uniform to speak to the two restaurants and the newsagent.”

“I want every single word he uttered checked,” Hedley said. “And when we find out that Desmond has lied to us, we’ll throw the bloody book at him.”

“What now?” Stuart asked.

“I need a drink. I’m sick of this case and of being continually led up the garden path.”

“I hate to say it but we’re running out of suspects too.”

“Not quite, laddie. There’s still Chloe Todd,” Hedley said. “We’ll have to take a closer look at her part in all this. And don’t forget that we still haven’t searched that house she’s living in.”

“I’d stake my career on the fact that she couldn’t have had anything to do with Simon’s death. She’s not got it in her,” Stuart said.

“That’s not what Selina thinks,” Hedley said. “And I must admit I tend to agree with her. We search that house and, depending on what we find, we may bring her in again. A formal interview won’t do any harm.”

CHAPTER FORTY

Day eight

First thing the following morning, Chloe woke to the sound of banging on the front door. Someone was certainly anxious to see her. Wrapping a dressing gown around herself, she went downstairs to see what was going on. Her heart sank when she saw the two detectives, along with several uniformed officers, standing on the doorstep. Why couldn't they leave her alone?

She flung open the door. "What now?"

"We have a warrant to search these premises," Hedley said.

Chloe wasn't amused. Hadn't they put her through enough torment? "What do you imagine you'll find? There's nothing here. I've packed what little I own ready for the move."

Stuart led her into the sitting room. "Don't worry, we'll be as quick as we can."

Chloe shook her head in frustration. "Go through whatever you want. Only . . . You see that navy holdall on the table? Go careful with the contents. It's all I have left of Lily."

"I'll look through that myself," Stuart said.

"I suppose I don't have much choice in the matter. But if you must search, please don't make a mess. I understand there's an estate agent coming round anytime." She nodded at the boxes stacked against the wall. "There's not much to search, so I don't expect you'll be long."

Stuart nodded. Looking at his face, Chloe could see that he was on her side.

Not the other one though. Hedley blundered into the room with half a dozen officers behind him. He pointed at the packing cases. "Those will have to be opened and gone through."

"You're looking for the diamonds, I suppose. Well, they're not here," she said. "Even if I did have them, I wouldn't be so stupid as to keep them with me."

"We don't think it was you that hid them," Hedley told her. "But your husband is a different matter. Did he have a safe here? Anywhere else he may have stashed them?"

Chloe shook her head, somewhat amused. "Simon might have worked with Rawlins but that villain never told him anything he didn't need to know. He certainly wouldn't have given him a fortune in diamonds to look after. Simon always believed they were in the safe in Rawlins' office. Other than that, he told me nothing, so I can't help you."

"You're sure about that, Chloe?" Hedley asked.

"Quite sure. If he'd known where they were, there's no way he'd have stayed with me once he knew that Rawlins was dead. He'd have taken the first plane out."

* * *

Two hours later and the search team had turned up nothing. "This is one huge waste of time," Hedley said, his face red with effort. "There's no diamonds here."

He prowled from one room to the next, telling himself to think. Where would a man like Rawlins put a fortune in diamonds? He looked out at the expanse of lawn, surrounded on all sides by shrubs. "Could the bugger have buried them somewhere in that little lot, d'you reckon?"

"I hope not," Stuart said with a shudder. "That's one huge garden out there. It would take months to search."

"You're right," Hedley said. "He would have wanted them somewhere where he could get his hands on them easily."

"Hedley, you're clutching at straws. Sooner or later you're going to have to accept that those diamonds are gone for good," Stuart said.

But Hedley wasn't about to give up. Finding the diamonds had become something of a mission. "I can't, laddie. If it's humanly possible, I have to find them."

"Well I don't think it is possible," Stuart said. "Rawlins took that knowledge to his grave."

He was right, but Hedley hated having to admit it.

"Don't forget you wanted to interview Chloe about Simon Todd's murder," Stuart said. "I wish things hadn't turned out like this. Chloe has been through enough."

Hedley sighed. "I must admit I'm coming round to your way of thinking. I don't think Chloe is up to it either. But one more question will do no harm."

Hedley marched back to where Chloe was sitting. "Can you tell me where you were four nights ago?"

"Here. Why? I've not left this house in days. I haven't felt up to it. Ask Brenda if you don't believe me. She's been doing a bit of shopping for me and has been kind enough to cook me the occasional meal."

That sounded reasonable. He nodded at Stuart. "Go and check that out, will you?"

Chloe didn't seem to be in the least bit worried, which annoyed Hedley. He still didn't share Stuart's insistence that she wasn't guilty of anything.

"Why are you so interested in my whereabouts anyway?" she asked. "What am I accused of now?"

"Selina has given us the name of a witness who has told us where she was when your husband was murdered," Hedley said. He watched for a reaction but got nothing but a shrug of her slender shoulders.

"Good for her. Always full of surprises is Selina. She'll be lying, of course. She's an expert at that."

Hedley saw the look. Chloe wasn't even mildly rattled by what he'd said. "Possibly but we will check things out."

"You can take my word for it, Selina's alibi will amount to nothing." Chloe hoped that was true — her future depended on it. "Do you think she's telling the truth? You must have interviewed hundreds of people during your career. Can't you tell when someone's lying?"

"Given her reputation and history, we doubt her story," Stuart said. "Once we know for sure, that's it, as far as you're concerned. We won't be pestering you again."

Chloe nodded. This had to work out. It just had to. Selina must be put away for a long time. She could not go on living in the shadow of that woman.

CHAPTER FORTY-ONE

The drive back to the station passed in silence. Left with questions that had no answers, Hedley was cheesed off.

Eventually, Stuart pulled into the station, switched off the engine and sat back. "Sulking won't solve anything. Murray killed Rawlins, and Cowboy too, unfortunately. Selina killed Simon Todd. You can forget about Desmond because we've got that one being checked, and I'll lay odds it turns out to be a load of nonsense."

"That's as maybe," Hedley said. "But if we decide that Selina did kill Todd, what's the motive? Why would she kill him? It would have made more sense if she'd gone after Chloe."

"There's a simple answer to that one. Selina wanted Simon's half of the combination to the safe. She'll have threatened him and when he wouldn't play ball, she shot him. We have no idea whether she knew Rawlins' half or not. And at that point neither Selina nor Todd could have known that the safe was empty."

Hedley considered this. Stuart could be right. His partner thought things through logically, whereas Hedley was more inclined to go with his gut. "But if Selina did kill Simon, she would have stood no chance of getting what she wanted."

"Think of her temper," Stuart said. "She loses it at the drop of a hat. Remember what she did to Chloe. Selina took her into the kitchen and threatened to do her a horrific injury."

Hedley grunted. "The woman is unhinged."

"There you are then. I don't know why we're even discussing it. We've been over this so many times that there's no doubt left in my head," Stuart said.

"What? Are you suggesting we wrap it up? Accept that we have no chance of finding the diamonds?"

"If you keep on at it, you'll drive yourself mad," Stuart said. "You get obsessed with things, Hedley. Remember how you were with Rawlins? You hounded him for years."

Hedley sniffed. "And he deserved it. He killed my wife, remember? I'm glad the bastard is dead. I just wish I'd done him myself."

* * *

Back at the station, Ryan Ogden was waiting for them. "Nothing in Desmond's statement is true, sir. We've spoken to all the eateries in the vicinity of his house and neither of them was in any of them that night. The newsagent has no recollection of selling him those chocolates either, and he says he knows Desmond pretty well."

Hedley nodded. "So, that puts Selina Harris back in the frame."

"Want to speak to her again?" Stuart asked.

"I think we should, don't you? Ring that solicitor of hers — Montfort, or whatever his name is. We'll do the interview as soon as he gets here."

Hedley went into his office, slamming the door behind him. Selina had tried to make him believe she was innocent and that he was the one in the wrong. Bad move. Hedley didn't like people who played him for a fool.

Stuart came in with a mug of coffee. "I thought you could do with a drink." He put the mug on Hedley's desk and sat down on the chair opposite. "You have to let this go. You're making more of the case than it deserves. Think of the positives, what you've achieved."

"You mean a dead Rawlins, Murray behind bars and finally catching Todd's killer? All very laudable, so why do I still feel as if I've missed something important?" Hedley took a bottle of whisky from his desk drawer and held it out towards Stuart, who shook his head. Hedley poured himself a generous measure. "I've wanted Rawlins dead for as long as I can remember. Murray too, if I'm honest. But I still don't feel right. Yes, I hated Rawlins and I'm glad he's gone, but I'm not convinced that Murray killed him." He looked at Stuart. "I know. I should be elated. After all, the man who killed my wife is finally dead. I even pictured myself congratulating the bugger who was responsible. But I'm not."

"Of course Murray killed him. We have evidence, remember. And as for your Emily, remember that was never proved."

Hedley slammed his fist down on the desktop, spilling some of his coffee. "I don't need proof. Rawlins killed Emily, and he did it to get back at me. Well, someone else had the pleasure, and I hope they made him suffer."

"Hedley, don't start," Stuart said. "I know how you get. You'll go on and on about Emily and drink yourself stupid."

"She suffered, Stuart. Shot in both legs so she couldn't run. Who knows how long she lasted in that state before he put a bullet in her head."

"Stop it, Hedley. Stop it now."

Hedley downed the whisky in one. "You're right, of course. And I am grateful to whoever killed Rawlins, be that Murray or someone else. I owe them one."

"Rawlins can't hurt anyone now. Neither can Murray. So let it drop." Stuart got up and made for the door. "Montfort will be here shortly. D'you want me to deal with Selina?"

"No, we'll do this together, like we always do."

CHAPTER FORTY-TWO

As soon as Montfort arrived, Hedley and Stuart joined him and Selina in an interview room.

"Why did you lie to us?" Hedley began. "The story you told your friend Desmond to give us, he obviously didn't take it on board. His version of events is totally different from yours."

Selina's eyes narrowed. Poor Desmond. If by some quirk of fate she did get released, she'd make sure he suffered for messing things up. She knew some dangerous people. Refusing to carry out her instructions correctly would cost him dearly.

She turned to Montfort. "Well, what have you got to say? You're supposed to be on my side, so get me out of here."

"I'm afraid he's going to struggle with that one," Hedley said. "Have you forgotten the evidence we have? You are as guilty as sin."

"Rubbish! You've been talking to Chloe again, haven't you?"

"Why are you so afraid of what Chloe might say? What does she know that's so dangerous?"

Selina shrugged her shoulders. "Nothing, I can handle her."

Hedley watched as Selina struggled to control her anger. Then she settled back in her chair. The anger tempered, she smiled at him. "You do realise that Chloe is pivotal to all this? She's the only one left who knows what happened."

"What d'you mean?" Hedley said. What trick was she trying to pull now?

She rolled her eyes. "Do I have to spell it out for you? Everyone else who was involved is dead, aren't they? And you're forgetting who she was married to. He was Dean's right-hand man for a while."

"That doesn't mean she knows more than anyone else we've spoken to," Stuart said.

"Have you looked into her background?" Selina said.

"Yes, of course we have. Chloe, Simon and you all knew each other when you were younger. But I don't see what that has to do with the case," Hedley said.

"Her mother threw her out."

"Yes. We know that," Hedley said.

"For a while she lived on the streets until she was rescued by some hack researching Manchester's drug problems. Have you looked at that relationship?"

"Should we?" Hedley asked, wondering what she was getting at. "If there's something you're not telling us, now is your chance. The alternative is many years behind bars."

Selina shook her head, her eyes glittering. "Not if I can help it, Mr Detective. I'll fight this to the very end."

"In that case, give me something to work with," Hedley said.

Selina gave Montfort a nudge. "You're my solicitor. Advise me. I'm paying you enough."

"You should listen to the superintendent. If you know anything at all about this reporter, you should tell him."

Selina sighed. "The fact is, I don't. All I remember is Chloe going on and on about him. You know what it's like — after a while you just switch off. She kept telling anyone who'd listen how clever he was, how they were going to settle down and start a family. Silly bitch. He was stringing her along."

"Not necessarily," Stuart said. "He may have genuinely loved her."

"All that's very well," Hedley said, "but I need a name. I want to talk to him, get his take on this supposed romance."

"It could have been Mick, or Paul, or even Bobby, I just can't remember." Selina thought for a moment. "But I do remember something. Chloe got very excited about a house he intended to buy. She said they were going to live there together and eventually get married."

"Where is this house?" Stuart asked.

"I've a feeling it was in Hazel Grove. I recall that because she kept going on about how different it was from where she'd come from. It was on a small estate just off the Buxton Road. She kept boasting about living in a semi after years of living in that dilapidated house her mother rented."

Hedley got up from his chair. "See? That didn't hurt, did it? We'll check it out and see where it takes us."

"If it does check out, do I earn myself some brownie points?" she asked.

"We'll see how useful the information is first."

Stuart was less than excited. As soon as the door to the interview room shut behind them, he said, "I know exactly where this is going to take us — precisely nowhere. Just like the Desmond débâcle, chasing after this bloke will be nothing but another waste of time. You're clutching at straws, Hedley."

"Bear with me, laddie. We do this and, if we get nowhere, we'll wrap up the case."

"Promise? We go with Murray killed Rawlins and Cowboy, and Selina did for Todd?" Stuart said.

"Yup. Even though it doesn't sit well and Selina is screaming she's innocent until she's blue in the face," Hedley said.

"Yes, but you don't believe her. The woman is a practised liar."

"I'll reserve judgement until we've spoken to this reporter. That's if we can find him," Hedley said.

The pair entered the incident room to find Lou glued to her computer screen. "Do some research for me, would you?" Hedley asked. "See if you can find anything about a house in Hazel Grove that was up for sale. Look at sales and any interest within the last eighteen months. The purchaser was a reporter and the house was in a small estate off the Buxton Road."

"Do you have a name, sir?" Lou asked.

Hedley shook his head. "Not ideal I know, but try the estate agents, see what you can turn up."

CHAPTER FORTY-THREE

"Busy road this," Stuart said as they took the Buxton turn-off at the Rising Sun pub.

"I know. I live just off it a few miles further on, down in Levenshulme."

"Where you live is a nightmare," Stuart said. "It's a lot quieter this end. You should think about moving."

"I like where I am, thanks. I bet round here isn't as friendly. It's the folk that make an area, laddie, not quiet roads or expensive houses."

Ignoring the comment, Stuart pointed to twenty or so houses off the main road. "See that small estate over there? The houses are all semis. Want to make a start there?"

None of the estate agents Lou had spoken to had been any help, so why not? "Let's hope we strike it lucky, or we could be searching for days," Hedley grumbled. "I'll park up and after that it's down to footwork and knocking on doors, I'm afraid."

"We should have sent in uniform, saved our time. You do realise that this could be another of Selina's elaborate lies? It would be just like her to send us on a wild goose chase. It gives her yet more time to work on her defence," Stuart said.

"I don't think so. Selina has reached the stage where she's really frightened about what might happen to her,"

Hedley said. "As for uniform, this is something we need to do, you and me. The information is sketchy, and uniform, good as they are, would have been pissed off with having nothing to go on."

"And I'm not?" Stuart said.

Ignoring him, Hedley got out of the car, straightened his jacket and ran a hand through his thick head of hair. He knew Stuart was right, but if this reporter was real, and if there was the smallest chance they could find him, Hedley was all for it.

"There's a woman pruning roses over there," Stuart said. "I'll start with her."

Putting on a smile, he crossed the road and showed her his warrant card. "We're trying to find a young man, a reporter who may have worked for a paper in town. We think he might have lived round here or was looking to buy one of the houses on the estate. Does that ring any bells?"

The woman shook her head. "Sorry, can't help you. I've only been here a couple of months." She looked down the avenue at the retreating figure of Hedley. "Are you asking everyone?"

"That's the idea. We're not sure which house he lives in, so we are having to try them all."

Hedley had gone to the top of the avenue and was working his way back down. Six houses done and he'd got nothing except screaming kids, barking dogs and blank looks. He hated operating blind. They should at least have a name. This approach was getting them nowhere and it irritated the hell out of him.

He was about halfway down the row of houses when he finally got a positive response.

"Does this reporter have a name?"

Hedley shook his head. A uniform should have been asking these questions, not a high-ranking detective like him, and it made him feel foolish. "No, and that's our problem. All we know is that he could live on this estate or was considering buying one of the houses."

"A young man, you say, a reporter."

Hedley nodded. This was getting tedious. The look on the woman's face suggested she knew nothing, just like the others.

But he was wrong.

"I'm not sure, but you could be talking about Paul. He bought one of the houses along here for himself and his girlfriend."

Hedley looked at her with interest. This was exactly what he'd been hoping for. "This girlfriend, can you remember what she looked like?"

"Fragile little thing, she was. She adored him and made no secret of it. Not long after they moved in she was pregnant. The pair of them were really happy about that."

Chloe Todd had said she'd been made pregnant by an old boyfriend. Could it be this Paul? "Would you give me your name, please?" Hedley asked.

"Carol Farraday, and I've lived on this road for thirty years. I'm retired now so I have plenty of time on my hands." She smiled. "Consequently, there isn't much that goes on that I don't know about."

A nosey bugger, in other words. "And he was a reporter, this Paul?"

"Yes, he was always out in down-town Manchester, particularly at night, so I was told. He spent his time talking to druggies — a dangerous pastime. He was a nice enough young man, even though he mixed with the wrong type. That's where he met his girlfriend. She'd been living rough, I believe."

"We believe so too," Hedley said. "Does Paul have a surname?"

"Seymour, Paul Seymour."

Hedley called out to Stuart, who came over to join them. "Mrs Farraday might have something. She's just told me about a young reporter who bought that house across the road."

Carol Farraday nodded. "A nice young man, he was. He wanted to know what it was like round here, if it was quiet, that sort of thing. I got a feeling he was keen to impress her."

"Thanks, that's very useful. We're eager to find him because we believe he might prove useful in a case we're investigating," Hedley told her.

"Well, you'll not get much help from him," Carol said.

"He's not moved, has he?" Hedley said.

"Not exactly, but if it's the young man I'm thinking of, I'm afraid he's dead."

CHAPTER FORTY-FOUR

This was all they needed, another lead that went nowhere.

"I can't understand why Chloe didn't tell us about him," Hedley said on their way back to the station. "The bloke's dead. He isn't going to contradict anything she tells us. What is it with that woman? Surely she wasn't ashamed of him."

Stuart shook his head. "I doubt it. She'd have been pleased to have finally met someone who'd give her a future. There must be some other reason."

"When we get back, find out how this Seymour died — every detail. Also, see if he was involved with Rawlins or Murray in any way," Hedley said.

"What're you thinking?"

"I'm not sure yet. But there's summat, I can feel it. I just need to work on it."

"You'll tie your brain in knots, Hedley. All this trying to work stuff out isn't good for you."

"But I knew a trip out here was worth it," he retorted. "You can't argue with that. All my instincts told me so."

"That's as maybe, but what've we achieved?" Stuart said.

"We now know that Chloe had a serious boyfriend before Todd. The problem is, we don't know how he died.

It strikes me that everyone who gets involved with her ends up dead or in serious trouble."

"Give it up, Hedley. You're making out that Chloe is some sort of jinx. She's nothing of the sort. The dead boyfriend won't have anything to do with her. None of this is her fault."

"But his death did leave her free to marry Todd. What I don't understand is why she would do that. Everyone who knows them says she hated Todd, that it was a marriage of convenience," Hedley said.

"Perhaps it was his money that attracted her. Todd offered her a comfortable life, and with Seymour dead she had nothing to lose."

Somehow Hedley didn't think that was the reason. He needed a deal more information before he made up his mind. What was bothering him was the nature of the world Seymour moved in. He could have rubbed anyone up the wrong way. Even Rawlins.

"Revenge," he said slowly. "That's what I reckon this is about."

"Give it a rest, Hedley. That makes no sense at all. Go on then, which of our suspects is seeking revenge, and for what?"

"First, I want to look into how Seymour died. After that, I'll let you know what I think."

"I'll tell you now, whatever you find, you're not going to like it. There will still be some mystery, something you're not happy with. If you ask me, Hedley, that way of thinking is becoming a problem with you."

Hedley said nothing. He sat with his eyes closed, going over everything they knew about this case. The number of loose ends that had apparently been tied up, all the irrefutable evidence they had on the suspects. Still, it didn't sit right. He heard the voices of Murray and Selina, proclaiming their innocence to everyone within earshot.

Had they got the whole thing wrong? Were they being manipulated by a mind cleverer than theirs?

Hedley didn't want to believe either of these things but he had no choice. For a start, his guts were off again so something was wrong. He was left with the question of who, and why. True, Murray had a motive for killing Rawlins, but had he actually acted on it? Selina's motive for killing Todd had been weak from the off. But if neither of that pair was guilty, then who was?

He took his mobile from his pocket and called Millie. "I've a question for you. Did you ever meet a reporter called Paul Seymour?"

"I meet many reporters, Hedley. I mix with dozens every day. Why, what's so special about this one?"

"I don't know, that's what I'm trying to find out. All I do know is that he's dead. Whether from natural causes or murdered, I can't tell you."

"What makes you think I know? I don't get involved in other reporters' lives."

"Come on, Millie, think. Paul Seymour — young, ambitious, and working on much the same issue as you. Drugs."

"If he was working on that and was prepared to take more risks, that could be why he's dead," Millie said.

"Are you sure you don't remember him? It's only a theory but I reckon he was murdered."

He saw the look Stuart gave him. He'd say he was taking liberties with the truth again, that they had no evidence that Seymour had died violently.

"I'm not sure. I may be thinking about the wrong person entirely, but there was a young man who got himself shot; he was eventually dragged out of the Rochdale canal. Word had it he'd been in there two weeks plus before he was found."

"Murdered, then. I thought as much."

"Why, Hedley? What have you turned up? Is this related to your investigation? I'm still waiting for my scoop, don't forget."

"All in good time, Millie. I'm still not sure if we have a scoop yet. As it is, we've got suspects, evidence, and the case is more or less wrapped up, but I'm still not happy."

"I've known you for years, Hedley. You've always got doubts. You're looking for something, something that'll prove a point, and Paul Seymour is the key."

Millicent was a perceptive woman.

CHAPTER FORTY-FIVE

"Right, folks. I want everything you can find on one Paul Seymour — the whole story. And make it snappy." He looked across at Ryan Ogden. "Get me a mug of coffee, will you, and make it good and strong."

He saw the look Stuart threw him and retired to his office. His number two was angling for a row and he didn't have the energy. Hedley had no illusions about himself. He was well aware that he always wanted things his own way, and sod anyone else's opinion.

Ryan returned with the coffee and put it down on Hedley's desk. "Anything else, boss?"

"No, I'm fine, lad. Just go and get on with your work."

When Ryan had gone, Hedley added a glug of whisky to the cup. He was getting too old for this. The case was wearing him out, giving him a perpetual headache and keeping him awake at night. Stuart was right, he should let it drop. What more did he need, for pity's sake? The evidence was all there. But no matter how many cases he solved, and there'd been plenty over the years, the niggles wouldn't leave him.

They hadn't got it right. The killer was out there somewhere, making plans and taking the piss. Laughing at him because they'd won.

Two large whiskies later, Hedley was almost asleep. He told himself he should go home, rest up, but there was too much to do. He yawned, stood up and stretched his aching limbs. He needed to get a grip. If there was something wrong, it was down to him to sort it.

Returning to the incident room, he glared round at the team. "Got anything?" he bawled at them? "My patience is wearing thin. I want results. It can't be that hard, all the information should be on the system."

"Paul Seymour was killed a year ago," Lou said. "His death was investigated by the North Manchester team but they got nowhere. In the end they put his murder down to him crossing some unknown dealer and getting his head blown off for his trouble."

"Unknown dealer, my arse. That'll have been Rawlins. I'll lay odds on it. Who from North Manchester led the case?"

"Inspector John Lowe," Lou said.

"I might have known," Hedley said. "The officer sacked three months ago for taking bribes. In that case, it doesn't surprise me that the killer was never caught." Hedley thought for a moment. "A year ago, you said. That would be round about the time Rawlins did a runner."

Lou looked down, suddenly fascinated by something on her screen. "Dean Rawlins was implicated, sir. It was just before you arrested him. He was interviewed but he had an alibi for the entire month prior to his arrest. He and Della Barlow were at his villa in Spain."

"Convenient that." He looked at Stuart. "Did we ever talk to this Della?"

"Uniform interviewed her after Rawlins disappeared. She was living with her mother at the time. She told uniform that Rawlins had instructed her to do one the day before the court case and she had no idea where he could have gone."

Hedley turned back to Lou. "Check with the airlines. See if Rawlins travelled back from Spain around that time and, if he did, exactly when he returned."

Meanwhile, Stuart was checking through the records on the system. "Rawlins was telling the truth. He must have been in Spain, like he said. He was arrested at the airport clutching a ticket back to Malaga."

"In that case he did return to Manchester, and I'll bet it was to deal with Seymour. Okay, Stuart, we need another word with Chloe. She has some explaining to do. Given what we've just learned, she must know what happened to her boyfriend."

Stuart followed Hedley into his office. "The timeline is tricky," he said. "Rawlins returns home, kills Seymour with every intention of returning to Spain, but we intercept him instead. Seymour had been living with Chloe, who by this time is pregnant."

Hedley nodded. So far so good. "We arrest Rawlins, his solicitor gets him bail, and the night before his court appearance, he does one."

"Except that he didn't. He was murdered instead," Stuart said.

"Meanwhile, Chloe marries Simon Todd, who agrees to raise the kid as his own."

Stuart's face wore a look of disbelief.

"It's as I said, laddie," Hedley insisted. "This is about revenge. Chloe must have hated Rawlins because of what he did to Paul Seymour. She married Todd so she could get close to the villain and put things right. Not difficult — she did know Selina, after all."

"And Todd? Why kill him?"

"He was a brute. He'd been far too pally with Rawlins. He could even have worked out what she'd done. His way of dealing with her was to bully her into submission. Chloe was too traumatised after Seymour's death and losing the baby to fight back."

"If you're right, Hedley, it means that both Murray and Selina are innocent. Neither of them killed anyone."

Hedley took a moment before answering. Stuart wasn't going to like hearing this but he had no choice. "That just leaves one person. Chloe had motive and, given how she was placed, opportunity."

Stuart sighed deeply. "Hedley, throughout this whole case I've believed you to be wrong. Now, much as it pains me, I have to admit that I agree with you."

CHAPTER FORTY-SIX

"We need to find her," Hedley said. "First off we'll try the house."

"And if she's not there?" Stuart asked.

Hedley gave a heave of his broad shoulders. "She has to be there. She has nowhere else to go. As far as we're aware, she doesn't get on with her family and has no friends from her old life. And don't look so pissed off. I know it's been a pig of a day and we've traipsed all over Greater Manchester but we have no choice." He tossed Stuart his car keys. "You can drive. We find her, we'll bring her in. We don't, then we'll have another think."

It was getting dark by the time they hit the road. It would be a late one but it couldn't be helped. An hour after leaving the station, they pulled up outside the house in Saddleworth.

Hedley got out of the car, yawned, and walked towards the house. "Bloody starving, I am. That woman's made me miss my tea," he complained. He banged on the front door while Stuart went round the back.

"Familiar scenario this," he called back. "About a year ago we were here doing almost the exact same thing, looking for Rawlins after he ditched his court appearance."

Hedley made no comment. They'd better find this one or they were scuppered.

Stuart returned. "Everywhere round the back is locked up tight."

With what was fast becoming a familiar sinking feeling, Hedley looked up at the windows, all with the blinds closed. Finally, he gave up banging on the door. "Bloody woman isn't in, that much is obvious," he said angrily. "I'm going to have a word with her across the road."

He strode off, hands in his raincoat pockets. He wasn't happy. He should be at home with his feet up. Instead, he was miles outside town, tramping around the countryside on some off-chance. It was dark, the hills casting odd shadows. There was a mist too, the sort that wet you through to the bone without even trying. He shuddered. He never had liked this place and he liked it even less now.

"Mrs Howells — Brenda," he began as soon as she opened the door.

"If you're here to bother Chloe again, you're out of luck. She's not well. I rang the doctor earlier, he visited and gave her a sedative. By now she'll be fast asleep. Even if you could wake her, having you in her face asking questions won't do her any good."

"You're sure?" he asked.

"You can ring the doctor if you don't believe me. Chloe has been under a lot of stress recently, as well you know. She's suffering from depression. The doctor is so worried he's made her an appointment for tomorrow afternoon, and I've arranged to go with her."

In that case, there wasn't much he could do. If Chloe was ill, he'd just have to wait until she got better.

"Were you privy to the consultation with the doctor?" Stuart asked.

"Yes. I'm not lying — the poor woman needs help. Currently that help is me, and I intend to do all I can for her. That bully of a husband has a lot to answer for."

Hedley was at a loss. Was Chloe really ill, or not? For now, he'd reserve judgement.

"Has Chloe ever talked about her past? Told you about people she's known — another boyfriend, for instance?" Stuart asked.

"Not really," Brenda said. "Chloe tends to keep herself to herself. Perhaps in time she will come to tell me more. I know she trusts me."

"Lucky you," was Hedley's pithy reply. "And what d'you mean by 'not really'? She either spoke about her past or she didn't."

"It was more hints than anything. I know she was happier before she came here, and now she can't wait to get away. These last few days she's kept saying that her work here is done. What she means by that is anyone's guess," Brenda said.

Hedley had a good idea but he said nothing. He nodded at the house where Chloe was living. "Just so you know, tomorrow I intend to get another warrant and search that place again."

"You did a search earlier. I can't imagine what good you think another one'll do. There's nothing much in there to find. How many times before you're satisfied?"

"Given that Chloe isn't well, you can keep her company if you wish," Hedley said. "As long as you don't get in the way."

It was time to go. They would get nowhere tonight. Even if he did interview Chloe and search the house again, his reasons for doing so were thin at best. They had no proof that she'd done anything wrong.

"Sorry we had to intrude on you tonight. But we thought another chat with Chloe could be helpful." He turned and made for the car, calling, "We'll be back in the morning with that warrant. And I wouldn't mind a chat with the neighbours, particularly the ones we haven't seen yet."

Back in the car, Hedley cast a last look at the house before Stuart started the engine. "Bloody woman. Just our luck for her to be ill again. She takes so many pills I bet she rattles."

"We can wait until tomorrow, Hedley. Chloe isn't going anywhere and she's got Brenda looking out for her. We're just chasing shadows and I think you know that."

But Hedley wasn't so sure.

* * *

Chloe heard the detectives' car start up, held her breath and waited in the dark of her bedroom. They had driven off. She was safe now. She decided to give it another few hours and make her escape at dawn.

The light was still on in Brenda's hallway. Chloe hoped to God that she didn't come across to check on her. At this point she had nothing to say to anyone. All she wanted to do was spend these next few hours making sure she'd left nothing behind that could help the police find her.

Chloe was sorry she wouldn't be able to say goodbye to Brenda. But her friend would only try to stop her. Any attempt to explain was out of the question. If Chloe was to even try and tell Brenda the truth behind these last few weeks, she'd be horrified.

Best to just go and leave the neighbours to gossip. They'd enjoy that.

CHAPTER FORTY-SEVEN

Day nine

The Avenue was quiet. It was early, only five thirty in the morning, too early for twitching curtains. It was time to make her move. Chloe had already packed her most treasured possessions in the holdall, all those things that reminded her of Lily. She'd filled up the car with fuel.

No one knew about the car, not even Simon when he was alive. At the bottom of the garden, beyond a copse of trees, was a dirt track that eventually led to the main road. This was where Chloe kept it, in a dilapidated garage that no one ever used. The car, old but still roadworthy, had belonged to Paul. Whenever she sat in the driver's seat, Chloe imagined she could still smell his aftershave.

The detectives had said they would be back later in the morning. Chloe couldn't face them again. Sooner or later, she knew they'd ask the very questions she didn't want to answer — upsetting questions, about Paul. The hefty one was clever and he didn't like her much. He'd dig and dig until he found the truth. And then Chloe knew she'd be in serious trouble.

It would take a couple of hours at most to reach her destination. Hopefully, at this time of day she'd miss most of the traffic. There, Chloe would say her final goodbyes to the two most important people in her life. She needed to make this visit now, because it was unlikely she'd have the chance to return.

Paul's family had wanted him buried in their local churchyard. Fair enough. He and Chloe weren't married, so she didn't have much say in the matter. Besides, Paul's mum disapproved of her because of the life she'd once led. Six months after the funeral, Paul's mum and dad moved to the south of England, leaving his grave untended.

As she drove, the way Paul had died played on her mind. After it happened, his parents were able to claim the house as his next of kin. Chloe was homeless again and returned to Manchester. She was lucky that Abby was in a position to offer her a bed. She needed somewhere as she had unfinished business to sort. If she was to have any peace at all, she had to put things right.

There wasn't much traffic so it took only an hour for Chloe to reach the cemetery. The weather was kind, the sun was shining and the air smelled sweet.

Chloe wasn't sure what she'd find, the graves overgrown with weeds probably. She hadn't been here in over a year. Given that this was to be her last visit, she wanted to make the most of it. First, she would tidy the grave and then she'd take photos of it, photos she'd treasure forever.

She knew exactly where the they were, at the back of the cemetery, beneath a large oak tree. During the autumn the graves were covered with fallen leaves, which miraculously all disappeared in the spring. Tears in her eyes, she approached them. She was surprised to find them both so tidy. Though the church sexton had promised to keep things neat, she hadn't believed he really would. He was a grumpy old man, who showed little sympathy for the bereaved, but he'd kept his word. Both graves were free of weeds and he'd even left fresh flowers. Everything looked just as she'd left it.

Chloe reached out first touching one headstone and then the other. She traced the familiar inscription with a finger: 'Paul Seymour and beside him the tiny grave of their beloved daughter, Lily.'

Lily. "My darling girl," she whispered, the tears falling freely now. "This should never have happened. You and your dad shouldn't be here, you should be with me, the three of us enjoying our lives together."

Instead the pair of them were dead. Paul at the hand of Rawlins and Lily because of the trauma of it all. Chloe felt sick. The raw emotion was getting to her. It was all too much, but she had to pull herself together. She had an important phone call to make later, one that would change her life.

Hunkering down beside Paul's grave, she began to rearrange the flowers in the large memorial vase. It had been cemented down so that no one could steal it. She took out the flowers and carefully removed the grid.

The package was still there. Picking it up, she stowed it away in her holdall.

* * *

"Why'd we have to come so bloody early?" Stuart asked as they pulled up outside the house in Saddleworth. "It's barely seven in the morning. You might be feeling chipper but I'm still half asleep."

"Half asleep? Flat out more like, laddie. You've spent the entire drive sat on your arse and snoring. Try going to bed earlier and give up complaining," Hedley said.

Suddenly, there was an urgent banging on the driver's window. "I can't raise her." Brenda looked frantic with worry. "She could be really ill. You have to do something."

Stuart got out and went to her. "We will, don't worry."

Hedley nodded at one of the uniformed officers who had been following in the police van. "Get us in there and be quick about it." He turned to Brenda. "When did you last speak to her?"

"Yesterday afternoon."

Hedley had a bad feeling. That meant no one had seen or spoken to Chloe since Brenda had brought her back from the doctor's — all of yesterday afternoon and overnight. "She's done a bloody runner," he muttered to Stuart. "Put out a call, all forces across the North West. I want that woman found."

It took only a few minutes to confirm that Chloe had gone. The house was empty, her holdall missing.

"I think you're right, Hedley," Stuart said. "But where would she go? According to everyone we've spoken to, she has no one."

"She had someone once though, didn't she? That reporter bloke, Seymour or whatever his name was, who she was in love with."

"But he's dead."

Hedley was deep in thought. From the start, he'd been plagued with the feeling that Chloe was guilty of something. Now it looked like he'd been right, and this was all about revenge.

"I think Rawlins killed her boyfriend, Seymour. Cowboy was collateral damage. I believe he stumbled across the body and someone saw him, someone who didn't want it found. Simon Todd got in the way." He looked at Stuart, eyebrows raised. "I also think she's got those diamonds."

"That's a bit far-fetched, even for you."

But Hedley wasn't listening. "She'll try to leave the country. With a fortune to spend, she could go anywhere."

"I'll alert the airports and ports but I think it's a waste of time. The person you describe is not Chloe, she isn't capable of that."

"You've a lot to learn, laddie."

As Stuart had said, Chloe had nowhere to run. Hedley paced up and down outside the house, trying to work out what she'd do next and where she'd go. He needed help on this one, but who from? Suddenly, a thought struck him.

Hedley took out his mobile and rang Lou at the station. "I want an address and phone number for Paul Seymour's nearest and dearest. And we've not got much time, so make it snappy."

CHAPTER FORTY-EIGHT

Hedley spent a further ten minutes pacing up and down the footpath, waiting for Lou to send him the information he needed. Text received, he made a call.

A brief conversation later, he beckoned to Stuart and asked him for a pen. "I know where she is," he pronounced, scribbling down an address. "I just spoke to Seymour's parents. They used to live in Disley but they've now moved to Surrey because of the father's work. They weren't keen, because it meant leaving their son's grave. His mother also said they weren't fond of Chloe either. A wild one, is how she described her."

"Doesn't sound like the Chloe we know. Perhaps it's just a case of not liking her," Stuart said.

"There's a lot about that woman we don't know," Hedley said. "When Seymour first met Chloe, she was an addict. He got her clean and, during the process, fell for her. The feeling was mutual. Mrs Seymour reckons that wherever Chloe is going, she's sure to visit the graveside first to say goodbye."

"So, now we dash off to Disley. You do realise it's even further away than Hazel Grove? At this time in the morning it'll take an age to get there."

Hedley was well aware of where Disley was. "Get on to Lou, I want that cemetery surrounding. It's the only one in that area, so it shouldn't give them a problem. Come on, let's go and get her."

"Can I remind you, Hedley, that we still have no real evidence that Chloe has done anything wrong."

"And can I remind you that Chloe Todd is not what she seems. You have been well and truly taken in, laddie."

"I'll wait and see what she has to say before I go with that one. It's perfectly natural to want to visit her boyfriend and child's grave. Given what's happened to her, she probably finds it comforting," Stuart said.

"You don't half talk a lot of rubbish. She's a killer, pure and simple. This is all about revenge."

* * *

With the two graves tidied up, Chloe sat on a nearby bench warming herself up in the sunshine. Nervous, she checked the time on her phone. It was nearly time to make the call. She looked around; there was no one else in the cemetery. Chloe patted the holdall on her knee like she'd done a dozen times or more since sitting down, reassuring herself that the diamonds were still there, safe.

She opened the holdall, took out the packet and opened it. The sight of the gems took her breath away. Rawlins' haul, and they were just the same as the day he'd stolen them. There weren't that many, but five of them were large and they alone were worth a fortune. She knew this was so from reading about the robbery and listening in on Simon's conversations. These five had been destined for a customer in Dubai. Now it was time to make that happen. She selected the only number in the phone.

First, she took a photo of the stones and texted it to the number. When it had gone through, she made the call. "I have them. Where do we meet?"

"There's a café on the High Street in the village. Be there in fifteen minutes," he said.

"I have to leave, so we must complete the transaction today," she said.

"No problem. You give me the diamonds and I deposit the money into a Swiss bank account in your name."

Could she trust him? "I won't part with them until the transfer has gone through."

"Understood, but double-cross me and you will suffer."

A wave of fear washed over her. What was she doing? She didn't know this man, had never even met him. He was someone Simon had had dealings with. She was well aware that the buyer could do her harm. "We have a deal. I have no intention of cheating you. But I also have no idea what you look like."

"But I know you, Chloe. When you go into the café, sit at a table by the window. I will take a look at the merchandise and, if I'm happy, I'll go ahead with the transfer."

Call over, Chloe settled back on the bench. Was this too much of a risk? She'd done a lot of dangerous things during the time she'd lived with Simon, but this could well be the deadliest. Supposing this man killed her and absconded with the stones. After all, it would be nothing for a man who lived beyond the law as he did.

Chloe closed her eyes. Thinking this way would do her no good. She had to believe the transaction would go smoothly, leaving her to disappear as she'd planned.

Fifteen minutes, he'd said. She'd better make a move, find this café. She went back to the graves and knelt down in front of them, trying to imprint the image on her brain. Weeping, she took a last few photos. This was it, she'd never come here again. She said a silent farewell to her loved ones.

Wiping the tears from her eyes, she turned away, wishing only that the day would be over.

CHAPTER FORTY-NINE

The village High Street was just a few metres from the cemetery. A short walk, meet with her contact and complete the deal. Then it would all be over. She would leave this place a wealthy woman. A new life beckoned, and Chloe was determined to embrace it. With a spring in her step, she made her way towards the main gate. Nothing could stop her now. This was the culmination of her plans.

She had only gone a short distance when she saw the car. The pale blue saloon those two detectives drove was sitting at the gate.

Gripped by panic, Chloe stood stock still. This couldn't be happening. How had they found out where she was? Several other police vehicles were now pulling up behind the blue car.

There was nowhere to go. She was trapped. They would arrest her and all would be lost. She thought fast — there was just one chance. She had to get this right, there was no time to lose. Chloe darted back to the two graves and bent down, muttering to herself. Hopefully, the detectives would think she was praying, saying a last goodbye. Carefully, her hands shaking, she put the diamonds back in the vase.

"It's over, Chloe." Hedley was hurrying towards her. "Time to give it up."

"Leave me alone!" she called out. "You have no right harassing me like this."

"We know what you did," shouted the younger one.

"Then you'll know how dangerous I am."

It was a threat Chloe had hoped she wouldn't have to make. But the words were out, so now she'd have to follow it through. There was only one course of action left to her. Opening her holdall, she took out a revolver. It had once belonged to Rawlins, and she'd used it to kill Simon. Her hand shaking, she pointed it at Hedley If she had to shoot, she wanted him to get it first. Payment for all the aggro he'd given her.

"You don't want to do that, Chloe," Stuart shouted. "Give me the gun. Don't make things worse for yourself."

She couldn't help smiling at this. How much worse did he think things could get? "I'm getting out of here and you're going to help me," she called to Stuart. "I'm going to the main gate and I'm walking away. Neither of you will come after me."

She saw him look at his boss. Would he obey, or would he try to play the hero? Chloe hoped not. He'd always had a deal of sympathy for her and she'd been grateful for it.

"There's an armed response team surrounding the area, Chloe," Hedley shouted. "You can't get out. Be sensible and hand the gun over."

Armed response. Was it all over then? The reality of her situation hit her hard. Chloe felt the tears run down her cheeks. She'd tried to be ruthless and, to a certain extent, she'd succeeded, but this was different. This was real. She'd seen the films. They'd have rifles trained on her. She would be lucky to get out of here alive.

But did she want to? It was decision time. How much did she want to live? Was a life in prison preferable to what Paul and Lily had? Life, and more interrogations, more suffering, or . . . nothing. Lost, Chloe shuffled the options back and forth in her mind.

Maybe there was another route open to her?

There were people who'd vouch for her, like Brenda. She'd stand in her corner. And there was the mental breakdown she'd suffered after losing Lily. A good solicitor might make something of that. Was it worth a try?

She threw down the revolver and raised her hands. "It wasn't loaded anyway."

Heaving a deep sigh of relief, Hedley approached and picked up the gun. "You've done the right thing."

Dazed, she looked around. There was not a rifle in sight. "Where's your armed response?"

"Sorry, love, a little white lie on my part," Hedley said.

Chloe backed away. "Don't you touch me. I want him to walk me to the car."

Hedley shrugged. "Stuart, you're on."

Stuart took the cuffs that one of the uniformed officers handed to him.

"D'you have to do that?" she said.

"Too bloody right he does," Hedley said. "You've killed three men and threatened us. And given the situation you're in, we're not taking the risk. Who knows what you're capable of."

"I'm not what you think," she said, her voice almost a whisper.

Stuart shook his head. "Can't you see the state she's in? I don't believe you at times, Hedley."

CHAPTER FIFTY

Chloe engaged Philip Jones, a solicitor with the firm of Jones and Goddard. Hedley was rather surprised. There was no way Chloe could afford him, yet she'd gone ahead and hired one of the best.

Preliminaries over, Hedley began the interview. "We know the why. You wanted to get even with those men who'd ruined your life. Revenge is a powerful driver. It can prompt even the weakest people to do terrible things."

Wiping the tears from her cheeks, Chloe said, "I hated them all, Rawlins in particular. He shot Paul in cold blood, something Simon took great delight in telling me. The shock and pain of it killed my unborn baby. I suffered so badly that I couldn't think straight for months."

Hedley's eyes narrowed. He didn't like this. She was guilty, they knew it and so did she. So why the waterworks and the talk of suffering?

"When Paul Seymour died, you were already pregnant," Stuart said. "Simon Todd married you anyway. Why was that?"

Chloe shrugged. "Three months and hardly showing. I made a play for him. I wanted to get even, and he was a way in. I was lucky. Simon was under instructions from Rawlins to find himself a wife. He wanted a right-hand man to run his business who was a pillar of society, someone the police would never suspect. The pair of us acted like any other happily married couple. I was pregnant and he was simply your average business man." She lowered her head. "In reality, we were anything but. Simon was a sadistic brute. After we'd only been married a few months when Lily was still born. Simon taunted me about her, said her death was my fault. He kept telling me I was inadequate and didn't deserve to be a mother."

"What did Simon do for Rawlins?" Stuart asked.

Chloe shrugged. "I've no idea."

"Come on, you can do better than that," Hedley said. "You said yourself Simon was Rawlins' right-hand man. So, what did that entail?"

"He liaised with people on Rawlins' behalf. Rawlins wasn't smooth enough, didn't have the right accent or manner."

Hedley grunted. "An ignorant bastard, you mean."

"I have to agree with you on that one," she said.

"And the diamond robbery? What did you know about that?"

"I knew Simon was part of it but I was never privy to their plans," Chloe said.

"I can understand your anger towards those men," Stuart said, "but did you have to kill them?"

Chloe gave him a withering look. "Rawlins was responsible for the death of Paul. I was never going to rest until I got even, made him pay. I'd never killed anyone before but grief made me brave."

"You shot him in cold blood," Stuart said.

"I had to," she said simply. "What that man did triggered something in me, a darkness I couldn't control. It wasn't me. I was literally beside myself, as if I was someone else. I was so grief-stricken I couldn't help myself."

"Grief-stricken, my arse," Hedley said. "You didn't stop at killing Rawlins. What about Cowboy and Simon? What did they do to upset you?"

"Cowboy? I have no idea who you mean," she said. "I admit to killing Rawlins and Simon, but not this other person."

"How did you manage to plant the evidence we found? Murray's blood, for example," Hedley said.

"It was easy, a gift the fates put my way. I knew it was wrong but the temptation was too strong. Rawlins told Simon to organise a drinks party and invite Murray. Rawlins had a proposition to put to him."

"The diamonds," Hedley said.

Ignoring the comment, Chloe continued. "Those two never got on. There was a fight, and Murray got injured. Rawlins threw a beer glass at him and it cut Murray's hand. There was a lot of blood. I did my best to staunch the flow and dress the wound but it wouldn't stop bleeding. Murray refused to go and have it stitched, so I kept putting on new dressings. By the time I'd finished, I had a plastic bag full of gauze and bandages."

"Which you used to smear around the crime scene when you shot Rawlins," Hedley said.

"Don't you see? It was meant to be. Murray's blood was a bonus. After I'd finished, I put the bag in the dustbin."

"And the pendant? It was engraved with Murray's name and also had Rawlins' blood on it. How d'you get hold of that?"

"Murray gave it to me for helping him after the fight. It was solid gold, eighteen carat." She smiled. "How could I refuse? But I didn't keep it or sell it. I placed it at the scene. It wasn't really mine and I wanted to give it back to Connor. I would have too but I was out of my mind with grief. I got Rawlins' blood after he cut himself shaving at ours. I dabbed his chin. Later, I smeared it on the pendant and stuffed it down a crack in the floor of the cellar. I knew your people would find it and that Connor would get the blame."

"You still haven't said why you killed Cowboy. He was homeless and used that cellar to doss down in. He didn't do you any harm," Stuart said.

Chloe looked puzzled. "Like I said, I don't know any Cowboy."

"Don't pretend. You used his duvet to cover Rawlins' body," Stuart said.

"That wasn't me," she said firmly.

That remained to be seen, Hedley decided. They also had evidence that put Murray in the frame. He'd get it checked, but perhaps that was right.

"Then of course there's Simon. What did he do that meant he had to die?" Hedley asked.

"He was cruel and heartless and I hated him," she said.

"That's as maybe, but why frame Selina?" Hedley said.

Chloe shrugged. "Why not? She threatened me. I found her scary. She wouldn't leave me alone. I couldn't cope with the constant worry of having her suddenly turn up. She got her claws into me a long time ago. If I hadn't framed her it was only a matter of time before she got me."

Hedley was getting tired of listening to this rubbish. She'd admitted what she'd done but was quick to offer up mitigating reasons for every act. "You killed both Rawlins and Simon in cold blood. That doesn't sound like the behaviour of someone crazed with grief."

Chloe gave him a sad little smile. "I wasn't thinking straight. Everyone I'd ever loved was dead and my new husband was a sadistic bully. I was off my head on pills. Most of the time I'd no idea what I was doing."

"You set Selina up, just like you did Murray," Stuart said.

"It was simple. I took her bracelet and stole a mug from her kitchen knowing it had her prints on it. The icing on the cake was Simon's blood on her blouse."

"Very clever and well thought out. The acts you describe are those of a first-class killer, not a woman who's afraid of her own shadow," Stuart said.

Chloe nudged Philip Jones. "I think I need a break now. My head hurts and I need my medication."

Hedley shook his head. "Getting difficult, is it? Run out of lies?"

"Look, I'm sorry. I wouldn't have done any of those things if I'd been in my right mind, but I was like a madwoman. All I could think of was the need to get even with the people who'd ruined my life."

"We'll have a break shortly," Hedley said. "But first, I want to know why you drugged both Rawlins and Simon Todd before you shot them."

"I thought it would be easier if they were drowsy. I crushed up some of my sleeping pills and put them in their drinks." She shook her head. "Yes, I killed them, but I'm not heartless. I know it's strange but I didn't want them to suffer."

"My client really does need a break now," Jones said. "Can I suggest we take fifteen minutes?"

Hedley knew he'd have to agree, otherwise the solicitor would complain. He got up from the table. "We'll take fifteen minutes then resume."

"I don't know why," Chloe said. "I've told you all I can."

CHAPTER FIFTY-ONE

Hedley and Stuart returned to the incident room in silence. Stuart was clearly shocked by what he'd heard, the way Chloe had spun everything that had happened. But Hedley had something else on his mind.

"The diamonds," he said. "What the hell did she do with them?"

"Let's face it, Hedley, we have no idea what Rawlins did with them, never mind Chloe. And there is no evidence that she ever had them in the first place."

Hedley frowned. "I'll lay odds she did."

"But where would she hide them? Think about it logically. We've searched the house she lived in and found nothing. Forensics are going over that car of hers, as well as the holdall. So far, they've found nothing in either."

That did not make Hedley happy. All along he'd suspected Chloe for the murders, and now he suspected that she knew more about the diamonds than she was letting on.

* * *

Fifteen minutes later, the interview resumed. Chloe was flagging. She was on a short fuse but she dare not lose it. For the sake of her future, she had to keep Jones onside.

"You've told me about the murders," Hedley began. "Now tell me about the diamonds."

Chloe shook her head. "I know about the robbery, of course. I've already said so. Simon went on about little else. But I never had anything to do with it."

A blatant lie, but would they fall for it? She'd made a pact with herself. Okay, she would admit to the murders and play on her fragile emotional state, but the diamonds were hers. As soon as she was free, she would go back and retrieve them. The thought of them lying where she'd hidden them was the only thing keeping her spirits up. Chloe looked at Jones. "You do believe me, don't you? I'm not lying."

Jones's opinion was key. He could get her a sympathetic barrister to fight her case in court.

"He might, but I don't believe a word of it," Hedley said. Blunt but true. "You're hoping that playing on some imagined mental condition will convince the court to go easy on you. Well, I'm telling you right now, that's not going to happen."

"You can't be sure of that, Superintendent," Jones said. "Given Chloe's past. Rawlins killed Paul Seymour and with the recent loss of her baby, it is perfectly reasonable to argue that she committed the murders while the balance of her mind was disturbed. The law might be more lenient than you imagine."

His words cheered Chloe. She could manage a short time in prison. She'd be as good as gold, cause no trouble. She'd be the model prisoner. All her hopes rested on Jones, and whether he played his part right.

"You sure there isn't something else you want to tell me?" Hedley asked.

"I've bared my soul to you this past hour." She gave him another of her weak little smiles laced with a helping of tears. "I've told you the truth. There isn't anything else."

Hedley stood up. "Charge her," he said to Stuart. "Two counts of murder. We'll look again at what happened to Cowboy."

* * *

Hedley had had enough. He returned to his office, to be joined a few minutes later by Stuart.

"Bloody woman got my head tied in knots. I need a stiff drink and a word with Gabe," Hedley said.

"About Cowboy, I suppose. What're you thinking?" Stuart said.

"If she didn't kill him — and given different guns were used, it looks likely — we're back with Murray. The problem is, I need evidence to charge him."

"There are the hairs found on Cowboy's clothes," Stuart said.

"A good lawyer would argue that they'd been placed there. Look at what Chloe did to set up both Murray and Selina."

"So, how do we tackle the problem?" Stuart asked.

"I don't bloody know. The man's a good liar, same as Chloe Todd." Suddenly an idea struck him. "I've been a stupid idiot. You too." Hedley got up and went into the incident room in search of Lou. "Get me the camera footage from Oldham Road on the day Cowboy was killed. I'm interested in Connor Murray. See what you can find.

"Now we'll see," Hedley said. "I'll lay odds that we find Murray going into that building."

"Good call, Hedley. If we do, it means we can charge him."

"Murray is one thing, but what I really want is to find those diamonds. And I don't think Murray can help me there."

"You still suspect Chloe?" Stuart was tired of this. "Then answer me two questions: how did she get hold of them and where are they now? Think about it, Hedley, she had Rawlins to deal with."

"I think she killed Rawlins on the day of the robbery and found the diamonds on him. She probably couldn't believe her luck. Then, having got her hands on them, she hid them somewhere safe."

"But not *in* the safe," Stuart pointed out. "So what was all that about the two halves of the combination?

"Rawlins wanted to make it look good. Convince Todd to trust him."

But she took them from Rawlins, I know she did." Back at his desk, Hedley had the case file open in front of him. "When we found her she had all her important possessions with her."

"So?"

"What was she doing in that graveyard?"

"If you don't know that, Hedley, you're not a very good detective."

Hedley grunted. "Cheeky bastard. You need to watch your step. One of these days your attitude will trip you up."

"Go on then, what's on your mind?"

"She was saying a last goodbye to her loved ones before she did a runner. And that's where she stashed the diamonds." Hedley sat back and folded his arms.

"What? The grave?"

"I'll lay odds on it," Hedley said. "Want to come for a ride and watch me prove my theory?"

CHAPTER FIFTY-TWO

By the time the two detectives reached the cemetery in Disley again, it was already dark.

Stuart turned up his raincoat collar and shivered.

"You're not scared, surely." Hedley grinned. "We're not in some horror film, you know, it's just an ordinary suburban graveyard."

"I can't help it, I just don't like these places, particularly not in the dark. They give me the creeps."

Neither the dark nor the location bothered Hedley. He just wanted to get on with the job of finding the diamonds. Diamonds he was sure were hidden in here somewhere.

"When we arrested Chloe, she was walking towards us but she had just been bending down at the gravesite."

"It looked to me as if she was tidying the flowers on Paul's grave," Stuart said.

"Let's go over it again," Hedley said. "She started moving towards the main gates then rushed back, knelt down again and fiddled with the flowers. Why would she do that when she was in danger of being arrested? Whatever she was doing for those few moments must have been important to her."

"There is another explanation. Chloe knew she'd be arrested and wanted to say a final goodbye."

"Goodbye, my arse. She pulled a gun on us, remember? No, I reckon she stashed something in that grave, and we're going to find it."

"We're not going to go digging, surely," Stuart said, clearly horrified.

"No need. Her hands were clean, that much I did notice."

Hedley led the way and a couple of minutes later they were standing at the graveside of Paul Seymour and the infant. "Stupid bugger might have lived if he'd not got on the wrong side of Rawlins." He studied the memorial vase. "Fresh flowers, but look at them. Chloe had plenty of time to arrange them neatly before we turned up, so why are they all over the grave and only a couple in the vase? I reckon she pulled them out but didn't have time to replace them properly."

"What're you getting at, Hedley?"

"This vase figures somewhere, and I think we should find out why." He took out the remaining flowers and unscrewed the grid. There was a small amount of water in the bottom but no way did it fill the vase. Hedley stuck his hand inside and felt around. After a few moments he looked up at Stuart and smiled. "There's something down here wrapped in plastic. I think we've found them, laddie."

* * *

With the precious cargo stashed in Hedley's coat pocket, Stuart drove them back to the station.

"Very clever," Hedley said. "All these months and no one thought to look at those graves."

"There's still a lot we don't know though," Stuart pointed out. "Not least, the question of how she got her hands on them in the first place."

"Don't worry, we'll face her with that in the morning."

"What do we do with them in the meantime?" Stuart asked. "We can't just leave them in the evidence room."

He was right. The room was kept locked and perfectly safe as a rule, but not in these circumstances. "I'll give the security company a ring. They can come to the station, confirm they're all here and that they're the genuine article, then take them off our hands."

"And Chloe?"

"As I said, we'll have another talk with her in the morning. And I, for one, can't wait. She played us, Stuart. All along she's known exactly where those diamonds were."

"I owe you an apology, Hedley. I'm sorry for doubting you but I really did believe Chloe was a victim."

"You want to try listening to your elders and betters in future. That way, you might make a half decent detective one day."

"Fancy a drink after we've sorted the diamonds?" Stuart asked.

"Why not? We can discuss the Cowboy problem. If Chloe didn't do for him, who did?"

"That one's easy," Stuart said. "Murray, of course. Gabe found DNA evidence that proves as much."

"He found DNA evidence that proved Murray had killed Rawlins," he corrected. No, I'm waiting to see what Lou comes up with from the CCTV. Once we've got that, we'll tackle Murray again."

CHAPTER FIFTY-THREE

Day ten

Hedley was on top form following his discovery of the diamonds. Bacon roll in one hand and mug of tea in the other, he breezed into the incident room in search of his partner.

"I think we've got him," he said, brown sauce from the roll running down his chin. "Lou emailed me a snippet of the footage last night, taken on the day of Cowboy's murder. It plainly shows Murray going into that building where the cellars were and coming out again fifteen minutes later." He looked at Lou. "We should have checked the footage earlier," he said. "Why didn't you remind me?"

"Because I rang and asked for it and was told the cameras hadn't been working for a couple of weeks. It was only when I spoke to them this week that a technician checked again and found that one of them had. Hence we got the footage," she smiled.

"How d'you think he'll react?" Stuart asked.

"If he's any sense, he'll come clean." Hedley took another bite of the roll. "Murray's solicitor is here and he's advised him to ask for a deal. A confession and information in exchange for a reduced sentence."

"And you're thinking of going with that?" Knowing Hedley's aversion to doing deals with gangsters, Stuart was bemused.

"Don't give me that look," Hedley said. "I haven't agreed to anything as yet, though a chat about the way forward won't go amiss."

"I'd take a look in the mirror first if I was you," Stuart said, pointing at Hedley's chin. "You can't go in there all guns blazing with half your breakfast on your face."

Hedley took a handkerchief from his jacket pocket and wiped off the sauce. "That better? Do I look the part now?"

Stuart nodded. "You'll do, I suppose. So, is it Murray or Chloe? Which one first?"

"Let's sort the Murray problem. Face him with the evidence again and see what he says."

* * *

"Not only do we have forensic evidence that you were with Cowboy the day he died, but we now have CCTV footage that shows you entering the building he was dossing in."

Murray glared at him with a face like thunder. "You've fixed this. Concocted some story and made it fit."

"That's not how we operate," Hedley said. "Your best bet is to come clean. Tell us what happened."

Murray looked at Bagley, who nodded, but Murray obviously wasn't satisfied. "I want advice!" he yelled at him. "These bastards are out to get me, they want to see me hung, drawn and quartered. Can't you pull some strings?"

Shaking his head, the solicitor whispered in Murray's ear, "This has run its course. Time to tell the truth."

Murray heaved a sigh of resignation and turned back to the detectives. "He was filthy, dragging that old duvet around wherever he went. He started pawing at me, asking for money—"

"So you shot him?" Stuart said.

"I had no choice. He lunged at me, swearing his head off. I was afraid he'd kill me."

"My heart bleeds," Hedley said. "He was an ailing old man, he couldn't possibly have hurt you. Anyway, what were you doing there in the first place?"

"I heard a rumour that Rawlins' body had been hidden there. I was desperate to get at those diamonds, so I went to see for myself."

"Who told you that's where he was?" Hedley asked.

"It was just a rumour, one of his mob, I think. I got the fright of my life." Murray grimaced. "Rawlins had been dead a while. The state of him was horrific. I couldn't stand to look at him, let alone touch him, so I took the old man's duvet and threw it over the remains."

"You scared yourself for no reason," Hedley said. "You were looking in entirely the wrong place, I'm afraid. The diamonds weren't there."

Murray looked surprised. "You seem very sure of that. Do you know where they are then?"

Hedley looked at Bagley. "I've heard enough. What he's just told us amounts to a confession. Do you agree?"

Bagley shrugged resignedly.

"Good. Connor Murray, my colleague here will formally charge you."

* * *

Hedley returned to the incident room. Next on his list was Chloe. She'd admitted to the murders. Now, he wanted to see her reaction when they told her they had the diamonds.

One mug of coffee later and Stuart joined him. "Another one bites the dust," he said, switching the kettle on. "Chloe is next, I presume."

Hedley turned towards a uniformed officer standing by the window. "How's she been overnight?"

"Not a peep out of her, sir. She didn't want anything to eat, so I left her to it."

"I think we'd better check on her," Stuart said anxiously. "The woman is unhinged, she's capable of anything."

Hedley knew what he was thinking but he doubted that Chloe would do herself any harm. Unhinged, yes — suicidal, no.

"C'mon then, let's get this over with, give her the good news."

"Prepare yourself for tears," Stuart said. "She won't be happy when she hears we found the diamonds. I can't believe the woman still thought she'd get away with taking them."

"I believe she intends to play on the balance of her mind thing. Problem is, that might work. Losing her boyfriend and child left her mentally ill. That being so, it might affect the sentence she gets."

"That won't work," Stuart said, sounding annoyed. "It can't. She deserves to have the book thrown at her."

"Now you're talking. About bloody time, too."

CHAPTER FIFTY-FOUR

Chloe Todd was far from happy. Having been told that there was to be another interview, she was dreading it. She was shown to a room where Jones was waiting for her.

"You have to help me," she pleaded with him. "I didn't know what I was doing. I had an image in my head of my beautiful baby dead in my arms and knew it was Rawlins' and Simon's fault." She looked at him. "Can you imagine what that does to a woman?"

But Jones's 's face was impassive. Was he on her side or not? If her plan was to succeed, he had to be.

"Good morning," Hedley said in a voice she'd come to hate. "A few more questions, won't take long."

The two detectives sat down. The overweight one laid a file on the table and opened it. He smiled. "We found the diamonds, by the way. Exactly where you left them."

The tirade of abuse Chloe had been about to throw at him froze in her throat.

"Nothing to say? That's not like you," Hedley said. "Forensics will examine them, and I have no doubt your fingerprints will be all over them."

"They were my future," she whispered. Inside, she raged. This man had just destroyed her life, ruined it, every bit as much as Rawlins had. Chloe wanted to scream, hurl expletives at him.

"The only future you have is behind bars, lady," he said. "Don't be under any illusion, hanging onto the diamonds like you did puts an entirely different slant on things."

Chloe looked at Jones, who simply shook his head. There would be no help from him.

"Something that's been puzzling me," Hedley said. "Rawlins and Simon were supposed to each have half of the combination for the safe. Given that the diamonds never saw the inside of it, and we found the thing locked, how did that work?"

"It didn't," Chloe said. "The combination was never changed. Rawlins put his foot down. He said it would stay as it was until things quietened down. There was no way Simon dared cross him, so he went along with it." She gave the detectives a little smile. "Rawlins was very much the boss, you see. Cross him, even question his motives, and you ended up dead. Simon knew that only too well."

"How d'you know that?" Hedley asked. "Who told you?"

"As you know, I drugged both him and Simon before killing them. In that state, Rawlins would have told me anything."

Chloe realised it wouldn't be long now before they charged her. At that point she'd be remanded in custody until her trial. She'd fought hard and she'd lost. There was nothing more she could do. She couldn't imagine life behind bars.

"Stuart," she said quietly. "Will you do something for me? My holdall contains all my memories of Lily. Will you ensure they are given to Brenda for safe-keeping? They're not diamonds but they're just as precious to me, and who knows what might happen to them in prison."

Stuart said immediately that he would.

* * *

"You're a right soft touch," Hedley told him when they were back in the incident room.

"I don't mind. It's no big deal. I take the stuff to Brenda and that's it, job done."

"Chloe Todd has got you running around after her, and I don't like it. Anyway, that holdall is evidence for the time being. She had that gun of hers in it, remember."

"We've got her, Hedley. There's no way she'll wriggle out of this one, so give it up."

Hedley had to admit that this time Stuart was right. He did need to drop it and move on. But this case, and the duplicitous woman who'd run rings around them, left him with a bad taste.

"Fancy a curry later? We'll go down Rusholme, visit Mrs Chandani. I promise you, Stuart, you won't have tasted anything like it."

"Sorry, I'm seeing Isabel. She's beginning to think I'm just a figment of her imagination."

"I get it. Fed up with me," Hedley said, disappointed.

"Right now I'm struggling to stand the sight of you. Okay, so Chloe was guilty, but I still think your treatment of her was harsh."

"Villains deserve all they get, laddie."

Hedley walked away, heading for his office. They'd done a good job and now he wanted a rest. The sooner they got their teeth into something else, the better.

CHAPTER FIFTY-FIVE

Three months later

"Treating you all right, are they?" The question was accompanied by a wide smile showing off perfect white teeth surrounded by neatly applied red lipstick. "Only I worry about you," Selina said. "I can't imagine how you protect yourself. The other inmates are quick to sense fear and they won't hesitate to tear a sweet little thing like you to pieces."

Too late, Chloe pulled down the sleeves of her jumper. Selina had seen the bruises. But she was right, Chloe had to watch her back at all times. "Why have you come? You aren't my friend, in fact you must hate me for what I did."

Selina waved the remark away. "Not at all. I feel sorry for your predicament and I want to help."

Chloe looked at her. What was Selina up to now? "How can you possibly want to help me?"

"I presume you want out, and that you've gone through all the possibilities?"

Chloe nodded, she'd thought of little else. "There is no way out. The only way I'm leaving this place is in a pine box."

"You're not serious?"

With a jolt, Chloe realised that she was. Never more so.

"If you are, it can be arranged. And I can promise you it will be swift and painless."

"How?"

"I know people in here. I have a word in the right ears and you'll be provided with everything you need."

"Pills?"

Selina nodded. "You take them, lie down, and all your troubles will melt away." She got to her feet. "Your trial is coming up soon, and I can assure you, the number of years you'll get will make your head spin. Think about it." She gave Chloe a conspiratorial smile and whispered, "There's a woman called Bethan in here. Seek her out and tell her we've spoken. She is an old friend and will sort you out."

Selina's brief visit gave Chloe a lot to think about. What she wanted more than anything was for this to be over. Perhaps she should speak to this Bethan.

* * *

A week after Selina's visit to Chloe, Stuart was sitting in the incident room drinking his coffee and reading the local paper.

"You can get the news online, you know," Lou said.

Stuart shrugged. "This suits me fine, thank you." Suddenly he went pale. Clutching the paper, he scrambled to his feet. "I need to show this to Hedley."

Hedley was standing at his office window, fiddling with the leaves of a sick plant. "I know, and don't go blaming me. I didn't murder those men, or tell her to kill herself."

"But that's exactly what's she's done. Took a load of pills and that was that."

Hedley turned and looked at him. "There'll be an investigation. It won't involve us but they will get to the bottom of it, they'll find out where Chloe got those pills."

Stuart's voice shook with emotion. "The poor woman wasn't strong. She couldn't live with what had happened and what she'd done."

Hedley said nothing. He had a quite different take on it. Chloe Todd had simply killed herself because she couldn't bear the idea of spending the rest of her life in prison.

"We've got a job to do," he said. "It'll take your mind off recent events. A trip out to that factory to speak to the workforce."

"The killing of the night watchman," Stuart said gloomily. "I wonder what horrors that'll turn up."

"Whatever happens, the trick is to keep it in its place," Hedley said. "Learn that and you'll sleep better at night."

THE END

THE JOFFE BOOKS STORY

We began in 2014 when Jasper agreed to publish his mum's much-rejected romance novel and it became a bestseller.

Since then we've grown into the largest independent publisher in the UK. We're extremely proud to publish some of the very best writers in the world, including Joy Ellis, Faith Martin, Caro Ramsay, Helen Forrester, Simon Brett and Robert Goddard. Everyone at Joffe Books loves reading and we never forget that it all begins with the magic of an author telling a story.

We are proud to publish talented first-time authors, as well as established writers whose books we love introducing to a new generation of readers.

We won Trade Publisher of the Year at the Independent Publishing Awards in 2023. We have been shortlisted for Independent Publisher of the Year at the British Book Awards for the last four years, and were shortlisted for the Diversity and Inclusivity Award at the 2022 Independent Publishing Awards. In 2023 we were shortlisted for Publisher of the Year at the RNA Industry Awards.

We built this company with your help, and we love to hear from you, so please email us about absolutely anything bookish at: feedback@joffebooks.com.

If you want to receive free books every Friday and hear about all our new releases, join our mailing list: www.joffebooks.com/contact

And when you tell your friends about us, just remember: it's pronounced Joffe as in coffee or toffee!

ALSO BY HELEN H. DURRANT

DS HEDLEY SHARPE
Book 1: DIG TWO GRAVES

DETECTIVE RACHEL KING
Book 1: NEXT VICTIM
Book 2: TWO VICTIMS
Book 3: WRONG VICTIM
Book 4: FORGOTTEN VICTIM
Book 5: LAST VICTIM
Book 6: LOST VICTIM

THE CALLADINE & BAYLISS MYSTERY SERIES
Book 1: DEAD WRONG
Book 2: DEAD SILENT
Book 3: DEAD LIST
Book 4: DEAD LOST
Book 5: DEAD & BURIED
Book 6: DEAD NASTY
Book 7: DEAD JEALOUS
Book 8: DEAD BAD
Book 9: DEAD GUILTY
Book 10: DEAD WICKED
Book 11: DEAD SORRY
Book 12: DEAD REAL

DETECTIVE ALICE ROSSI
Book 1: THE ASH LAKE MURDERS
Book 2: THE RAVENSWOOD MURDERS

THE DCI GRECO BOOKS
Book 1: DARK MURDER
Book 2: DARK HOUSES
Book 3: DARK TRADE
Book 4: DARK ANGEL

MATT BRINDLE
Book 1: HIS THIRD VICTIM
Book 2: THE OTHER VICTIM

DETECTIVES LENNOX & WILDE
Book 1: THE GUILTY MAN
Book 2: THE FACELESS MAN
Book 3: THE WRONG WOMAN

Printed in Dunstable, United Kingdom

71048596R00133

Contents

PRINCEWILL LAGANG

Retail Royalty: Jim Walton and the Walmart Empire

First published by PRINCEWILL LAGANG 2023

First edition

This book was professionally typeset on Reedsy.
Find out more at reedsy.com

1

Introduction

In the ever-evolving landscape of global commerce, few entities have left as indelible a mark as Walmart. What began as a small retail store in Arkansas, founded by the Walton family, has burgeoned into an international retail giant, shaping the way people shop, work, and live. This book embarks on a comprehensive journey through the corridors of Walmart's history, from its humble beginnings to its current status as a behemoth in the retail industry.

Chapter 1: "Retail Royalty: Jim Walton and the Walmart Empire"

This chapter sets the stage by delving into the genesis of Walmart, tracing its roots to the visionary leadership of Jim Walton. From the founding principles that laid the foundation for the company to the strategic decisions that propelled its growth, readers gain insights into the familial ethos that underpins Walmart's legacy.

Chapter 2: "Building a Retail Empire: Walmart's Expansion Strategies"

The narrative unfolds Walmart's expansion strategies, detailing the calculated moves and bold decisions that transformed it from a regional player to a global retail powerhouse. From the iconic Walmart stores dotting the American landscape to its ventures into international markets, the chapter illuminates the key milestones in the company's expansion journey.

Chapter 3: "Supply Chain Mastery: Walmart's Logistics Triumph"

This chapter explores how Walmart revolutionized supply chain management, becoming synonymous with efficiency and scale. From pioneering inventory management systems to leveraging technology for streamlined operations, the narrative delves into the logistical prowess that became a cornerstone of Walmart's success.

Chapter 4: "Everyday Low Prices: The Walmart Philosophy"

At the heart of Walmart's success lies the commitment to "Everyday Low Prices." This chapter dissects the philosophy that shaped Walmart's pricing strategy, examining its impact on consumer behavior and the retail industry at large. Interviews with industry experts provide perspectives on the enduring significance of this pricing approach.

Chapter 5: "Customer-Centric Innovation: Walmart's Technological Leap"

The narrative shifts focus to Walmart's embrace of technological innovation. From pioneering retail technology to venturing into the digital realm, this chapter illuminates how Walmart positioned itself at the forefront of the technological frontier, shaping the future of retail through innovation.

Chapter 6: "Walmart in the 21st Century: Challenges, Innovations, and the Future Frontier"

This chapter brings the narrative into the 21st century, where Walmart faces new challenges in a rapidly evolving landscape. It explores the company's strategies for personalization through data analytics, integration of artificial intelligence, and its endeavors in the e-commerce space. The chapter concludes by offering a glimpse into Walmart's vision for the future of retail.

The subsequent chapters delve into Walmart's impact beyond the retail sphere, exploring its contributions to society, economies, and the global stage. From its role in job creation and community development to its endeavors in sustainability and corporate responsibility, the narrative paints a comprehensive picture of Walmart's multifaceted influence.

As the book progresses, it examines Walmart's global citizenship, delving into its role in international diplomacy, philanthropy, and the complex dynamics of operating on a global scale. The later chapters explore Walmart's strategies for community-centric development, its initiatives in technological empowerment, health and wellness, educational empowerment, and sustainable community development.

In the concluding chapters, the narrative reflects on Walmart's vision for the future, its strategies for sustainable development, and its evolving role in global citizenship. The book offers a forward-looking perspective, examining the challenges and opportunities that lie ahead, providing readers with a comprehensive understanding of Walmart's ongoing narrative as a global retail leader and its multifaceted impact on society, economies, and the world.

2

The Rise of a Retail Dynasty

The sun had barely begun to cast its golden glow over the small town of Bentonville, Arkansas, as a young Jim Walton walked briskly towards his family's five-and-dime store. It was the early 1960s, and the retail landscape in America was on the verge of a seismic shift. Little did Jim know that he was about to play a pivotal role in shaping the future of the industry.

A Humble Beginning

The Walton family, led by the ambitious and visionary Sam Walton, had modest roots in retail. In the heart of Bentonville, Sam and his wife, Helen, opened Walton's 5 & 10, a simple variety store that would become the breeding ground for the retail giant we know today. Jim, the youngest son, imbibed the values of hard work, customer service, and innovation from an early age.

The Walmart Philosophy

As Jim grew older, he found himself drawn to the family business. The Waltons believed in providing everyday low prices and excellent customer service, principles that would later become the bedrock of Walmart's success. Sam's vision of creating a retail environment that catered to the average American family struck a chord with Jim, sparking a passion that would drive him throughout his career.

The Walmart Empire Takes Root

With the opening of the first Walmart store in 1962 in Rogers, Arkansas, the family laid the foundation for a retail empire that would span the globe. Jim, then in his early twenties, played an integral role in the expansion of the business. He immersed himself in every aspect of the operation, from managing inventory to understanding the intricacies of supply chain management.

Challenges and Triumphs

The journey to retail dominance was not without its challenges. Walmart faced criticism for its aggressive expansion strategies and impact on small-town businesses. However, Jim Walton, along with his siblings and the Walmart team, navigated these challenges with resilience and adaptability. The company's commitment to innovation, epitomized by its early adoption of technology and data-driven decision-making, set it apart in an ever-evolving retail landscape.

A Legacy in the Making

As the 1970s unfolded, Walmart's influence grew, and Jim Walton's role within the company became more prominent. The family's wealth expanded exponentially, but their commitment to the values instilled by Sam remained unwavering. The small-town five-and-dime had transformed into a retail powerhouse, and Jim was at the forefront, steering the company towards even greater heights.

Chapter 1 lays the groundwork for the epic tale of Jim Walton and the Walmart Empire. From the humble beginnings in Bentonville to the global retail giant that would revolutionize the industry, this chapter sets the stage for a narrative of ambition, innovation, and the indomitable spirit of a family that became retail royalty.

3

The Visionary Leadership of Jim Walton

A Shift in Leadership

As the 1980s dawned, the retail landscape continued to evolve, and so did Walmart under the visionary leadership of Jim Walton. Sam Walton's passing in 1992 marked a pivotal moment for the company. The youngest Walton sibling, Jim, stepped into the role of Chairman and CEO, inheriting not only the title but also the responsibility of sustaining and expanding the empire.

Embracing Change

Jim Walton's leadership style differed from his father's, yet it retained the core values that defined Walmart. Recognizing the changing dynamics of consumer behavior, Jim spearheaded initiatives to modernize the company. Under his guidance, Walmart embraced technology, implementing computerized inventory systems and leveraging data analytics to streamline operations and enhance customer experience.

Global Expansion

With Jim Walton at the helm, Walmart's expansion transcended national borders. The company ventured into international markets, setting up stores in South America, Europe, and Asia. The relentless pursuit of growth and market dominance reflected Jim's determination to carry the Walmart brand to every corner of the world. This global expansion brought both opportunities and challenges, as Walmart adapted its strategies to diverse cultures and economies.

Social Responsibility

Jim Walton's leadership extended beyond the boardroom. Recognizing the impact a retail giant could have on communities, he championed social responsibility initiatives. Walmart became a leader in sustainability efforts, committing to reduce its environmental footprint and promote ethical sourcing practices. The company's philanthropic endeavors, under Jim's guidance, aimed to address pressing social issues, further ingraining Walmart in the fabric of the communities it served.

E-Commerce Revolution

As the 21st century unfolded, Jim Walton navigated Walmart through the digital revolution. Acknowledging the rise of e-commerce, he led the company into the online realm, strategically acquiring and integrating e-commerce platforms. This shift reflected Jim's ability to adapt to changing consumer preferences while staying true to Walmart's commitment to affordability and accessibility.

Challenges on the Horizon

Despite the continued success, Walmart faced its share of challenges under Jim Walton's leadership. The company grappled with controversies surrounding labor practices, criticism of its impact on small businesses, and legal issues. Jim's ability to address these challenges with transparency and adaptability would shape the narrative of Walmart's role in society.

Chapter 2 explores the transformative era under Jim Walton's leadership. As Walmart evolved into a global powerhouse, Jim's strategic vision, commitment to innovation, and emphasis on corporate responsibility played pivotal roles in shaping the company's identity. The chapter sets the stage for the complexities of leadership and the ongoing pursuit of retail excellence in an ever-changing world.

4

Navigating Turbulence: Walmart in the 21st Century

The Digital Frontier

As the 21st century progressed, the retail landscape faced unprecedented disruption, and Walmart found itself at the forefront of the digital revolution. Chapter 3 delves into the challenges and triumphs as Jim Walton steered the company through the complexities of the digital frontier.

E-Commerce Dominance

Under Jim's leadership, Walmart intensified its focus on e-commerce, recognizing the seismic shift in consumer behavior. Strategic acquisitions, technological investments, and a revamped online platform propelled Walmart into direct competition with digital giants. The battle for e-commerce supremacy became a defining chapter in Walmart's evolution.

Innovation and Technology

Jim Walton's commitment to innovation became evident in the incorporation of cutting-edge technologies. Robotics, artificial intelligence, and data analytics transformed the supply chain, inventory management, and the in-store experience. Walmart's ability to harness technology not only improved operational efficiency but also elevated the overall customer journey.

Challenges and Controversies

With the digital transformation came a new set of challenges. Chapter 3 explores the controversies that arose, including concerns about data privacy, cybersecurity, and the impact of automation on employment. Jim Walton faced scrutiny from both the public and regulatory bodies, testing the resilience of Walmart's reputation and its ability to adapt responsibly to the changing technological landscape.

Labor Practices and Social Impact

Walmart's size and influence brought increased scrutiny on its labor practices. Jim Walton, recognizing the importance of a satisfied and motivated workforce, implemented initiatives to improve employee benefits and working conditions. The chapter delves into the delicate balance between shareholder expectations, social responsibility, and the evolving expectations of a conscientious consumer base.

The Global Stage

As Walmart continued its global expansion, Jim Walton faced geopolitical challenges and shifting economic landscapes. The chapter explores the delicate dance of navigating international markets, trade tensions, and adapting the Walmart model to diverse cultural and regulatory environments.

Sustainability Commitments

Jim Walton's dedication to social responsibility extended to environmental sustainability. Walmart, under his leadership, set ambitious goals to reduce its carbon footprint, promote renewable energy, and enhance sustainability throughout its supply chain. The chapter unfolds the company's journey toward becoming a leader in corporate environmental responsibility.

Legacy and Future

As Chapter 3 draws to a close, it reflects on Jim Walton's legacy. The narrative explores how his leadership, marked by technological innovation, social responsibility, and global expansion, shaped Walmart into a resilient and adaptable retail giant. The closing pages set the stage for the challenges and opportunities that lie ahead in the ever-evolving world of retail and e-commerce.

5

Walmart in the Community: Philanthropy, Challenges, and Corporate Evolution

Community Engagement

Jim Walton's leadership extended beyond the walls of Walmart stores. This chapter explores the company's commitment to community engagement and philanthropy, examining the initiatives aimed at making a positive impact on the communities Walmart served.

Local Initiatives

Recognizing the importance of being a responsible corporate citizen, Walmart, under Jim Walton's guidance, launched a series of local initiatives. These ranged from supporting local schools and healthcare facilities to promoting small businesses within the communities where Walmart operated. The chapter sheds light on the challenges and triumphs of aligning corporate goals with the unique needs of diverse communities.

Disaster Relief Efforts

Walmart's logistical prowess became a beacon of hope in times of disaster. The chapter delves into the company's rapid response to natural disasters, showcasing its ability to mobilize resources and provide critical aid. Jim Walton's commitment to disaster relief initiatives highlighted Walmart's role as a corporate entity with a social conscience.

Evolving Retail Dynamics

As the retail landscape continued to transform, Walmart faced new challenges and competitors. The chapter explores the rise of online retail giants, changing consumer preferences, and the efforts made by Jim Walton and his team to keep Walmart at the forefront of the industry.

Omnichannel Strategy

To adapt to the evolving retail dynamics, Walmart embraced an omnichannel approach. The integration of in-store and online experiences aimed to provide customers with seamless shopping options. This chapter analyzes the intricacies of implementing such a strategy and the impact it had on Walmart's market position.

Competition and Collaboration

Walmart faced stiff competition from both traditional retailers and emerging e-commerce players. The narrative unfolds the strategies employed by Jim Walton to maintain Walmart's competitive edge, including strategic partnerships, acquisitions, and innovations in product offerings. The delicate balance between competition and collaboration shaped the retail giant's trajectory in an increasingly interconnected market.

Reflections on Leadership

Chapter 4 reflects on Jim Walton's leadership style as it evolved through the years. Interviews with colleagues, industry experts, and those within the Walmart community provide insights into the personal and professional growth of Jim Walton, painting a portrait of a leader who navigated the complexities of corporate America with resilience and adaptability.

Succession Planning

As the chapter concludes, attention turns to the future. Succession planning and the question of who will carry the torch for the Walmart legacy are explored, offering readers a glimpse into the ongoing narrative of Walmart's corporate journey.

Chapter 4 weaves together the threads of community engagement, corporate evolution, and the dynamic retail landscape, presenting a comprehensive picture of Walmart's role in society and its ongoing commitment to adapting in an ever-changing world.

6

Legacy Unveiled: The Enduring Impact of Jim Walton on Walmart

Shaping a Lasting Legacy

As Jim Walton's tenure as the leader of Walmart entered its later years, Chapter 5 delves into the lasting impact he left on the company and the retail industry as a whole. This chapter explores the culmination of a lifetime dedicated to transforming a small-town variety store into a global retail powerhouse.

Leadership Transition

With the passage of time, the inevitability of a leadership transition loomed. Chapter 5 explores the intricacies of Jim Walton's decision to step down from his role as the leader of Walmart. Interviews with key figures shed light on the considerations, challenges, and emotions involved in passing the torch to the next generation of leaders.

Continuity and Change

The narrative unfolds the strategies employed by Jim Walton to ensure a smooth transition while preserving the core values that defined Walmart. The delicate balance between continuity and the necessity for strategic evolution is examined, providing insights into how the company maintained its identity while adapting to new leadership.

The Next Generation

As a new era dawned, the focus shifted to the next generation of the Walton family and Walmart leadership. Chapter 5 introduces readers to the individuals poised to carry forward the Walmart legacy. Their visions, strategies, and approaches to leadership are explored in the context of the challenges and opportunities facing the retail industry.

Innovations in Retail

The chapter delves into the ongoing innovations within Walmart, showcasing how the company continues to stay at the forefront of retail trends. From advancements in technology to sustainability initiatives, the narrative illustrates how Walmart remains a dynamic force in the ever-evolving retail landscape.

Global Expansion Strategies

Under the new leadership, Walmart's global footprint continued to expand. The narrative takes readers on a journey across continents, exploring how Walmart adapts its strategies to diverse markets while maintaining a commitment to providing affordable products and uplifting local economies.

Reflections on the Walmart Legacy

Chapter 5 invites reflections from industry experts, employees, and community members on the enduring legacy of Walmart and the Walton family. The impact of the company on communities, economies, and the retail industry as a whole is examined through the lens of those who have witnessed its evolution.

The Walmart Effect

The chapter examines the phenomenon known as the "Walmart effect" — the wide-ranging economic and social consequences of Walmart's presence in communities. Interviews and case studies illustrate how the company's influence shapes local economies, employment landscapes, and retail ecosystems.

Epilogue: The Ever-Expanding Horizon

As Chapter 5 concludes, an epilogue sets the stage for the ever-expanding horizon of Walmart and the retail industry. The narrative hints at the challenges and opportunities that lie ahead, inviting readers to contemplate the enduring legacy of Jim Walton, the Walmart empire, and the ongoing narrative of retail royalty.

7

Walmart in the 21st Century: Challenges, Innovations, and the Future Frontier

Evolving Consumer Dynamics

As the 21st century progresses, Walmart finds itself navigating a retail landscape marked by rapid technological advancements, shifting consumer behaviors, and global uncertainties. Chapter 6 explores how the company continues to adapt, innovate, and address challenges in this dynamic environment.

Personalization and Data Analytics

The chapter delves into Walmart's strategies for personalizing the shopping experience through advanced data analytics. From targeted marketing to personalized recommendations, the company embraces technology to create a more tailored and efficient customer journey.

Artificial Intelligence and Automation

Walmart's commitment to innovation unfolds as the narrative explores the integration of artificial intelligence and automation in various aspects of the retail process. From smart inventory management to cashierless checkout experiences, the chapter illustrates how Walmart leverages cutting-edge technologies to stay ahead.

E-Commerce Expansion and Competing in the Digital Arena

As e-commerce continues to reshape the retail landscape, Walmart remains a major player in the digital arena. The chapter outlines the company's strategies for expanding its online presence, competing with tech giants, and meeting the demands of an increasingly digital-savvy consumer base.

Ecosystem Expansion and Partnerships

Walmart's efforts to create a comprehensive retail ecosystem are explored. From partnerships with tech companies to acquisitions that complement its business model, the narrative sheds light on how Walmart strategically positions itself in the broader digital marketplace.

Navigating Global Challenges

The chapter addresses the geopolitical challenges and global uncertainties that impact Walmart's operations. Trade tensions, supply chain disruptions, and economic fluctuations all contribute to a complex landscape that requires strategic decision-making and adaptability.

Sustainability and Corporate Responsibility

As societal expectations for corporate responsibility rise, Walmart continues to lead in sustainability initiatives. The chapter explores the company's commitments to environmental stewardship, ethical sourcing, and social responsibility, showcasing how Walmart strives to be a positive force in the communities it serves.

Renewable Energy and Climate Action

Walmart's efforts to transition to renewable energy and reduce its carbon footprint are highlighted. The chapter delves into the company's initiatives to combat climate change and the role it plays in shaping sustainable practices across the industry.

The Future of Retail: Walmart's Vision

The chapter concludes by providing a glimpse into Walmart's vision for the future of retail. Interviews with current leaders, industry analysts, and stakeholders offer insights into how the company envisions adapting to emerging trends, fostering innovation, and maintaining its position as a global retail leader.

Tech-Driven Customer Experiences

Walmart's future initiatives in enhancing customer experiences through technology and innovation are explored. From augmented reality shopping experiences to advancements in supply chain transparency, the narrative paints a picture of Walmart's commitment to staying at the forefront of the retail frontier.

Ongoing Commitment to Affordability

Amidst all the technological advancements, the chapter emphasizes Walmart's unwavering commitment to providing affordable products and everyday low prices. Interviews with executives and customers provide perspectives on how Walmart's dedication to accessibility remains a cornerstone of its identity.

Chapter 6 serves as a comprehensive exploration of Walmart's ongoing journey in the 21st century, tackling the challenges, embracing innovations, and envisioning a future where the company continues to shape the retail landscape.

8

Walmart's Impact Beyond Retail: Social, Economic, and Global Influence

Social Impact: Walmart and Local Communities

This chapter delves into Walmart's multifaceted impact on local communities. From job creation to philanthropy, the narrative explores the ways in which Walmart shapes the social fabric of the areas it serves.

Employment Opportunities

Walmart's role as a major employer is examined, shedding light on the economic opportunities the company provides in various communities. Interviews with employees offer personal perspectives on the impact of Walmart on livelihoods and local economies.

Community Development Programs

The chapter highlights Walmart's community development programs, focusing on initiatives aimed at education, healthcare, and small business support.

Case studies illustrate how these programs contribute to the well-being and growth of communities.

Economic Influence: Walmart's Ripple Effect

Walmart's economic influence extends far beyond its stores. The narrative explores the ripple effect of Walmart's operations on suppliers, supply chains, and the broader economy.

Supplier Relationships

The chapter delves into the dynamics of Walmart's relationships with suppliers, from local businesses to international manufacturers. Interviews and case studies provide insights into the challenges and opportunities for businesses in the Walmart supply chain.

Small Business Impact

Walmart's impact on small businesses is examined, addressing both the challenges faced by local retailers and the opportunities for entrepreneurs to connect with the Walmart marketplace. The narrative explores the delicate balance between corporate growth and supporting small business ecosystems.

Global Influence: Walmart as a Corporate Citizen

Walmart's global reach has implications beyond national borders. This chapter explores the company's role as a corporate citizen on the global stage.

International Partnerships and Collaborations

Walmart's collaborations with international organizations and governments are highlighted. From global sustainability initiatives to partnerships fostering economic development, the narrative examines how Walmart leverages its influence for positive change.

Cultural and Social Adaptation

The chapter delves into the complexities of Walmart's presence in diverse global markets. Cultural adaptations, localization strategies, and the impact on local economies are explored through case studies and interviews with experts.

Challenges and Criticisms: Navigating Controversies

Walmart's immense influence has not been without controversy. This chapter addresses the criticisms and challenges the company has faced, from labor practices to environmental concerns, and explores how Walmart responds to these issues.

Labor Practices and Employee Welfare

The chapter examines controversies related to labor practices and employee welfare, shedding light on Walmart's efforts to address these concerns through policy changes, employee benefits, and engagement initiatives.

Environmental Concerns and Sustainability

Walmart's environmental impact is explored, focusing on controversies surrounding sustainability practices. Interviews with environmental activists and experts provide perspectives on the challenges and advancements in Walmart's journey toward greater sustainability.

Legacy Beyond Retail: Reflections on Walmart's Influence

As the chapter concludes, it reflects on Walmart's enduring legacy beyond the realm of retail. Interviews with scholars, analysts, and community leaders offer diverse perspectives on how Walmart has shaped social, economic, and global landscapes.

Lessons Learned and Ongoing Evolution

The narrative closes with reflections on the lessons learned from Walmart's journey and the ongoing evolution of the company's role as a major global influencer beyond the traditional boundaries of retail.

Chapter 7 serves as a comprehensive exploration of Walmart's impact on society, economies, and the global stage, examining the multifaceted ways in which the company influences the world beyond its storefronts.

9

Walmart and the Future: Innovations, Challenges, and Continuing the Legacy

Embracing Technological Frontiers

As Walmart moves forward into the future, this chapter explores the company's commitment to staying at the forefront of technological innovation. From artificial intelligence and automation to augmented reality, the narrative unfolds how Walmart continues to leverage cutting-edge technologies to enhance the customer experience and streamline operations.

AI-Powered Customer Insights

The chapter delves into how Walmart utilizes artificial intelligence to gain deeper insights into customer preferences and behaviors. Personalized shopping experiences, targeted marketing, and anticipatory services are examined as integral components of Walmart's tech-driven future.

Automation in Supply Chain and Fulfillment

The narrative explores the integration of automation in Walmart's supply chain and fulfillment centers. From robotics in warehouses to autonomous delivery vehicles, the chapter illustrates how Walmart embraces automation to improve efficiency and meet the growing demands of e-commerce.

Sustainability and Ethical Practices

Building on the sustainability initiatives explored in earlier chapters, this section provides an in-depth look at Walmart's ongoing commitment to environmental stewardship and ethical business practices.

Circular Economy Initiatives

The chapter examines Walmart's efforts to move towards a circular economy, emphasizing waste reduction, recycling programs, and responsible product lifecycle management. Interviews with sustainability experts and company executives provide insights into Walmart's role as a leader in corporate environmental responsibility.

Ethical Sourcing and Fair Trade

The narrative explores Walmart's initiatives to ensure ethical sourcing and fair trade practices throughout its supply chain. Case studies and interviews with stakeholders shed light on the challenges and successes in promoting responsible business practices globally.

Diversity, Inclusion, and Social Impact

As societal expectations evolve, this chapter explores Walmart's endeavors to foster diversity and inclusion within the company and its impact on the communities it serves.

Workplace Diversity and Inclusion

The narrative examines Walmart's initiatives to create a diverse and inclusive workplace. From diversity hiring programs to fostering an inclusive corporate culture, the chapter delves into how Walmart is addressing the complexities of diversity and inclusion in the 21st century.

Social Impact Programs

Walmart's ongoing commitment to social impact programs is highlighted, including initiatives related to education, healthcare, and community development. The chapter explores how these programs contribute to Walmart's broader mission of making a positive difference in the world.

E-Commerce Evolution and Omni-Channel Strategies

As e-commerce continues to evolve, this chapter provides insights into how Walmart adapts its strategies to remain a key player in the digital marketplace.

Seamless Omni-Channel Experiences

The narrative explores how Walmart integrates online and offline channels to provide customers with seamless shopping experiences. From in-store pickup to digital loyalty programs, the chapter showcases Walmart's efforts to create a cohesive omni-channel retail environment.

Innovations in Online Retail

The chapter delves into ongoing innovations in Walmart's online retail platforms. From virtual storefronts to interactive shopping experiences, the narrative illustrates how the company remains agile in meeting the evolving expectations of digital-savvy consumers.

Navigating Global Challenges

As Walmart operates on a global scale, this section addresses how the company navigates geopolitical challenges, economic uncertainties, and global disruptions.

Supply Chain Resilience

The chapter explores Walmart's strategies for building a resilient supply chain, particularly in the face of global disruptions such as pandemics, natural disasters, and geopolitical tensions. Interviews with supply chain experts and company leaders provide perspectives on the complexities of managing a global retail network.

Economic Development and Localization

Walmart's role in economic development and localization strategies is examined. The narrative explores how the company adapts its business model to diverse markets, fosters local economic growth, and navigates the nuances of operating in different cultural and regulatory environments.

The Next Generation of Leadership

As Walmart continues to evolve, the chapter looks at the next generation of leaders within the company and the Walton family.

Succession Planning and Corporate Governance

The narrative provides insights into Walmart's succession planning strategies and corporate governance practices. Interviews with current leaders and industry experts shed light on how the company ensures continuity while fostering innovation and adaptability.

The Walton Family Legacy

The chapter explores the roles of the Walton family in shaping the future direction of Walmart. From philanthropy to strategic decision-making, the narrative illustrates how the family legacy continues to influence the company's values and vision.

Conclusion: A Continued Journey

Chapter 8 concludes by reflecting on Walmart's continued journey into the future. The narrative offers a synthesis of the innovations, challenges, and legacy explored throughout the book, providing readers with a comprehensive understanding of Walmart's ongoing narrative as a global retail leader.

10

Walmart and Society: Reflections on a Transformative Partnership

The Walmart Effect on Communities

This chapter explores the intricate relationship between Walmart and the communities it serves. It examines the social and economic impacts of Walmart's presence, considering both the positive contributions and challenges that arise in local communities.

Job Creation and Economic Stimulus

The narrative delves into the role of Walmart as a major employer and economic stimulus in various communities. Interviews with local business owners, employees, and community leaders provide diverse perspectives on the ways in which Walmart shapes local economies.

Small Business Dynamics

The chapter examines the dynamics between Walmart and small businesses in its vicinity. Case studies and testimonials shed light on how local enterprises navigate the challenges and opportunities presented by the presence of a retail giant.

Beyond Retail: Walmart's Cultural Influence

Walmart's influence extends beyond commerce and into the cultural fabric of society. This section explores how Walmart has become ingrained in the daily lives and cultural narratives of people across the globe.

Walmart as a Cultural Icon

The chapter reflects on how Walmart has become more than just a retail destination, evolving into a cultural icon. From portrayals in popular media to its role in shaping consumer behaviors, the narrative examines the multifaceted ways in which Walmart is embedded in contemporary culture.

Community Engagement and Cultural Programs

The chapter highlights Walmart's community engagement programs and cultural initiatives. From supporting local arts to promoting cultural events, the narrative illustrates how Walmart contributes to the cultural vibrancy of the communities it calls home.

Sustainability, Responsibility, and Environmental Impact

Building on earlier chapters, this section provides an in-depth exploration of Walmart's commitment to sustainability and corporate responsibility, emphasizing the company's impact on the environment.

Renewable Energy and Green Practices

The narrative examines Walmart's strides towards renewable energy and environmentally friendly practices. Case studies and interviews with environmental experts provide insights into the challenges and successes of Walmart's sustainability journey.

Responsible Supply Chain Management

The chapter explores how Walmart addresses environmental and ethical concerns within its supply chain. From responsible sourcing to minimizing waste, the narrative illustrates how Walmart navigates the complexities of global supply chain management with an eye on sustainability.

E-Commerce and the Digital Divide

This section delves into the role of Walmart in bridging or contributing to the digital divide, exploring how the company's digital initiatives impact access to information, technology, and opportunities in various communities.

Digital Inclusion Programs

The chapter examines Walmart's initiatives aimed at fostering digital inclusion. From providing affordable technology products to supporting digital literacy programs, the narrative illustrates how Walmart contributes to reducing the digital divide.

Challenges of Digital Accessibility

The chapter also addresses the challenges associated with digital accessibility, exploring how disparities in technology access and digital literacy can create barriers for certain communities. Interviews with experts and community members shed light on these complexities.

Corporate Accountability and Ethical Governance

This section delves into Walmart's corporate governance, accountability measures, and efforts to maintain ethical standards in its operations.

Transparent Business Practices

The chapter explores Walmart's commitment to transparent business practices. From financial disclosures to ethical guidelines, the narrative examines how the company upholds accountability and fosters trust among stakeholders.

Ethical Decision-Making in a Global Context

The narrative delves into the challenges of making ethical decisions in a global business context. Interviews with corporate ethics experts and insights from within Walmart's leadership shed light on the complexities of maintaining ethical standards across diverse markets.

Walmart's Educational Initiatives

As a major player in the business landscape, Walmart also invests in educational initiatives. This chapter explores the company's contributions to education, ranging from employee training programs to support for educational institutions.

Employee Training and Development

The narrative examines Walmart's commitment to employee training and development programs. From leadership academies to skill-building initiatives, the chapter illustrates how Walmart invests in its workforce and contributes to individual professional growth.

Educational Partnerships and Philanthropy

The chapter also explores Walmart's educational philanthropy and partnerships. Case studies and interviews with educational leaders provide insights into the ways in which Walmart supports educational institutions and initiatives.

The Changing Face of Retail: Walmart's Vision

This section provides a forward-looking perspective on how Walmart envisions its role in the ever-evolving retail landscape.

Innovations in Retail Technology

The narrative explores Walmart's visions for the future of retail technology. From augmented reality to virtual shopping experiences, the chapter offers insights into how Walmart anticipates and embraces technological advancements.

Continued Global Expansion

The chapter reflects on Walmart's plans for continued global expansion. Interviews with international business experts and company executives provide perspectives on how Walmart envisions its presence in diverse markets in the coming years.

Conclusion: A Symbiotic Relationship

Chapter 9 concludes by reflecting on the symbiotic relationship between Walmart and society. The narrative offers a synthesis of the impacts, challenges, and innovations explored throughout the book, providing readers with a comprehensive understanding of the dynamic and evolving partnership between Walmart and the communities it serves.

11

Walmart and the Next Horizon: Charting a Course for the Future

Navigating Uncharted Waters

As Walmart stands at the threshold of a new era, this chapter explores the uncharted waters of the evolving retail landscape, examining the challenges, opportunities, and strategic imperatives that lie ahead.

Shaping the Post-Pandemic Landscape

The narrative delves into how Walmart, like all businesses, navigates the post-pandemic landscape. From changes in consumer behavior to the acceleration of e-commerce, the chapter examines how the company adapts its strategies to meet the demands of a rapidly evolving world.

Health and Safety Considerations

The chapter explores Walmart's ongoing commitment to health and safety, considering how the experiences of the pandemic influence the company's approach to providing a secure shopping environment for customers and a safe workplace for employees.

The Intersection of Technology and Retail

As technology continues to reshape the retail industry, this section examines Walmart's strategies for leveraging emerging technologies to enhance the customer experience and streamline operations.

Artificial Intelligence and Machine Learning

The narrative explores how Walmart harnesses the power of artificial intelligence and machine learning to gain deeper insights into consumer behavior, optimize inventory management, and personalize the shopping experience.

Blockchain and Supply Chain Innovation

The chapter delves into Walmart's exploration of blockchain technology and its potential applications in supply chain management. Interviews with industry experts and company leaders provide insights into how Walmart envisions the future of transparent and efficient supply chains.

Strengthening Global Partnerships

This section explores how Walmart continues to strengthen its global partnerships, considering both the challenges and opportunities presented by international markets.

Trade and Geopolitical Considerations

The chapter examines how geopolitical tensions and trade dynamics shape Walmart's global strategies. Interviews with international business experts shed light on the complexities of navigating the global stage in an era of evolving political and economic landscapes.

Cultural Adaptations and Localization

The narrative explores how Walmart adapts its business model to diverse cultural contexts. From tailoring product offerings to embracing local traditions, the chapter provides insights into how Walmart fosters cultural sensitivity in its global operations.

Sustainability as a Strategic Imperative

Building on earlier chapters, this section examines how sustainability continues to be a central pillar of Walmart's corporate strategy.

Net Zero and Carbon Neutrality Goals

The chapter explores Walmart's ambitious goals for achieving net-zero emissions and carbon neutrality. Interviews with sustainability leaders and environmental experts offer perspectives on the challenges and innovations associated with these targets.

Circular Economy Initiatives

The narrative delves into Walmart's efforts to embrace a circular economy. From product design to waste reduction, the chapter illustrates how Walmart contributes to the transition towards a more sustainable and circular approach to consumption.

E-Commerce Evolution and Retail Innovation

As e-commerce remains a driving force in the retail landscape, this section explores how Walmart innovates its digital platforms and online experiences.

Seamless Omni-Channel Integration

The chapter examines how Walmart further integrates its online and offline channels to provide customers with a seamless and unified shopping experience. From digital loyalty programs to interactive in-store technologies, the narrative illustrates Walmart's commitment to omni-channel retailing.

Emerging Trends in Online Retail

The chapter explores emerging trends in online retail and how Walmart positions itself to stay ahead of the curve. Interviews with e-commerce experts and technology innovators offer insights into the future of online shopping and digital retail experiences.

Corporate Social Responsibility in a Changing World

This section examines how Walmart continues to evolve its corporate social responsibility initiatives to address pressing societal challenges.

Diversity and Inclusion Advancements

The narrative explores how Walmart enhances its diversity and inclusion initiatives. From workforce representation to community engagement, the chapter illustrates how Walmart remains committed to fostering an inclusive and equitable corporate culture.

Social Impact Programs and Philanthropy

The chapter delves into Walmart's ongoing social impact programs and philanthropic endeavors. Case studies and testimonials highlight the tangible ways in which Walmart contributes to social welfare and community development.

The Next Generation of Leadership

As leadership transitions occur, this section examines how the next generation of leaders within Walmart shapes the company's vision and strategies.

Leadership Perspectives

The chapter provides insights from the next generation of leaders within Walmart, offering perspectives on their vision for the company's future. Interviews with executives and key decision-makers shed light on the strategic direction that will guide Walmart into the next era.

Innovation from Within

The narrative explores how Walmart fosters a culture of innovation from within its ranks. From employee-driven initiatives to internal innovation programs, the chapter illustrates how Walmart taps into the creative potential of its workforce to drive positive change.

Conclusion: Writing the Next Chapter

Chapter 10 concludes by reflecting on the themes, challenges, and opportunities explored throughout the book. The narrative offers a synthesis of Walmart's journey, providing readers with a forward-looking perspective on the company's role in shaping the future of retail and its continued impact on society.

12

Walmart and the Social Fabric: Nurturing Community Bonds in the Future

Community-Centric Strategies

As Walmart looks to the future, this chapter explores the company's evolving strategies to strengthen its ties with local communities. From community engagement programs to inclusive initiatives, the narrative examines how Walmart continues to play a pivotal role in nurturing community bonds.

Locally Tailored Offerings

The chapter delves into how Walmart tailors its product offerings and services to meet the unique needs of diverse communities. Interviews with community leaders and business owners provide insights into the collaborative efforts between Walmart and local stakeholders.

Small Business Support Programs

The narrative explores Walmart's continued commitment to supporting small businesses. From incubator programs to initiatives that promote local entrepreneurship, the chapter illustrates how Walmart fosters economic growth and resilience within communities.

Technological Empowerment at the Community Level

As technology becomes increasingly integral to community development, this section examines how Walmart empowers communities through digital initiatives and technology partnerships.

Digital Literacy and Access Programs

The chapter explores Walmart's initiatives aimed at improving digital literacy and access in local communities. Case studies and interviews with community leaders highlight the transformative impact of such programs on individuals and businesses.

Technology Partnerships for Community Development

The narrative delves into Walmart's partnerships with technology companies to address community challenges. From smart city initiatives to digital infrastructure projects, the chapter illustrates how Walmart contributes to the technological empowerment of communities.

Health and Wellness Initiatives

In the wake of global health challenges, this section explores how Walmart integrates health and wellness initiatives into its community-centric strategies.

Accessible Healthcare Services

The chapter examines Walmart's efforts to make healthcare services more accessible within communities. From in-store health clinics to telehealth partnerships, the narrative illustrates how Walmart contributes to community well-being.

Public Health Partnerships

The narrative explores Walmart's collaborations with public health organizations. Interviews with healthcare professionals shed light on the ways in which Walmart supports public health initiatives and emergency preparedness at the community level.

Educational Empowerment for All

This section delves into Walmart's initiatives to empower individuals through educational programs, contributing to the development of skills and knowledge within communities.

Lifelong Learning Programs

The chapter explores Walmart's commitment to lifelong learning. From employee training initiatives to educational resources for community members, the narrative illustrates how Walmart fosters continuous education within its sphere of influence.

Educational Infrastructure Support

The narrative delves into Walmart's support for educational infrastructure. Case studies highlight partnerships with schools, colleges, and vocational training centers, showcasing how Walmart contributes to building a foundation for educational success.

Sustainable Community Development

As sustainability takes center stage, this section examines how Walmart integrates environmental and social sustainability into its community development initiatives.

Sustainable Infrastructure Projects

The chapter explores Walmart's involvement in sustainable infrastructure projects. From renewable energy initiatives to eco-friendly community spaces, the narrative illustrates how Walmart contributes to environmentally conscious community development.

Socially Responsible Investments

The narrative examines how Walmart directs its financial investments toward socially responsible projects. Case studies highlight community development funds, affordable housing initiatives, and partnerships that contribute to the social fabric of communities.

Inclusive Employment Practices

This section explores Walmart's commitment to inclusive employment practices, fostering diversity and equal opportunities within its workforce.

Diversity Hiring and Training Programs

The chapter examines Walmart's initiatives to promote diversity in hiring and employee training. Interviews with human resources professionals provide insights into the challenges and successes of fostering an inclusive workplace culture.

Community Workforce Development

The narrative delves into Walmart's role in community workforce development. From job fairs to vocational training programs, the chapter illustrates how Walmart contributes to building a skilled and diverse workforce within local communities.

Social Impact Measurement and Reporting

In an era of increased corporate accountability, this section explores how Walmart measures and reports its social impact within communities.

Impact Metrics and Reporting Practices

The chapter examines the metrics and reporting practices employed by Walmart to measure its social impact. Interviews with sustainability and corporate responsibility experts provide perspectives on the challenges and importance of transparent impact measurement.

Stakeholder Collaboration for Impact Assessment

The narrative explores Walmart's collaboration with stakeholders for comprehensive impact assessments. Case studies highlight instances where community members, NGOs, and local authorities actively contribute to the evaluation of Walmart's social impact.

Shaping the Next Chapter Together

As the chapter concludes, it reflects on the collaborative efforts between Walmart and communities to shape a collective future. The narrative offers a synthesis of the strategies, partnerships, and initiatives explored throughout the book, providing readers with a forward-looking perspective on the evolving relationship between Walmart and the communities it serves.

13

Walmart and Global Citizenship: Navigating a Complex World

International Diplomacy and Trade Relations

This chapter explores Walmart's role in international diplomacy and trade relations as the company navigates the complexities of a globalized world.

Economic Diplomacy

The narrative examines how Walmart engages in economic diplomacy, shaping trade policies and fostering international economic cooperation. Interviews with trade experts and government officials provide insights into Walmart's influence on global economic relations.

Trade Partnerships and Alliances

The chapter delves into Walmart's partnerships and alliances with international organizations and trade groups. Case studies illustrate instances where

Walmart collaborates with global stakeholders to address trade challenges and promote fair business practices.

Philanthropy on a Global Scale

As a global corporate citizen, Walmart's philanthropic initiatives extend beyond national borders. This section explores the company's impact on global humanitarian efforts.

International Disaster Relief

The chapter examines Walmart's role in international disaster relief efforts. From providing aid during natural disasters to supporting refugee communities, the narrative illustrates how Walmart contributes to global humanitarian initiatives.

Global Health Initiatives

The narrative delves into Walmart's contributions to global health initiatives. Case studies highlight partnerships with international health organizations, showcasing how Walmart addresses health challenges on a global scale.

Addressing Global Challenges

This section explores how Walmart tackles pressing global challenges, including climate change, poverty, and inequality.

Climate Action on a Global Scale

The chapter examines Walmart's global efforts to address climate change. Interviews with environmental leaders and case studies illustrate how Walmart contributes to international initiatives aimed at mitigating the impacts of climate change.

Global Poverty Alleviation

The narrative explores Walmart's role in global poverty alleviation. From ethical sourcing practices to community development projects, the chapter illustrates how Walmart contributes to reducing poverty in diverse global contexts.

Human Rights and Ethical Supply Chains

As ethical considerations become increasingly important, this section delves into Walmart's commitment to human rights and ethical supply chain management on a global scale.

Ensuring Ethical Sourcing

The chapter examines Walmart's efforts to ensure ethical sourcing across its global supply chain. Interviews with human rights advocates provide perspectives on the challenges and advancements in promoting ethical business practices.

Combating Forced Labor and Exploitation

The narrative delves into Walmart's initiatives to combat forced labor and exploitation within its supply chain. Case studies highlight instances where Walmart takes a stand against human rights abuses and works to create a more ethical and transparent global supply network.

Cultural Sensitivity and Global Operations

This section explores how Walmart navigates cultural sensitivities and adapts its operations to diverse cultural contexts around the world.

Localization Strategies

The chapter examines how Walmart employs localization strategies to adapt its business model to different cultural norms. Interviews with international business experts and case studies illustrate instances where Walmart successfully navigates cultural diversity.

Respect for Local Traditions

The narrative delves into Walmart's approach to respecting and preserving local traditions. From marketing campaigns to product offerings, the chapter illustrates how Walmart incorporates cultural sensitivity into its global business practices.

Global Workforce Dynamics

As a multinational corporation, Walmart manages a diverse and extensive global workforce. This section explores how the company addresses the unique dynamics of its global employee base.

Cultural Inclusivity in the Workplace

The chapter examines how Walmart fosters cultural inclusivity within its global workforce. Interviews with employees from different regions provide insights into the challenges and successes of building a diverse and harmonious workplace.

Cross-Cultural Leadership Development

The narrative explores Walmart's strategies for developing cross-cultural leadership. Case studies illustrate instances where Walmart invests in leadership programs to cultivate a cadre of leaders capable of navigating the complexities of a global business environment.

Technology Transfer and Innovation Exchange

This section explores how Walmart contributes to technology transfer and innovation exchange on a global scale.

International Technology Partnerships

The chapter examines Walmart's international technology partnerships. From collaborations with tech companies to joint ventures with local innovators, the narrative illustrates how Walmart fosters technology transfer and innovation in diverse global markets.

Global Innovation Hubs

The narrative delves into Walmart's establishment of global innovation hubs. Case studies highlight instances where Walmart collaborates with local talent and resources to drive innovation and technological advancements in various regions.

The Future of Global Citizenship

As the chapter concludes, it reflects on the evolving landscape of global citizenship and Walmart's role in shaping a responsible and ethical future on a global scale. The narrative offers a synthesis of the global initiatives, challenges, and opportunities explored throughout the book, providing readers with insights into the complexities of navigating a complex and interconnected world.

14

Summary

In this comprehensive exploration of Walmart's impact on the retail landscape, society, and global affairs, the book unfolds across twelve chapters, each delving into a distinct facet of the retail giant's journey. From the foundational narrative of Jim Walton and the rise of the Walmart Empire to the ongoing challenges and innovations of the 21st century, the book navigates through the intricate layers of Walmart's legacy.

The chapters progressively unfold, providing insights into the leadership transitions, global expansions, and technological advancements that have shaped Walmart's trajectory. The narrative delves into the company's commitment to sustainability, corporate responsibility, and the enduring impact it has on local communities. Each chapter paints a vivid picture of Walmart's role as a global influencer, exploring its relationships with suppliers, the complexities of its global operations, and the challenges it faces in the ever-evolving retail landscape.

As the book progresses, it examines Walmart's initiatives in e-commerce, artificial intelligence, and automation, showcasing the company's commitment to staying at the forefront of technological innovation. The narrative also reflects on the social, economic, and cultural impact of Walmart on local communities, shedding light on the intricate dynamics of its relationships with small businesses, its role in job creation, and its cultural significance.

Chapters dedicated to Walmart's global influence provide an in-depth look at the company's role in international diplomacy, trade relations, and philanthropy. The book addresses Walmart's contributions to global humanitarian efforts, its initiatives in climate action, and its commitment to ethical sourcing and human rights.

The later chapters delve into Walmart's strategies for community-centric development, exploring how the company empowers local communities through technological initiatives, health and wellness programs, and educational empowerment. The book also explores Walmart's role as a global citizen, addressing the challenges of cultural sensitivity, ethical supply chains, and the dynamics of its diverse global workforce.

The concluding chapters offer a forward-looking perspective, examining Walmart's vision for the future, its strategies for sustainable development, and its evolving role in global citizenship. The narrative reflects on the challenges and opportunities that lie ahead, providing readers with a comprehensive understanding of Walmart's ongoing narrative as a global retail leader and its multifaceted impact on society, economies, and the world.